ROMAN SAVAROVSKY

THE
LAST PALADIN

To all the Gifted of this world!

Roman Savarovsky

BOOK 1

MAGIC DOME BOOKS

The Last Paladin
Book #1
Copyright © Roman Savarovsky 2025
Cover Art © Alexander Rudenko 2025
Cover designer: Vladimir Manyukhin
English translation copyright © Julia Fouche 2025
Published by Magic Dome Books, 2025
ISBN: 978-80-7702-274-3
All Rights Reserved

TABLE OF CONTENTS:

CHAPTER 1

"WELL, WELL, LOOK WHO WE HAVE here, you little pest." I cracked my neck with a grin. "Looks like I finally got you."

Barefoot and draped in a tattered cloak, I stood in the heart of the desert, with sandstorms raging around me, swallowing the sky in a thick, swirling haze. But within the storm's eye, just ahead, was a barely visible, round opening in the ground — a tiny hole, maybe four inches across. Just big enough for a rodent or, in this case, the fat little Spatial Worm I'd been hunting for the past year.

Tracking down the only living thing in a dead, barren world isn't easy.

As it happened, this creature was my one way out of the Portal, where a pack of traitors had lured me with their deception. Did those arrogant fools really believe they could be rid of me that easily?

The leaders of the Empire's Top Ten Clans had long since given up trying to kill me in the open. Instead, they thought if they trapped me in this desolate elemental world of Time, I'd simply vanish, never to return.

Ha. They wish.

I'll give them credit — this attempt was certainly their most inventive. Ten years of plotting, three floors of the Tower blown to pieces, four thousand bodies left in the rubble. All that just to trick me into a Portal-trap and seal the way out.

Those highborn idiots are going to get the shock of their lives when I show up at their doorstep.

This time, their little games went too far. Those arrogant Princes will pay. They'll answer to me personally.

They could have taken a shot at me; I didn't care. All they did was disgrace their Clans and throw away their men. Let the brats have their fun. But killing old Aks... I'll never forgive them for that.

With that thought, I crouched down, pressing my hand against the small opening, and closed my eyes.

The Spatial Worm was close. The cowardly creature that had run from me across this entire world was now desperately trying to burrow deeper. I could sense its fear, its frantic urge to escape.

But it was too late to run, little one.

"Consume," I whispered.

Darkness surged from my hand, reaching the panicked creature in under a second. The deafening scream of a dying beast rang in my ears, followed swiftly by silence, and then... nothing but darkness.

* * *

Traveling through Portals isn't exactly a pleasant experience, let me tell you. Your physical body dematerializes, its information threads through the void between worlds, and then reassembles on the other side. It's rough on the mind and your energy balance.

And if you're using just the remains of a sealed Portal, a pinch of off-world worm, and raw elemental force to get through, the experience gets even less enjoyable.

My vision blurred, my head pounded like someone had hammered it twice, and every cell in my body ached from exhaustion.

But it was worth it!

Because instead of those cursed dunes and endless dead sand, there were trees all around me! Real, green, living trees!

The scent of pine hit me like a slap, the sound of rustling leaves — which I hadn't heard in a year — was pure bliss to my ears, and a cool breeze brushed across my face.

Absolute heaven.

"Home, sweet home," I murmured, smiling as I got to my feet.

Instinctively, my hands reached for the broad leaf of a nearby plant, where a few drops of water gleamed. Just enough for a single sip, but it revived me a bit.

My tired mind started remembering what life felt like.

With that small bit of moisture, and the realization that my third attempt at returning home had finally worked, all my pain faded away. I stretched with a contented sigh, took a deep breath of the clean forest air of my world, and dusted off my black cloak, the only item to survive a year's worth of close encounters with the Element of Time.

That ruthless force had turned everything it touched into lifeless white sand, so none of my other belongings had made it through. A sudden influx of oxygen snapped my brain back into action, leaving only a slight weakness, hunger, and an annoying dryness in my mouth — nothing a good meal, some solid sleep, and a couple of quarts of prime imperial liquor couldn't fix.

"Although this might be harder to restore," I muttered with a touch of frustration as I activated the elemental Seal.

A year in the insatiable desert of Time had drained my connection to my native Element of Darkness down to nearly nothing, and that rough inter-world crossing had consumed the last dregs of my energy.

All I had left were crumbs — barely enough to fuel anything useful. Great.

This was going to take more than a day to recover. Forget a day; it would take years of hard work and clearing Portals to restore what I'd lost. And believe me, the Princes responsible for this mess were going to answer for every drop of my valuable off-world energy that had gone to waste.

"I'll have to use the Tower's Source," I concluded reluctantly.

The magisters are going to chew my ear off again.

Marcus, you need to be more economical!

Marcus, that energy belongs to all humanity!

Marcus, you've left twenty floors in the dark again!

But when it comes to sealing the toughest Portals and replenishing the Great Source more than the rest of humanity combined, the old cranks couldn't care less.

With that thought, I released the Seal and looked around.

Were trees in the Empire always this huge?

For the last couple of years before being trapped, I'd done nothing but jump from Portal to Portal, with breaks for food, sleep, and the occasional romance. I'd started to know some foreign worlds better than my own — the very one I was supposed to protect.

Right now, though, I couldn't begin to guess exactly where I was.

The trees were so monstrously tall that I couldn't see the sky, let alone the Tower of Argus — the greatest achievement of humanity and a flawless landmark, nearly three thousand feet tall. I'd been counting on spotting it on the horizon.

I hadn't expected my improvised Portal crossing to deposit me directly into my bed on the ninety-ninth floor, but I didn't think it would drop me far from the Tower either. Home had to be close.

All that was left was to figure out which direction to go.

And just then, I heard the sound of an engine in the distance.

People — always a good sign. They might not feed me, but at least they could point the way. Truth be told, I missed human voices, too. After a year in the desert world, it wasn't the Element of Time that brought me closest to death but sheer boredom.

"Maybe they'll even have shoes..." I muttered, glancing down at my bare feet.

The sound of the engine grew louder, and a few seconds later, weaving skillfully between the massive trees, a vehicle with a battered imperial crest came into view.

Only, the vehicle looked... strange.

It was a black, angular pentagon with an open cabin and a long bed, but the oddest part was that it didn't have any wheels. Or rather, it did, but they were arranged horizontally and didn't touch the ground.

"Out of the way, you bum!" a burly driver with a wild look bellowed.

The strange, elongated pickup swerved slightly

to the left, making no move to slow down.

Not very polite.

Then again, I did look like a complete vagrant — a scraggly, dehydrated body, unshaven face, covered in sand, and with a torn cloak hanging over my bare chest.

Recognizing me as the First Paladin of Argus was out of the question.

In the truck bed, I spotted three more men, all in combat gear, and one of them manning a silver gun that vaguely resembled the imperial "Aron" machine gun.

Two of the soldiers glanced at me briefly with disinterest, but one, dressed in armor with a red star insignia, cupped his hands around his mouth and shouted, voice raw with urgency,

"Run, man! Save yourself!"

Why was he yelling? He nearly lost his voice.

He should have been paying more attention to his surroundings. A barely noticeable stone fin protruding from the ground was moving directly toward the pickup's path.

I almost felt sorry for the poor guys. They had hardly any elemental response. The squad was clearly not from a Gifted Clan. What bad luck to run into a B-class portal creature outside the Tower's perimeter.

With a dull thud, something from underground sent the pickup flying, spinning in midair before crashing down on its side.

The soldiers in the bed were flung in all directions.

Only the driver, held in place by a safety frame, stayed inside the cabin. The machine gunner fared the worst — he was thrown the farthest and became the first victim of the Stone Serpent.

The thirty-three-foot portal creature burst from the ground, swallowing the poor man whole.

He didn't even have time to scream. But his surviving comrades quickly climbed on top of the overturned pickup like it was a lifeboat.

The Stone Serpent roared, revealing a wide maw lined with two hundred metal teeth, each capable of chewing through a tank.

The guttural growl echoed through the forest, but the creature didn't seem eager to attack the remaining soldiers just yet.

The overturned pickup had an elemental power generator on board. Stone Serpents hate electricity more than anything and wouldn't go near it, let alone eat it, which meant...

"Well, hello there, friend," I said with a smile, looking at the giant stone face that had turned toward me. "And how did you end up here?"

The creature's amber eyes locked onto me with intense focus. Broad stone plates laced with flexible copper insets twisted along the length of its thirty-three-foot body in an elaborate pattern. A sharp fin protruded from its forehead, and its metal teeth gleamed menacingly.

This was a rare and deadly creature, usually found only in Portals of the Earth Element, and it didn't often venture beyond them.

How on earth did it get past the Tower's defenses and end up here? Where were the guards these idiot Princes were supposed to have posted to intercept threats? How had other Paladins allowed a breach outside Argus's perimeter? And if they did mess up, where was the cleanup crew?

So many questions, and no answers...

As I pondered how the Stone Serpent had gotten here, it lost patience and lunged at me with a hiss.

Leaving a deep furrow in its wake and snapping branches, the beast gathered speed and leapt.

Impatient thing.

"Up we go." I exhaled sharply, jumping ten feet into the air and catching hold of a branch.

One measly energy point spent from my scarce reserves, but it was worth it. The Stone Serpent didn't have time to react to my maneuver and slammed headlong into a massive tree trunk.

A loud, clanging sound echoed through the area as the dazed creature recoiled to the side.

Perfect opportunity for an attack — too bad I didn't have a proper weapon at hand.

Finding nothing better nearby, I reached for the closest branch and yanked it. It didn't budge!

"What the hell..." I muttered, only now noticing a faint elemental aura radiating from the tree. "Well, that's interesting." I smirked, gripping the branch with both hands.

A couple of sharp kicks, another *erg* spent, and now I had a three-foot-long wooden shaft with tiny metallic flecks embedded in it.

There was no time to figure out how an off-world elemental tree had sprouted in the middle of Imperial lands. I took aim at the dazed serpent and hurled the shaft.

The makeshift weapon landed directly in the creature's amber eye, sending it into a frenzy as it began thrashing its stone tail wildly against the tree. The now one-eyed Stone Serpent was so intent on felling the poor tree that it didn't notice me slipping down and rolling to the side.

The creature's vision worked in such a way that when one eye was damaged, the other temporarily went blind. So I had a bit of time to prepare a proper attack, but I didn't have enough energy for a lethal strike.

"What am I supposed to do with you now?" I scratched my head, watching as the persistent, blind serpent continued its furious battle with the tree.

It even seemed like it was winning, with splinters flying everywhere.

A voice suddenly called out from behind me, sharp and urgent. "Hey, man!"

I lazily glanced over my shoulder to see an interesting sight.

The burly driver, having apparently forgotten that he'd nearly died moments ago, was laughing at the serpent's stupidity. It seemed he was wholeheartedly rooting for the tree in this strange duel.

His younger, lanky colleague was taking in the scene a bit more soberly, watching with wide, terrified eyes. But it didn't help much; he was frozen in place, too scared to move a muscle.

The one shouting was an older, sturdily built man with graying hair, clad in black armor with a red star on the shoulder. Most likely the leader of this odd squad. At least, he was the only one in the trio who stayed fully focused.

"Need some help?" I asked.

"Actually, it's the opposite..." The older man bit his lip, visibly wrestling with himself.

I could see it in his eyes — if not for his injured leg, his depleted energy, and the two greenhorns behind him, this warrior would have charged straight into battle with the serpent without a second thought.

That kind of courage deserved respect. Not every commoner has that kind of bravery.

"Well, spit it out." I sighed. "That serpent won't stay dazed for long."

"I was going to ask for your help..." he finally decided, "our combat elementalist was the first one the creature swallowed, and only he could keep it distracted. But you look like a capable man, someone who can handle it. We just need three minutes... to get the vehicle back upright."

"Why didn't you flip it over right away?" I shook my head. "You might have gotten away in time."

"Well..." the older man murmured hesitantly, glancing away. "We thought it would eat you first."

"And now you're worried I'll just run off." I smirked.

"You'd be within your rights to." The older man

nodded seriously. "I'm just laying it out as it is, man. If you decide to leave, we're done for. The serpent's blind, but not deaf. If we start up the transport, it'll sense the vibrations and attack. And without the vehicle, none of us will last an hour in this forest. But if you lead the serpent away, we'll come back for you. Without its eyes, the creature won't be fast. We can make it."

A Stone Serpent roaming free... an elemental tree in the heart of the Empire... and a commoner warrior seriously hinting that this serpent wasn't the only danger lurking in the forest... Was I really home?

Well, one problem at a time. And the most pressing one right now was a thirty-three-foot stone menace, which had finally felled its tree opponent and was now scanning the area for a new target.

Of course, I had no intention of running away.

Imagine that — a Paladin fleeing from a portal creature. Ridiculous.

Granted, there had been a few tactical retreats back when I was young and green — say, seven years ago — but let's not dwell on that.

"Alright, old man," I agreed, "you'll get your three minutes."

"Really?" he asked, his eyes widening in disbelief.

"Really," I confirmed. "You got a weapon?"

"Y-yeah," he stammered, glancing around wildly until his eyes landed on the lanky young colleague.

Without a second's hesitation, the warrior deftly yanked a longsword from the boy's belt and tossed it to me.

I caught the "gift" and gave it a spin in my hand, sizing it up.

Earth-forged metal, not Portal-infused. Balance is mediocre, and the elemental conductivity is garbage. The sort of thing you'd give to kids in a sandbox, but hey, better than nothing.

"It'll do." I nodded and took off in the opposite direction from the pickup.

"How could you just give him my family sword!" a voice wailed behind me.

"What 'family' sword? You won it in a card game!"

"And I was planning to pass it down to my son!"

"You don't have any kids!"

"To my future kids!"

"Shut up, Martyn, and start flipping! One... two... lift!"

I didn't hear the rest, because the serpent's furious hiss drowned out all other sounds in the area.

It had finally spotted me.

I thought I'd have to step on its tail to get its attention.

The creature narrowed its one good eye at me menacingly and charged.

"Again, without any preparation?" I said, shaking my head disapprovingly. "No respect for your opponent."

I ran a fair distance, then stopped and turned to face it.

I had misjudged the serpent. This time, it was moving cautiously. It didn't charge straight in but kept two-thirds of its body safely underground.

Satisfied that I was staying put, the Stone Serpent began circling me like a shark, sending surges of earth my way from a distance.

I dodged easily, gripping the sword in a reverse hold, and waited.

Then the forest echoed with the roar of engines. The serpent slowed, clearly hearing that its prey was trying to escape, but didn't break its circle.

Of course, the vengeful creature knew I was the one who'd gouged out its eye, and it wouldn't leave until it settled the score.

But it had no intention of letting the others go either. So, it picked up speed, closing the circle's radius.

The waves of earth kept battering me, trying to knock me down, but I held my balance until, suddenly, the creature's tail tip shot up right beneath me.

I dodged to the side, letting the metal spike pass in front of me, but the serpent had anticipated that and struck my supporting leg, sending me sprawling to the ground.

A sharp, guttural hiss erupted from the creature. "*Hssssaaahh!*"

Its open maw loomed over me, but the faint smile on my face went unnoticed by the half-blind serpent as it lunged down with its massive, multi-ton frame.

* * *

"N-Nick, why are you stopping?" Martyn's voice cracked with panic. "Floor it!"

"No orders to leave," Nick replied coolly, his broad shoulders giving a slight shrug as he continued to watch, entranced, as the Stone Serpent rocketed into the air and crashed down on the strange vagrant they'd encountered in the dead forest.

"It's over!" Martyn spat bitterly. "The guy's toast... and he destroyed my sword, too, the bastard!"

But the order to leave never came. Retired Imperial Service Captain Edward continued to watch in silence, observing what seemed to be the end of the battle between man and beast.

"Are you messing with me, old man?" Martyn snapped, grabbing the captain by the collar. "He's dead! Dead! Let's go!"

"No, kid," Edward replied firmly, easily brushing the boy aside. "I gave my word that we'd pick him up."

"There's no one left to pick up!" Martyn shouted, his frustration boiling over. "That thing ate your vagrant! Don't you care that my sword was sacrificed for nothing?"

"He's moving," Nick noted quietly, missing how the scrawny kid slipped past him and, with all his might, stomped on the gas pedal.

The engine roared, but the vehicle didn't budge an inch.

The vehicle's propulsion system required elemental energy input, which Martyn didn't have to begin with. He'd joined the squad after swiping an old map from a drunk aristocrat a month ago, only to discover that its information was way outdated, leading his first real foray at age fifteen slightly off course.

"We're all gonna die..." Martyn muttered in despair, sinking to his knees. His terrified gaze shifted to the living mountain of stone and earth, which was indeed moving slowly, heralding their imminent doom.

But five seconds passed without an attack. Another five seconds, and suddenly, a human hand burst out of the mass of rock and soil.

In dead silence, the trio watched as the human figure emerged, like some corpse rising leisurely from the grave.

The familiar vagrant stood up and brushed himself off. Dirt, blood, and the creature's insides slid off his tattered cloak without leaving a single stain. Not a scratch marred the man himself.

"Where's my sword?" Martyn asked, alarmed at the sight of the man's empty hands.

"Screw your rusty sword," Nick muttered, picking his jaw up off the floor. "I want a cloak like that..."

"Wanna try taking it from him?" Edward said with a smirk.

“N-no, I’d rather stay alive,” the driver said quickly, shaking his head, watching in awe as the vagrant, with an unbothered half-smile on his face, walked towards them.

CHAPTER 2

KILLING THE STONE SERPENT cost me four *ergs*, and it refilled my reserves by only six.

Not much to brag about.

Sure, I could've drawn out another ten units of energy from its dead body, but that would've taken at least half an hour, which I didn't have.

I took the gray-haired man's warning about the forest's dangers seriously. I could feel it myself — the danger in the air. My instincts, honed by battle, were sharply attuned to my surroundings.

The flora around me seemed earthly at first glance, but a closer look revealed that every tree, leaf, and blade of grass was tainted by off-world elemental energy. The corruption ran deep and had been there for quite a while, which just didn't add up in my mind.

"Welcome aboard," Edward greeted, extending

a hand to help me into the truck bed. Then he gave Nick the signal, and the pickup sped off.

"Thanks for the sword," I said, settling onto the side bench.

"No big deal." He shrugged, sitting across from me.

"It is a big deal!" Martyn protested with a scowl. "I only got it back from the grinder yesterday, wrapped the hilt in leather, and added a cool engraving!"

"Engraving, you say? You didn't mention that," Edward raised an eyebrow in mock surprise. "And what did it say?"

"'Martyn, Scourge of the Valleys!'" Martyn blurted out passionately, and the pickup exploded with laughter.

Neither Nick nor Edward spared the young one, and even I couldn't suppress a smile. Martyn, though, pouted and turned away, trying to hide his reddened face.

Ah, youth. Once, I too burned with that kind of reckless enthusiasm — until around age eight, anyway. Those were the days... until old Aks had mercilessly beaten that childish nonsense out of me, along with anything else that held me back from getting stronger.

"Don't worry about the sword," Edward said, catching his breath from laughing. "Consider it payment for the help. We wouldn't have made it out without you."

"I'm not used to running; I was just protecting my own life." I shrugged.

"Even so!" Edward retorted. "In doing so, you saved three lives. And I always repay my debts. My misguided grandson Martyn paid with his sword for the life you saved. The man at the wheel is Nick, and his contribution to you is a free ride in this beauty, and here's my part."

With that, Edward handed me a worn tactical backpack.

"This belonged to Greg, our elementalist. May he rest in peace. He won't need it anymore, but you might," he said with a sad smile.

Not quite understanding, I opened the backpack and couldn't help but smile. For a down-and-out guy like me, this was the perfect gift.

"Nothing fancy, but it's clean," Edward said with an air of importance. "Should fit you well enough, too. You'll also find a canteen of water, some rations, a couple of bandages, a compass, a bit of money, and some other odds and ends."

"Thank you." I nodded gratefully and started changing.

Parading around in a stiff, scratchy cloak was no fun, so I gladly pulled on some normal, soft clothes underneath. The chill in the forest was bad enough to freeze everything off.

I got to work on the rations right away, washing them down with half the water in the canteen. Life instantly felt two times better. A hot shower would make it perfect.

"You're welcome." Edward waited patiently until I finished. "You saved our lives; it's the least I could do. Sorry, but it's all we have, as they say."

"It's more than enough," I assured him, munching on a biscuit.

"That's good to hear." He smiled. "By the way, name's Edward. You can just call me Cap."

"Marcus." I introduced myself belatedly.

"Hey, good to meet you, Marcus!" Nick waved. "Man, you took down that beast like a pro! Gives me chills just thinking about it! How'd you do it?"

"Experience," I replied with a shrug.

"So, you're a combat elementalist," Edward mused with respect. "Sorry, I didn't realize at first. Your eyes look too normal for a Gifted."

"My connection to the Element has weakened," I said honestly.

Edward frowned slightly but kept his thoughts to himself.

"Yeah, right." Martyn scoffed. "Everyone knows a Gifted's eyes never lose their color! He killed the creature by pure luck and now he's playing it up..."

I ignored the young one's outburst. I had no desire to convince him otherwise. He was young — life would teach him soon enough.

My thoughts were much more focused on where we were headed.

I'd thought I might recognize the area once we got farther, but the gloomy forest landscape showed no sign of changing. This strange elemental forest stretched endlessly in all directions...

"So how'd you end up alone in a place like this, Marcus?" Edward asked cautiously after a pause.

It was only natural that my appearance and behavior would raise questions and reasonable suspicions. After all, to them, I was a stranger — even if I'd saved their lives.

"Closing a Portal," I replied, almost truthfully.

I wasn't planning on being too open, but I couldn't remain completely silent either. I had too many questions about what was happening around me, and to get answers to even some of them, I couldn't be seen as a threat.

"On your own?" Edward looked me over with a skeptical smirk.

"There were three of us initially," I explained, "but in the end, I was the only survivor."

As old Aks liked to say, "Honesty is the quickest path to respect." And my old mentor knew his way around these things far better than I did.

"I see." Edward nodded sympathetically. "My condolences, Marcus. Losing people is always rough. Greg was a hired elementalist, and I'd only known him for two weeks, but I can still see that serpent devouring him alive every time I close my eyes. But that's just part of our lot."

"Closed many Portals, have you?" I asked.

"Heh, no, not us commoners," Edward replied with a sad smile. "When I served in His Majesty's Imperial Guard, my job was to cover the noble backsides of those who closed Portals. So, are you from a clan or are you a free agent?"

What a strange distinction.

Truthfully, I was neither.

My first impulse was to tell him that I was the

First Paladin of the Argus Order, but something held me back, and I stayed silent.

Not because I feared Edward might be linked to those who'd trapped me — no. I was confident I could handle all three of them if necessary. The issue was something else.

It just felt... wrong, somehow. In fact, everything around me felt off. Take this corrupted forest, for example, which just kept going and going.

Where did it even come from? Sure, the Order might have missed one off-world tree, maybe even a dozen. But an entire forest?

I couldn't wrap my head around it.

"If you don't want to answer, I won't press," Edward said, interpreting my thoughtful silence in his own way. He tapped a strange device on his wrist, and a holographic map appeared in front of him.

Interesting. A precision Light Element artifact in the hands of a commoner? Then again, after seeing a levitating pickup powered purely by elemental energy, I was getting harder to surprise. Just another oddity.

The glowing lines on the hologram gradually formed a map of the area. I recognized it with some relief as my homeland — though lacking any roads, settlement names, or other markers.

In the northern part of the map, I could make out the silhouette of the Great Tower... wait, moving away?

"Aren't we heading toward the Tower?" I asked, slightly puzzled.

"The Tower? Definitely not," Edward said, tearing his eyes away from the map. "We got closer to it than anyone has in years, and it was all for nothing," he added, giving Martyn a displeased look.

"Oh, come on, guys!" Martyn threw up his hands. "You saw the cave yourselves! It exists! How was I supposed to know the creatures' range had shifted!"

"You could have known because it's always shifting, and your map is a hundred years old!" Edward chuckled, though not unkindly. His annoyance seemed more directed at himself for failing to foresee the risk, resulting in the loss of one of his men.

"Hold on." I frowned slightly, noticing our location marker drifting further south. "What did you mean when you said we were closer to the Tower than anyone?"

"I meant exactly that," Edward replied with a wry smile, pressing a few more buttons on his device.

The holographic map zoomed out and filled with three colors — green, yellow, and red.

"Take a look," Edward continued, pointing to the moving dot. "We'll soon leave the Red Zone, an area confirmed to be infested with portal creatures. The only ones who venture in here are clan raids armed to the teeth or crazy folks like us trying to catch a bit of luck. And since the Princes' Council has its annual summit today, it's unlikely any clan members are closer to the Tower than we are."

Edward seemed to have finished speaking, but I kept staring at the massive Red Zone centered on the Tower. The area looked like it spanned about thirty-eight thousand six hundred square miles. And it was all overrun with portal creatures? Was this some kind of joke?

Curiosity welled up inside me, but outwardly I showed no reaction. They were already looking at me warily.

Sure, I could try to force the information out of them, but that wasn't my style. These people hadn't wronged me; I'd need to find another way.

"What about the people who live in the Tower?" I couldn't resist asking at least one question.

There were at least thirty-five thousand people within the Argus perimeter — the Council of Magisters, the Paladins, Order members, scholars, mentors, staff, followers, and their families…

"Did you get hit on the head with a rock or something? The Tower's uninhabited. There's no one there, and there never has been," Edward said firmly, folding up the map.

"My great-grandfather told me that long ago, mighty warriors lived there," Nick chimed in excitedly. "They mastered the Elements, closed Portals with a single look, and could destroy thousands of creatures with a snap of their fingers!"

"And I heard a Demon-God lives there," Martyn blurted out, "leading an invasion from hell! That's why the strongest Portals open near the Tower, and the creatures gather around it. They're protecting their creator!"

"That's all nonsense." Edward waved it off. "When I was a kid, my grandmother told me aliens dropped the Tower from the sky as punishment for humanity's sins. Are you going to believe that too?"

"Well." Nick chuckled. "Maybe it's true. Though I like the Northerners' version better. They believe the Tower is the afterlife, where fallen warriors go when they die. They sit there in safety, feasting and celebrating. Now that's romantic!"

"Yeah, I could go for a feast myself right now," Martyn said, drooling. "Tender meat, fresh garlic bread, and cold cider!"

"And a naked girl by your side," Nick added.

"Make it two!" Martyn nodded enthusiastically, flopping onto his side with a dreamy grin.

"And what would you do with them, you little fool?" Edward sighed. "Still wet behind the ears, and already thinking about women…"

The conversation gradually faded, replaced by silence.

The vehicle moved along smoothly. Dense forest alternated with clearings and sparse groves. The gloomy daylight took on a bluish hue. From the hill we'd just climbed, I could barely make out the distant spire of the Argus Tower.

The crown jewel of human achievement and the sole reason why humanity had been able to resist countless off-world creatures for centuries. Not just resist — the Great Source of the Tower had been capable of storing energy from other worlds, allowing humans to use that energy against their invaders, giving them hope of one day ending the threat for good.

And now the Great Source was lost. What had you humans done while I was gone...

In the calming silence, broken only by the steady hum of elemental engines, I finally put together one last, crucial question in my mind.

A question that, once answered, could explain all the strange things happening around me.

A question to which, I was already beginning to suspect, I knew the answer.

"Tell me, Edward... what year is it?"

CHAPTER 3

"YOU SURE YOU DIDN'T HIT your head?" Edward, who had been dozing, gave me a concerned look.

"I'm fine," I replied calmly. "I just spent a long time in that Portal."

"Yeah, that's obvious," Martyn quickly chimed in with a snide remark, earning a painful elbow to the ribs from his grandfather.

"It's the year 2723," Edward finally answered. "September."

So there it was. While I spent a year looking for a way out of that trap, nearly seven hundred years had passed here.

No wonder the world had changed. And clearly not for the better, considering humanity had somehow lost control of the Great Tower.

But, strangely, this thought didn't sadden me. Nor did it make me angry.

I wondered why.

Maybe, deep down, I felt that humanity — the same humanity that had betrayed me — deserved these consequences?

Who knows.

One thing was clear: getting into the Tower wouldn't be simple, even if I wanted to. The Stone Serpent was right on the Red Zone's edge, and I'd barely had enough energy reserves to bring it down. And it was far from the most dangerous off-world creature out there.

With my energy source depleted and my connection to the Element practically non-existent, I wouldn't get far.

Sure, I could break through if I really wanted to... but what would I find in the Tower?

Other than old Aks, I had no family, and I had no idea what had happened to the world in my absence. How long ago was the Tower lost? Why? Did any of the Order survive? Was the Great Source still intact?

Rushing in without information would be foolish. But if I couldn't return to the Tower, then where was I supposed to go?

In seven hundred years, generations had come and gone. And there was no one left to avenge old Aks. Everyone I'd known was long dead.

But then, that meant... no one who had known me was alive either.

The thought washed over me, bringing a strange wave of relief. For the first time in my life, I felt a heady sense of freedom.

Could it be that, after twenty years of endless battles, I was truly free of the burdens imposed on me?

Free from the weight of expectations, the guilt, and the responsibility for humanity that had been my constant companions since I was five years old, when the Order's magisters identified my Element as Darkness and proclaimed me the chosen one.

Since that day, everyone had cared only about two things: whether I would save the world or destroy it.

How I felt or what I wanted didn't matter to anyone.

"So, where are we headed, Cap?" I asked.

"To Fort-Hell, didn't I say?" Edward replied, scratching his head.

"Must've been lost in thought and missed it," I said, stretching my stiff neck. "Fort-Hell, then. And that would be...?"

"You're not local, are you?" Edward asked, though he didn't seem particularly surprised.

"Well, let's just say I lived north of here," I replied, glancing toward the Tower.

"Knew it! I knew you were from the North!" Martyn sprang up. "Everyone north of the Tower is crazy!"

"And how would you know, you idiot?" Edward sighed heavily. "You've never even seen one, and the first Northerner you meet just saved your life."

"Anyone could've done it with my sword!" Martyn scoffed.

"So why were you standing there with wet

pants?" Nick laughed.

"It was the rain! It was wet out there! Wet, got it!" Martyn shouted, his voice cracking as he slunk back into the corner.

The rest of the journey passed quietly.

Martyn was going out of his way to prove his usefulness, Edward was teaching the boy a few life lessons, and Nick occasionally threw out sarcastic comments as he skillfully navigated through the dangerous territory.

We didn't encounter a single portal creature on the way, though I spotted plenty of traces of their presence.

As I learned later, Nick was following a carefully calculated safe route. One wrong move or turn could have led us straight into a deadly ambush, but our driver was the best pilot south of the Tower, and crossing the Yellow Zone was child's play for him.

I couldn't tell how many hours had passed, but we arrived while there was still daylight.

The sun was just starting to dip below the horizon when massive stone walls appeared up ahead. Made from elemental stone, they were incredibly strong and curved outward to form the Third Outer Ring.

People had built these walls centuries ago to keep escaped portal creatures contained within the Tower's vicinity and prevent them from reaching the cities.

They'd been successful to varying degrees. Each year, the Red Zone grew larger, and the first two rings of walls, closer to the Tower, had been lost forever.

I gathered this much from fragments of my companions' conversations.

Wide gates made of elemental metal let us through into the perimeter. I had to admit, the fortifications were solid. Six watchtowers, a reinforced bastion, and two dozen elemental combat installations on the walls gave the place an imposing look. Not many portal creatures could survive under such concentrated fire.

Behind the gates, we entered a full-scale military settlement with dozens of fortified buildings and a vast training field. A quick glance told me there were about two hundred Imperial soldiers stationed here. Interestingly, only about ten of them seemed to be capable elementalists.

Not the best defense for a frontline outpost. But the soldiers' equipment was impressive. None of the weaponry looked familiar, but the elemental energy surrounding the place was substantial.

Passing through the checkpoint required an inspection, but it took less than a minute. As soon as the guards confirmed that Edward's squad was returning empty-handed with nothing to tax, they quickly lost interest in us.

"Four went out, four came back, no undeclared cargo," a slick customs officer in glasses announced dryly, scribbling on his tablet before slapping his hand on the pickup. "Welcome to Fort-Hell, gentlemen."

With his words, the barrier lifted, and we were

free to exit the military settlement. After five minutes of winding along a deserted mountain road, the pickup stopped at a narrow fork.

"Well, Marcus, this is where you go on alone," Nick said in his deep voice. "The entrance to the city is just down that road."

"Not heading that way yourselves?" I asked out of courtesy as I slung my backpack over my shoulders.

"We've got some other business to take care of," Nick replied without much enthusiasm.

From their grim expressions, I gathered their business wasn't pleasant, but I had no intention of prying. These people had already done more for me than I'd expected, and I was grateful.

"Be careful out there, Marcus," Edward said, clapping me on the shoulder. "Fort-Hell is the largest logistics hub in the south, but there's always a shortage of labor and funding. If they find out you're a refugee without documents, they'll work you to the bone, likely to death, before they let you go. I don't know what it's like up north, but down here, don't expect much fairness. Strength rules the south."

"Charming customs you've got." I smirked, hopping down from the truck. "I'll keep it in mind. Thanks."

"No problem." Edward waved it off. "My conscience would eat me alive if the man who saved my life kicked the bucket before I do."

"Yeah, do us a favor and try not to die, Marcus," Nick added. "Cap's lost too many good men as it is, and old men shouldn't be burying the young."

"You won't have to bury me; I promise," I said with a nod, waving them off.

"That's good to hear," Edward said, smiling from the retreating pickup.

They seemed to have urgent business, as Nick floored it like he was expecting a chase. Though, maybe that was just his driving style. You barely felt the speed inside the vehicle.

Now alone, I stretched my shoulders and started walking toward the city.

My mood was unexpectedly light. Without the weight of responsibility, it was easier to breathe, as if I were on vacation — for the first time in my life. I wondered, what do regular people do to relax?

With those thoughts, I climbed a hill, and below me, the city came into view.

"Wow." I whistled, taking in the massive buildings illuminated by hundreds of lights.

The city was surrounded by a fan of various fortifications along its approach routes to slow down the advance of creatures, giving the residents a chance to escape and the military time to respond.

Fort-Hell stretched out in a wide semi-circle, split down the middle by a broad central street.

The city was much larger than I'd expected — three, maybe five times the size of my home base, Argus Castle, which lay at the foot of the Great Tower.

And yet, regular people lived here, right next to the Red Zone, without fear.

In my day, there were no large settlements near the Tower, aside from Argus Castle. Large gatherings of people attracted portal creatures like a magnet, and protecting crowds of civilians was no easy task.

There hadn't even been a small village here in the past. But now, look — an entire Imperial city with fortified perimeters, an industrial sector, large residential areas, and even a railway.

The brightest lights were in the city center, so that's where I headed. But from here, the wide road split into three narrower ones, each winding down through dense forest with significant elevation changes.

How was I supposed to know which road led to the center? There were no signs. I stood there for a few moments, reasoning that the central road would logically lead to the heart of the city, then set off down it.

The sun had set beyond the horizon, and the trees on either side blocked my view, so I just stayed on my chosen path, whistling as I went.

The vegetation around me was untainted, so the only threat on the way was boredom.

If only I could stumble upon a real Portal, kill a few hundred creatures, recharge my energy reserves, strengthen my connection to the Element, and shake off the boredom. Just to remind my body what it felt like to fight to the death.

A year in the dead desert had made me forget

that exhilarating rush of battle and adrenaline. I missed it. The skirmish with the serpent had only whetted my appetite.

"And I wouldn't mind a bite to eat, either," I muttered, rubbing my rumbling stomach as I finally approached the city.

But judging by the dim lighting, the long concrete fence, and the smoking chimneys off to the side, I realized that this road hadn't led me to the center after all.

"Show me," I commanded, raising my hand.

A small dark wisp emerged from my palm and transformed into the shape of a butterfly, which fluttered up into the air.

The butterfly was slow, had no combat capabilities, and disappeared as soon as I glimpsed the direction to the main street. Not much of a scout, but I wasn't willing to spend more than one unit of energy.

The area I was in was off the main streets and bordered the industrial zone. The scenery matched: dark, damp alleys, grime, rot, and the stench of a hundred decaying bodies blended into a single, picturesque image.

Annoying, yes, but it couldn't ruin my mood or dampen my growing hunger.

All I needed was to find my way out of this maze to the main streets, where I could surely find food and a place to spend the night.

With that thought, I crossed another narrow alley, turned right, and stopped.

Three thugs with toothless grins were walking

toward me.

"Well, look what we've got here. Seems we picked the right time for a stroll," the one in the center rasped, clearly the ringleader.

"Yeah, but not such lucky timing for you, kid," the bald brute on my left said, cracking his knuckles for emphasis.

"Heh-heh," added the third, a big-eared lackey who pulled a dagger from under his jacket.

"Oh!" I exclaimed cheerfully. "Just who I needed! I got lost in these alleyways. Mind pointing me toward the main streets?"

The three snickered as they drew closer. The leader stayed in front of me while the bald one and the lackey flanked me, already eyeing my belongings.

"Of course we'll help. Why wouldn't we?" the leader chuckled hoarsely. "We'll even carry your things for you, right, boys?"

"Right, right," his friends agreed eagerly.

At that moment, the bald one suddenly grabbed my backpack, pulling me toward a fist armed with brass knuckles. I shrugged off the weight, dropped to a crouch, and let the blow sail over my head.

Then I straightened quickly, bringing the edge of my hand down onto his throat. He collapsed to the ground, clutching my backpack.

"You bastard!" the big-eared lackey squealed, lunging at me with his knife.

Too slow and too clumsy. I easily deflected his hand and drove my knee into his stomach, the crunch of ribs confirming he was out of the fight.

The leader was the only one left standing. His grin was gone, but he wasn't running.

"Have you lost your mind, idiot?" he rasped, glancing back. "Do you even know who I am?"

"I do." I nodded, slipping my backpack back on and stepping forward. "A dead man."

The leader flinched. The corner was far, and fighting clearly wasn't on his mind anymore.

"H-how… dead man…" he stammered, backing away.

His eyes darted to his fallen friends, and a flicker of envy crossed his face as he realized they'd survived by acting more boldly than he had.

"Well, it's simple." I sighed, drawing a finger across my throat. "A dark alley, anything can happen."

"Wait, wait, wait…" the would-be thug babbled in terror, dropping to his knees, realizing escape was hopeless. "Y-you wanted the center, right? I'll show you! I know the way! I know every inch of this place! They call me 'the Head' for a reason!"

"You'll guide me? With a broken leg?" I said with a smile.

"W-what? My leg's fine…" he started, confused, but then his eyes widened as he caught on.

What else could he expect? As old Aks used to say, "The leader bears triple responsibility for his subordinates." I'd learned that lesson the hard way through sweat and blood. Now it was my turn to pass the light of knowledge to others.

"A-a map!" he croaked hopefully, pulling a

crumpled sheet of paper from his jacket with trembling hands. "Here... we're right here..."

Seconds later, a black marker appeared in his hand, and he hurriedly traced a zigzag line across the wrinkled map, mumbling to himself before proudly handing it to me with a toothless grin.

"The black dot is us, and this line's the quickest way to the main street. Just ten minutes! And if anyone stops you on the way, say you're a friend of the Head, and everything'll be just fine! I swear!"

"So, 'the Head,' huh?" I mused, twirling the paper in my hand.

The crumpled sheet turned out to be a decent map of this part of the city, marked with several notes in the margins.

"Won't your pals kill you for spilling the details, Head?"

"N-no..." the thug drawled, rising slowly. "I'm, uh... a cartographer..." he declared with a look of importance. "Grew up here. Nobody knows the south like I do. I've got, uh... empirical memory!"

"Eidetic," I corrected.

"Yeah, that's it." He nodded vigorously. "I drew that map in half an hour today."

"They call you the Head for that?"

"Nah," he said, scratching the back of his head. "Once, a brick fell on my head... and, well... it broke, but I didn't even notice. Just brushed it off and kept walking. So they gave me the name."

"I see." I nodded knowingly, tucking the map into my pocket. "Then I'll deal with you according to your name."

"Wait, what do you mea—"

He didn't finish. A quick hook to the eye slammed his head into the corner of the building, and he dropped to the ground, unconscious beside his buddies.

The blow had been hard, but he didn't even bleed. A solid skull, indeed.

When he came to, he'd probably thank me. Even if he was valuable as the gang's "cartographer," returning unscathed after his buddies nearly got killed would spell trouble.

With the map, it was easy to escape the dark maze of alleys; it took no more than ten minutes. Any portal creatures that managed to get into the city would have a hard time finding their way to the residential areas.

Emerging onto the main street, I felt as if I'd entered another world. Everything around me was alight and shimmering with thousands of lights. Elegant buildings in strange shapes lined the wide stone-paved street in neat rows.

Brightly reinforced facades, windows resembling slits for archery, solitary balconies fitted with combat installations instead of flowers.

Yet the place buzzed with life, and dozens of colorful signs beckoned passersby. There were quite a few people around, dressed... diversely.

Some in business suits, others in shorts and shirts, some in military gear. The bright city center lured all its residents like moths to a flame. The sheer flood of new information left me a bit overwhelmed.

But my stomach quickly reminded me of my priorities, rumbling loudly.

Just then, the smell of freshly baked bread wafted over, but my gaze was suddenly fixed on a black and gold emblem painted in the shape of wings. It had been crudely slapped over an old wooden sign bearing the worn word Tavern.

Thoughts of food immediately faded into the background. The emblem was the mark of my old Order of Argus.

CHAPTER 4

THE OLD TWO-STORY TAVERN looked completely out of place amidst the fortified giants surrounding it. Small and weathered, it was like a blot of grime on a pristine white dress, standing out awkwardly against the lively street's polished facade. Yet, people had learned to tolerate its presence — and the crooked emblem on its sign, familiar to any Paladin or servant of the Argus Order.

Though the symbol of the Order was faded and skewed, it was unmistakably there.

The floorboards creaked, announcing my entrance. My eyes, adjusted to the bright outdoors, squinted in the dimness of the Tavern's first floor, lit by a single, flickering bulb.

"Welcome," muttered the man behind the bar, casting me a dour look. He stood behind a plain wooden counter, once a proper bar, now stripped

bare with shelves cleared and no tables around —
a sure sign they hadn't served a meal here in ages.

"The bar's two alleys down," he added, voice as
unwelcoming as my bedraggled appearance probably warranted.

"I need a place to stay the night," I said, lowering my bag as a sign I wasn't about to leave.

The man looked me up and down. "Three hundred," he announced, nodding toward a corner
where mattresses lay strewn across the floor, half
of them occupied by sleeping figures.

Three hundred for a grimy mat, moldy walls,
and the lingering odor of the street? I'd just as
soon sleep outside.

"Got a room with a real bed?" I asked, though
not very hopefully.

"Two thousand," he replied immediately, curt
and unwilling to haggle.

He had me figured out as a non-local without
other options, and he was right. The five one-thousand bills I'd found in my bag were all I had. Not
much, but better than nothing.

Accepting that he wouldn't deal with a scruffy
drifter like me, I counted out two thousand and
laid them on the counter.

He raised a brow in mild surprise but didn't
show it. Once he realized I had cash, his disdain
was tempered with a glint of interest.

"That's quite an emblem on your sign," I said
casually, taking advantage of his softening atti-
tude. "What's it mean?"

"Beats me. It was there when I was born," he

said, flipping open a worn ledger. "Got your papers?"

"I'm afraid I lost them."

He shut the book, frowning. "Then it'll be four thousand."

I nearly choked at the audacity of it, but my desire for a bed outweighed my urge to throw punches.

"Got hot water?"

"Shared shower upstairs," he replied.

"Fine," I agreed and exchanged the four bills for a key.

"Room eleven," he said, a bit more cheerfully.

"That emblem really does look familiar," I remarked, spinning the key idly in my hand. "A noble family crest, maybe?"

"Nah, we're just regular folk," he said, warming up after receiving the money. "The place has been handed down through the family for generations, always with that sign. Might have meant something once, but now it's just an old scrawl. My dad tried to paint over it once, but my grandpa nearly blew a gasket."

"Killed him over a scribble?" I chuckled, slinging my pack over my shoulder.

"Said we'd be cursed and punished by our ancestors if we covered it up." He shrugged. "Old fool, probably just senile."

"You had a wise granddad," I said with a grin.

"No, my dad was right. I'll paint over it the moment I can afford it." He sighed with disdain and hurried off.

Odd fellow. Didn't even give me his name. With service like this, it was no surprise his business was barely hanging on.

From our brief conversation, I'd gathered that the Order was long gone — or, at least, unrecognizable from the Order I'd once known. Still, it seemed some of them had managed to escape from Argus.

I'd secured a place to sleep, but my growling stomach still demanded attention. After a hot shower, a shave, and a quick change, I came downstairs feeling refreshed.

My tattered black cloak stood out, so I wrapped it around my right arm beneath my shirt. Leaving my only remaining possession in the room wasn't an option.

"A hot shower...that's the life," I murmured with satisfaction as I descended the stairs.

Especially after a year of wandering.

In that dead desert, I'd have given more than just four crumpled bills for a chance to wash. Money didn't mean much to me in my former life — Paladins of the Order had never lacked for it. In the Order, what mattered was strength, and it was rewarded so richly it could have sustained a hundred lifetimes.

"Glad you liked it," the innkeeper replied, a bit more welcoming now. He looked neater, sporting a bow tie and a name badge that read "Simon."

"Hey, Simon," I said, leaning on the counter. "Know where a guy might find some nobility in this town?"

"Nobility?" His eyes widened. "Why... would you want to know?" He inched back slightly.

"Oh, just for a chat." I waved a hand. "The Princes must pass through here sometimes, right?"

"Princes?" Simon looked even more astonished. "Now and then, but..."

"But?" I pressed him with a steady gaze.

"That kind of information is... sensitive," he said, recovering his composure. That mercenary glint was back in his eye.

"Not free, then." I sighed, eyeing the last thousand in my pocket. No — this one was for food. I'd figure out the answers the old-fashioned way.

"Fine. Can you at least tell me where I can eat?" I asked, narrowing my eyes. "Not a crumb in here, and I need somewhere loud and crowded."

"Try the roadside stands on Fifth Street," he said knowledgeably. "Big places won't let you in without papers, and newcomers are better off avoiding unguarded places."

"I think I'll risk it." I ignored his advice. "What's the busiest unguarded spot?"

"The Duck's Nail, down the southern alley past the church," Simon said reluctantly.

"Perfect, thanks, Simon," I said with a grin and stepped out into the cool night air.

The refreshing breeze was a balm to my senses. Now all I needed was a meal, some rest, and a tipsy noble willing to share how the world had ended up in this state. After that, I'd have time to figure out my next move.

As old Aks used to say, "No good decision ever comes on an empty stomach."

* * *

Simon paced nervously in the back room, unable to settle down. It had only been a little over an hour since that strange newcomer had walked into his establishment. He'd looked like a typical vagrant, just another broke wanderer. Simon saw it right away — the man didn't have much money. But what caught Simon off guard was how easily he'd agreed to pay. A bed in this town would have been hard to find even for two thousand imperial coins, and yet this stranger had handed over four thousand without a word of protest!

Simon had nearly bitten his own tongue, realizing he'd overcharged out of sheer greed...but the stranger didn't even blink. He'd even gone off to shower on his own, like some kind of fool.

Sure, he hadn't brought much with him. But Simon was already envisioning a nice little profit — at least twenty thousand from the Imperials — for a young, healthy captive like this one. And then, things took a turn for the better, promising him an even greater payday.

"Tim!" Simon called, breathless with excitement, the moment the dial tone turned to his friend's voice.

"It's Senior Sergeant Tim, if you please," Tim's voice replied with a chuckle. "What's up? Thought we'd squared away everything with your last order."

"Things have changed." Simon steadied his voice, hiding his nerves. "Price just went up."

"Don't push it, man." Tim's tone turned cold. "We can always leave you high and dry, you know. See how long that dump of yours lasts without us."

"You don't understand." Simon gave a huff of nervous laughter. "He's not just some runaway. The guy's Gifted!"

"Gifted? Didn't you say his eyes were normal?"

"Sure, the eyes, yeah. But the sedative water didn't even faze him. Stood under the spray for thirty minutes, and he's still wide awake."

"Did you remember to turn the artifact on?"

"Don't insult me, Tim!" Simon snapped. "I've been in this business for years! And on top of that, the counter's built-in paralytic didn't work on him either. He leaned right on it, not a twitch."

"Hm, interesting... A rogue Gifted without a clan amulet or papers. Any idea where he's from?"

"No clue. He didn't say. But I've never seen him in town before, and he's been asking strange questions."

"Alright, I'll pull a team together. Is he still there?"

"No, he went off to the Duck's Nail," Simon admitted, a bit embarrassed.

"You let him walk out?" Tim demanded. "They'll kill him there! Or worse — what if he runs?"

"He's not going anywhere," Simon assured him. "Paid for the night and left his stuff in the room. I checked."

"Alright, we'll be there by morning. If he's half as valuable as you say, you'll be dealing with Senior Sergeant Tim from now on! An undocumented Gifted like that is worth his weight in gold — prime slave material!" Tim laughed at his own joke. "Plus, we'll get you a new artifact. The 'Wyvern's Tear' should have even a water elementalist nodding off in no time."

"Maybe the charge is just low," Simon agreed, "but this one walked out of here like a new man — he was even more energized than before!"

"Let him enjoy his last free night, then." Tim chuckled, then hung up.

Simon kept pacing, heart racing with anticipation. He could practically feel the weight of the money waiting for him in the morning.

* * *

In my time, every Imperial inn, no matter how rundown, offered at least basic food for guests. Here, all I'd gotten was the name of a place to go ask for food — and only because I'd pried it out of the owner. This world truly was going to the dogs.

Strolling down the bustling main street, I scanned the buildings around me. Just as Simon had said, nearly every place had armed guards stationed outside, checking documents as people entered. At least the weasel hadn't lied about that.

After turning off the main drag and walking for another ten minutes, I found myself standing before an attractive white building. It had long, darkened windows, sliding doors made of elemental metal, and a sign that glowed with multicolored lights. It looked leagues better than Simon's dingy Tavern, with no guards in sight, so I headed inside.

As soon as I stepped through the doors, I was hit by a wall of noise from the crowd. The interior was simple yet tasteful, with sparse furnishings to maximize the open space. It was packed, with over a hundred people of all sorts milling about. Clearly, the place was popular.

Spotting an empty seat at the bar, I headed straight for it — an ideal vantage point to observe the locals.

My gaze swept over the crowd, searching for anyone useful. To my disappointment, I didn't see many Gifted, nor did I notice any aristocrats. The nobility, it seemed, preferred more exclusive venues. Most of the patrons here appeared to be mid-level criminals, a step above the trio of street thugs I'd encountered earlier.

My sharp hearing picked up snatches of conversation, but the topics were the same old drivel: money, women, monsters, and murder. Nothing I didn't already know and nothing useful to me. Just as I was about to write the place off, she walked in.

Tall, young, and clearly aristocratic, with a piercing gaze lit by Gifted energy, she turned heads as she entered. Her mere presence was enough to send shivers through the crowd and beads of sweat down foreheads, though everyone did their best to act like she wasn't there.

A young waiter, bound by duty, rushed to greet her and led her to a table in the far corner. She wore a loose sweater and jeans, but her every movement commanded attention. Even from behind, she was a striking sight.

Gracefully, she made her way to a corner table by the window, settling into the seat as if she owned the place.

I didn't take my eyes off her as I raised a hand to call the bartender.

"Welcome to the Duck's Nail, sir," he greeted me politely.

Now this was service. Simon could've learned a thing or two from him. It was good to see service hadn't entirely disappeared in this world. No questions about papers, no judgment, no greed — just a genuine willingness to serve.

"Hey there. Two beers, please."

The bartender followed my gaze to the woman and gave a slight shake of his head. "I wouldn't, if I were you."

"Oh?" I asked, amused. "She's the perfect reason for me to be here."

"I doubt she'll agree, sir. Unless your goal is to leave this world prematurely," he replied without missing a beat.

I laughed. "Not a chance. I just got back!"

The bartender didn't laugh with me. He simply shrugged. "That'll be a thousand imps," he said, setting down two mugs of imperial pale ale.

"A thousand..." I sighed, handing over my last

bill. Looked like a proper meal wasn't happening tonight after all.

At least I had some rations back in my room. Strange to think I'd ever find myself short on money. Tomorrow, I'd have to figure out a way to earn some. For now, I'd settle for buying the lady a drink.

"Although," the bartender added, his tone shifting, "if you're bold enough to offer her that drink, I'll cover the cost — not just for these, but for anything else you two order."

His voice wavered slightly, and a flicker of amusement played at the corners of his mouth. Bored, was he? Trying to entertain himself at my expense? Fine. I'd planned to approach her any-way.

"Deal." I nodded, picking up the mugs and heading straight for her table.

A true Paladin never shies from danger — whatever form it takes.

CHAPTER 5

I FOLLOWED THE SAME PATH the aristocratic beauty had taken not long ago. But unlike her, I didn't enjoy the courtesy of indifference. People stared openly, whispered among themselves, and some even started making bets on my lifespan.

A delegation from the eastern territories, perched on the second floor, panicked and hurriedly made their way out.

Strange folk.

Back in my day, commoners also feared the nobility, but not this much.

"May I sit?" I asked as I reached her table, catching her assessing gaze.

Then I calmly sat across from her and took a sip. Imperial pale ale hadn't lost its charm in the past seven centuries. Pure bliss.

"And where, pray tell, did I give you permission?" she asked, feigning displeasure.

"Of course you did." I nodded and smiled. "With your eyes."

"You must be mistaken." She barely managed to hide her amusement.

"I think not," I replied, sliding her the second mug of ale.

"If you think you can buy my company with beer, then you're either a fool or a madman," she said, tossing her thick hair with an air of superiority.

"Beer is merely a gesture of courtesy," I said with a shrug. "It's not right to drink alone at the table, is it? If you'd prefer something else, just say the word."

"I doubt you could provide what I truly desire," she replied, scrutinizing me skeptically.

To be fair, I didn't exactly look the part of the Empire's mightiest Gifted, a man with a nine-digit account at the Order's bank. And, well, I wasn't that man anymore.

Still, status and wealth were transient things. My knowledge and skills hadn't vanished. Nor had my taste for the finer things in life.

"You shouldn't judge a book by its cover," I said reproachfully, taking another sip.

"Hmm," she countered with a playful glint in her eyes, "but isn't that precisely what you did when you approached me?"

She was having fun. To her, this was nothing more than an amusing game — one she believed she could end at any moment. How naive.

"Not at all. Don't get me wrong; your 'cover' is stunning. But I approached you because of what lies beneath," I said, meeting her piercing jade gaze. "I came here with a purpose, and among everyone present, you alone are capable of giving me what I need."

"You're quite bold for a man with a death wish," she said with a chuckle, taking a sip of the ale I'd offered.

I couldn't see the bartender's face, but the sound of shattering glass behind us suggested he'd noticed.

"You can call me Marcus," I said, giving her a slight nod.

"Thanks for the beer, Marcus. But I'm afraid there's no need for me to remember your name." She smiled faintly, shifting her gaze past me.

At that moment, a towering figure appeared by my side.

Sitting with my back to the entrance, I hadn't noticed the arrival of another noble Gifted.

A hulking brute clad in full elemental metal armor stood glaring at me, radiating raw anger that boiled beneath layers of enchanted steel.

"My apologies for keeping you waiting, Princess," the armored man said obsequiously, before turning his blazing eyes on me. "And you. Leave. Now."

"How rude," I replied, moving my chilled ale out of the heat radiating from his armor. "The lady and I haven't finished our conversation."

"I said... Leave. This. Instant!" he growled, his

voice seething as he brought a heavy gauntleted hand down on my shoulder.

But before he could finish grinding out his words, the metal glove on his hand crumbled into ash with a crackling hiss. He recoiled in horror.

"You bastard!" he roared, losing control and reaching for the sword at his waist.

"Albert, stop!" The commanding voice of the young woman rang out, and the walking suit of armor reluctantly let go of his weapon.

It was an impressive blade of true elemental steel — a testament to the skills of the Empire's smiths. Good to know quality craftsmanship had survived the centuries.

"You're not as simple as you seem," the aristocrat said, her gaze sharper now. "Marcus... that's quite an unusual name. Do you have a family name?"

"Just Marcus. And since we're on a first-name basis now, might I have yours?" I asked calmly, ignoring the audible grating of metal nearby. Someone needed to oil that tin can.

"Oh? So you truly don't know who I am?" She leaned forward, intrigued. "How fascinating... And where exactly are you from, Marcus?"

"The north," I replied, sticking to my cover story.

"The north..." she repeated, tasting the word as she gestured for her armored companion to leave us and bring something to the table.

"But, Princess..."

"Do as I say!"

"Yes, ma'am..." he muttered reluctantly, clanking his way to the bar.

For such a massive hunk of metal, he moved remarkably quietly. I had no doubt he'd be a formidable opponent in battle. Even the combined might of all the local criminal bosses wouldn't leave a scratch on him.

And as for the aristocrat herself? Her elemental resonance was at least two, maybe three times stronger than his.

Impressive. In my time, Gifted like her were the ones protecting ordinary people.

So why, then, was the city wall defended by nothing but disorganized men armed with pseudo-elemental gear?

"I am Victoria of House Lugovsky, heir to the Clan of Nature," she declared triumphantly, clearly expecting a reaction.

I didn't so much as blink, which seemed to irk her. Though, I must admit, I hadn't anticipated meeting a direct descendant of the Ten Elemental Princes on my first day back — especially one from the clan responsible for trapping me.

"A pleasure," I replied evenly. "What brings a princess to a place like this? Even as a newcomer, I can tell there are far more suitable venues for someone of your stature."

"The beer here is excellent," Victoria said with a smile, taking another sip.

At that moment, a waiter arrived with utensils and two intricately plated dishes of aromatic appetizers.

"And the lamb in honey glaze is the best in town," she added. "You must try it when it arrives."

"Thank you, but I'll have to decline," I said, ignoring the gnawing emptiness in my stomach.

"A shame," she said, tossing back a bite-sized bruschetta topped with caviar. "You won't find delicacies like these anywhere else. Most of the dishes were prepared especially for me."

"I fear my pride wouldn't allow me to let a lady pay for my meal," I said politely.

"How quaint. And isn't that young bartender footing the bill for our tab?" she asked, her eyes sparkling mischievously.

"You've got sharp ears," I noted, impressed. "But I imagine that poor fellow couldn't settle a bill like this in a year, let alone a night. I wouldn't want him hanged for debt because of me."

"Old-fashioned, chivalrous, and considerate," she mused, her grin widening. "An extraordinary combination for a commoner. Tell you what, Marcus. Would your pride allow an exchange?"

"An exchange of what?" I asked, raising an eyebrow.

"Information. That's why you came here, isn't it? With just enough coin to buy entry," she said confidently, batting her lashes with feigned innocence.

"Not only beautiful but clever too," I observed. "A dangerous combination. No wonder everyone here is afraid of you."

"Oh, Marcus, they don't fear me for my mind." Victoria waved dismissively, adjusting her glowing jade earrings — crafted from elemental metal.

A weak Gifted would be dead within hours of wearing such artifacts, but the off-world energy only seemed to amplify her strength.

"And that's their mistake," I replied, ignoring the display. "So what could possibly interest a young noble like you in someone like me?"

"What lies beneath your shirt," she said with a provocative smile.

"Oh?" I leaned forward. "Now who's trying to buy whom?"

"Tempting as that might be..." Victoria licked her lips, "I was referring to the off-world fabric on your right arm."

"It's not for sale," I said, leaning back, suppressing the grin threatening to form.

The bait had been taken. Even if I were to leave silently now, she wouldn't let me go. That's how spoiled aristocrats worked — they always got what they wanted.

"Of course it's not for sale," the princess purred with a deliberately mournful sigh. "Besides, I doubt I'd have the funds for such a purchase right now. An artifact capable of slicing through an active Metal Element barrier without its owner's will in a single breath... that's priceless. I'd be content with answers to my questions in exchange. Where did you find it?"

"I took it off someone within a portal." I played along with her game.

"And where is this person now?" Victoria couldn't suppress her curiosity.

"Dead," I answered coldly. "Is that a problem?"

"Oh, not at all." She dismissed the notion with a wave of her hand, as if it were nothing. "In the Portals, the ancient law of the strong rules. Not for me to question it. What element powers your artifact?"

"Dangerous."

"I noticed," she replied, biting her lip. Victoria leaned in, using every ounce of feminine charm she had. She leaned forward, giving a tantalizing view beneath her sweater. Her hand slid over mine, breath quickening, her jade eyes sparkling with mischief. The world seemed to hold its breath.

Her fingers reached for the edge of the fabric wrapped around my right wrist, the fabric of my cloak's sleeve poking out slightly.

"I wouldn't advise that," I said with a smile but didn't pull away.

Victoria hesitated. The playful light in her eyes flickered. For a moment, doubt crept in. Then self-preservation won over curiosity, and she withdrew her hand, retreating.

Just then, a commotion erupted at the entrance. I turned, certain of the source — an agitated walking suit of armor making his way toward us, dragging a wiry youth in its iron grip.

"Hello again, Scourge of the Valleys!" I said cheerfully, waving.

"You... you... what?" the boy stammered, wide-eyed.

"You two know each other?" Victoria's surprise was evident.

"Not really," I said, giving the boy a sympathetic look.

His expression was a chaotic blend of righteous fury and abject terror. The suit of armor behind him, blocking his escape route, wasn't helping matters.

Martyn managed to compose himself enough to speak.

"That's unfair! You promised! You lied!" he shouted at Victoria before turning to me. "And I don't care that you killed the serpent! It was my sword! So its remains are mine too!"

Ah, he really should have kept his mouth shut.

Victoria listened in cold silence before standing. Her face was an emotionless mask, but a raw surge of elemental power radiated from her, leaving no doubt about her mood.

Martyn's mouth clamped shut, and he shrank into himself, gripping his cap tightly, eyes downcast.

"You tried to sell me someone else's kill?" Victoria's voice was cold.

"But..."

"To me, the Princess of the Nature Clan? You would make me an accomplice to a crime and stain my family's honor? Do you take me for a black-market merchant?" Her voice grew more dangerous with every word.

"Martyn shrank further, as if trying to disappear.

"But it was my..." he whispered, cut off by a punch from the armored guard.

"Get him out of my sight," Victoria ordered dismissively.

The guard lifted Martyn by the scruff and dragged him toward the door.

"Aristocrats always keep their word! You promised… Promised!" Martyn's cries faded as the door closed.

Victoria smoothed her hair, sat back down, and focused her attention on me again.

"On behalf of the Nature Clan, I apologize for that unfortunate incident," she said, bowing her head slightly. "Had I known from the start that the kill belonged to you, I would, of course, have dealt with you directly."

"Honestly, I have no idea what you're talking about," I said, shrugging.

"The Stone Serpent you killed. Or did the boy lie about that too?"

"No, he didn't lie. I did kill the serpent. But I had to leave its body behind in the forest. I don't consider anything left behind as my property."

"Think of it as you will, Marcus, but according to Imperial law, for the first twenty-four hours, only you have the right to its remains."

Interesting. This must be new; back in my time, all portal spoils were under the exclusive jurisdiction of the Order.

"If that's the case, I'd be happy to sell you the rights — and at a generous discount." I winked.

Martyn had unknowingly given Victoria a sense of guilt, easing my task. I'd have to thank him for that later. Not that the princess would have slipped off my hook now anyway.

"A discount?" Victoria asked playfully. "What have I done to earn such an honor?"

"By being such delightful company to relieve my boredom," I replied with a smile just as a large serving of dishes arrived, including the praised portal lamb in honey sauce.

The rest of our conversation followed the same pattern. Victoria kept up her flirtatious banter, clearly determined to hold my attention, while her hulking armored companion seethed silently from a few feet away.

I, meanwhile, savored the evening, truly basking in what felt like the first day of a long-awaited break.

In exchange for disclosing the location of the serpent's remains, I gladly accepted an assortment of exquisitely prepared dishes. Not only did they satisfy my ravenous hunger, but they were far tastier than I had expected.

Having survived countless Portals, I'd eaten more than my share of off-worldly meats, but my crude campfire cooking couldn't compare to the artistry of these local chefs. The lamb in honey glaze was a revelation — delicious enough to become an addiction.

"Well, if business is done," I said with a courteous smile, rising from my seat, "I think I'll take my leave. Before your twitchy metal friend completely loses his composure. It'd be a shame to ruin such a fine establishment."

"How dare you..." The armored behemoth leapt

to his feet, but one sharp glare from Victoria's jade eyes had him rooted to the spot.

Like a trained dog, honestly. I wondered if he'd hold a grudge — track me down by scent all the way to the Inn. What a pain that would be.

"You're right, Marcus," Victoria said with a sigh, standing up as well. "The tension here is palpable. But our business isn't entirely finished." Her voice took on a playfully wounded tone as she adjusted my collar. "You've left some of my questions unanswered... and you haven't yet received what you came for."

"You're not wrong," I said, meeting her gaze with just the right amount of charm. "I thought it might be... difficult under the current circumstances."

"Then let's change them," she replied instantly, seizing the opening I'd given her. "A private meeting. Just the two of us. We'll... exchange information."

"No reason to refuse," I said lightly.

With a provocative smile, Victoria retrieved a tiny jade stone from her neckline and slipped it into my shirt pocket.

"Midnight. Grand-Hell Hotel, Room 707," she whispered into my ear before striding away without a backward glance.

Her obedient metal companion followed close behind, not without casting one last murderous glare in my direction.

I ignored the buzzing whispers and astonished stares that swirled around me, instead pulling the

stone from my pocket and examining it thoughtfully.

A fragment of the Great Source — I'd recognize
it anywhere.

CHAPTER 6

A little later
Grand-Hell Hotel
Room 707

"YOU'VE COMPLETELY LOST your mind, my lady, inviting that commoner here!" Albert thundered, barely restraining himself from smashing everything around him.

"Watch your tone when you're speaking to your princess!" Victoria scolded him. "And don't break anything — my guest will be here soon!"

Albert Forgedon was one of the strongest warriors of the Metal Clan, but his lineage was too far removed from the ruling hierarchy, which is how he came to serve as the personal bodyguard of the princess of the allied Nature Clan. The young and exceptionally talented girl had extended favor to his obscure family, and she had every chance of becoming the leader of the entire Nature Clan in the near future. For that reason, Albert had gladly sworn to serve and protect Victoria.

Albert tried not to dwell on the fact that he had to report all of her actions to his superiors. Intrigue and politics held little interest for him. If the Prince declared it necessary for the clan's welfare, Albert wouldn't question it.

All he truly cared about was the safety of the princess entrusted to his care. The thought of a commoner laying hands on his precious charge filled him with a burning rage. He knew how many noblemen the young princess had rejected over the past five years — himself included!

"Why are you even in my room?" Victoria demanded, pausing as she rifled through the wardrobe.

In her right hand, she held a pair of red lace panties; in her left, a semi-transparent green brassiere. For a split second, she considered asking for advice but quickly dismissed the idea, lamenting again that her bodyguard was not a woman.

"To... protect your honor!" Albert straightened stiffly, making a visible effort not to look at the array of lingerie scattered around. "And to stop you from making a terrible mistake."

"You are not here to pass judgment on my decisions," Victoria said sharply, resuming her search for the perfect outfit.

Albert seethed inwardly, thinking he still had to report everything to her father and his clan's leader, but he said something else aloud.

"Why have you even arranged this meeting, my lady? And why would you give a commoner the Clan Shard? What if he simply runs off with it?"

"He won't," Victoria stated confidently. "And as for why... the answer is staring at you from your own hand."

Albert glanced shamefacedly at the gaping hole in his once-perfect elemental armor — a hole he still hadn't been able to mend. The reminder of the pauper's audacity rekindled his fury.

"It was an accident," Albert growled, tucking his hands behind him.

"That's exactly why, dear Albert, with all your strength, you're merely a bodyguard for a princess from a different clan," Victoria said with a mocking smile. "That was an artifact — and quite possibly a relic of the Fallen Order."

"That can't be!" Albert sputtered, unoffended by her words. "Relics of the Order haven't been found for a century!"

"He found one," the princess replied coolly. "And I want to know where."

This admission momentarily doused Albert's jealousy. If there was even the slightest chance it was a relic, they couldn't afford to lose it. But why pursue this matter this way? Why not simply capture the commoner on the street and torture the information out of him?

Even after five years as Victoria's bodyguard, Albert still couldn't understand the logic behind her plans.

"Very well, but I'll be in the next room, just in

case," Albert insisted.

"Absolutely not, you pervert!" Victoria snapped, hurling a shoe at him.

The heel clanged off the golden helm of Albert's elemental armor, which he never removed in front of others, as per the ancient traditions of his clan.

"He might notice and decide not to come!"

"A commoner?" Albert scoffed.

"A commoner who can wield a relic," Victoria reminded him.

"Fine," Albert conceded reluctantly. "And what do you wish me to do?"

"Prepare for an expedition beyond the wall. We depart at dawn. I need those remains. Understood?"

"You want me to leave the hotel and leave you alone?"

"You're the one who called him a commoner." Victoria shrugged, her eyes blazing with wild jade energy. "Or do you think I can't handle him myself?"

Albert, ever the perceptive bodyguard, recognized the limit of his princess's patience and wisely backed down.

"As you command," he said with a bow and quickly left the room.

"Whew," Victoria said with a relieved sigh as the door finally closed.

Finding the elusive Stone Serpent on her first day at the frontier was an unprecedented stroke of luck! It was for this purpose she had come here in secret. Her father knew where she was but, due to the Summit of the Princes, couldn't keep a constant watch over her.

This summit was her only chance to see her plan through. In three days, the front-line clan troops would return to Fort-Hell, making her scheme impossible!

For now, she only had Albert watching her — and his intellect wasn't enough to unravel her strategy. A strategy that required the Stone Serpent's remains.

According to that peculiar commoner, the remains were undamaged. Unbelievable fortune that, just a day ago, Victoria could only dream of.

Yet, as she sifted through her wardrobe, she couldn't understand why she wasn't rushing out immediately. Why wasn't she racing toward the precious remains?

Was it only about the relic? The odds it was truly a relic were slim.

Or was it... him? The dangerous thought wormed its way into her mind before she forcefully slapped it away.

No! Men had never been at the forefront of her concerns. The welfare of her clan had always been, and always would be, her top priority.

"The relic. Yes," Victoria declared aloud with conviction. "It's all about the relic!"

Pulling herself together and selecting her attire, she hurried off to shower. Midnight was less than an hour away.

* * *

"It gets curiouser and curiouser," I said, quoting one of old Aks's favorite sayings.

The tiny jade stone flipped between my fingers like a coin, and the simple motion somehow kept passersby at bay. I had noticed the peculiar reaction it elicited ever since the restaurant.

The sight of it made everyone suddenly polite, friendly, and... frightened. Even the bartender who had lost a bet to me could barely meet my gaze.

Still, when he learned he only had to cover the first two mugs of ale on the tab, he practically sang with relief and bombarded me with thanks. He returned my thousand with shaking hands and vowed I'd always have the best table reserved for me in that establishment.

Nice touch. The food there was amazing.

Truthfully, I would've forgiven him the thousand if it weren't for future plans. I felt uneasy without at least some coins in my pocket. Besides, he had practically dared me to take it.

As for the shard itself, I had a few theories on how it ended up in the clan's possession.

Two possibilities, really.

Either the Order of Argus cracked open the core of the Great Source and distributed the shards among the Princes when they lost the Tower...

Or the Princes had taken them by force.

Given that the Order's existence seemed all

but forgotten, even in a Tavern bearing its emblem, the latter seemed more likely.

In the current circumstances, that wasn't necessarily a bad thing. The shard was essentially a miniature Great Source. It could accumulate off-world energy and adapt it for human use.

If many of these shards remained in human hands, the loss of the Tower might not have been as devastating as I thought.

This particular shard was brimming with Nature's Elemental Energy, glowing a vivid jade green. Its energy circulated flawlessly, making it an extremely potent generator of elemental particles.

Achieving such perfect stability and clarity from off-world energy was no easy task.

The shard's craftsmanship was undeniably the work of a true master, one on par with the Order's magisters. I'd give anything to meet such a craftsman. Not only had this mystery expert managed to enhance the shard's efficiency to perfection, but they had also embedded a protective mechanism within it — a forced discharge triggered upon any attempt to forcibly drain its energy.

I could bypass this defense if I wanted, but I had no intention of damaging such fine work. Besides, Nature Energy was foreign to me; too much of it would be wasted, and I've never been one for squandering resources.

Old Aks taught me early on to value every speck of off-world energy humanity managed to harness.

"Marcus!" a familiar voice jolted me from my reverie.

"Hey, Cap," I said with a grin, casually flipping the shard into my chest pocket.

"It really is you!" Edward exclaimed, clapping me on the shoulder.

"Yeah, still kicking, as you can see," I said with a nod. "Listen, you showed up at just the right time. You know where the Grand-Hell Hotel is?"

"Of course," Edward said, narrowing his eyes, "but wouldn't you prefer somewhere a bit more modest?"

"Oh, it's not what you think," I said with a smirk. "I've got a lady to visit. Just point me in the right direction."

With those words, I handed him the crumpled map I'd acquired in an alley scuffle. I had no other means of navigating the city.

"A lady, huh?" Edward drawled, amused as he tapped the building's location on the map.

It was right in the heart of the main street, a ten-minute walk from the Tavern.

"Say, Marcus, where'd you find this map?" Edward asked curiously.

"Picked it up somewhere." I waved dismissively. "Why?"

"Because," Edward said, his eyes narrowing, "it marks the lair of Beast."

"Beast?" I echoed, puzzled.

"Not a creature — Beast," he corrected. "It's short for Beran Astor. A powerful Gifted, once a warrior of the Earth Clan. Now? He dabbles in illegal trade, using his talent to create hidden paths beyond the wall and breaching its integrity. He's been sentenced to death in the Empire in absentia. There's a hefty reward for information about him, and judging by the ink on this map..."

"It was drawn today," I confirmed.

"Well, starving won't be a concern for you now." Edward shook his head with a begrudging smile.

"That's convenient," I remarked, "since I've grown fond of the local cuisine. But what's got you so armed to the teeth at this hour?"

Edward's gear was far more combat-ready than during the last foray beyond the wall. Three firearms, full pouches of supplies, a dagger at his shin, a serrated sword on his back, even a belt of grenades emitting a potent elemental aura.

"Oh, it's... for self-defense," he stammered.

"Against what? A tank battalion?" I laughed.

"Don't worry about it, Marcus. We've seen worse," Edward said with a sigh. "Besides, it'll probably come to nothing. We'll hole up in the bunker for a week, tell some stories, drink some vodka. If only we could find Martyn. He's disappeared again, the little rascal."

"I saw your Martyn," I said with a nod. "At the Duck's Nail."

"That little—" Edward spat angrily. "Picking now to relax!"

"You misunderstand, Cap. He wasn't relaxing," I said sympathetically, and quickly recounted what had transpired at the restaurant.

The irritation in Edward's eyes turned to concern, then outright panic. The man looked like he might turn even grayer on the spot.

"Why did he... we could've waited... found the money," he muttered, barely holding back tears. "I forbade that idiot from even thinking of selling today! But he... I failed him, Marcus. Forgive an old man..."

"I don't hold a grudge, Cap. Even if he sold the coordinates, it's just money. You were there, too. You have a claim."

"Technically, we don't... laws were broken. He went straight to the princess, that fool! Anyone else, maybe we could smooth things over... but with her," Edward said, slumping, his face lined with despair. "They'll kill him... and it's my fault."

"Yours?"

"Yes... because of me and Nick, the kid did it. We came back from a foray empty-handed, with a damaged vehicle... left us saddled with debt. Nick wanted to sell the transport, but Martyn snapped! He screamed that without wheels, we were finished... and he was right, of course. But the debt had to be paid. We planned to sit somewhere safe, think things through... but Martyn..."

"Couldn't hold back and decided to fix it himself." I sighed.

"Thought he was grown..." Edward said, nodding sadly.

"Cap, what's the reward for your Beast?"

"Depends on the buyer... better with—" Edward began, but fell silent when he felt the paper slip into his hands.

"Enough to cover the debt?" I asked, watching his stunned expression.

"More than enough… I know trustworthy buyers who pay less than the Imperials but right away…" Edward's voice broke as he choked back a sob.

"Good. Take it — you need it more."

"I can't accept this for free!" Edward protested, clinging to the last shreds of his pride.

"It's a trade." I smiled, eyeing his gear. "For your grenade belt."

"What do you need grenades for?" Edward asked, bewildered.

"Oh, a certain establishment's service didn't meet my expectations."

"Service, huh… you realize those could level half a block, right?"

"Don't worry, I know how to handle them. So, do we have a deal?"

"If it's a trade… fine," Edward said, shaking my hand eagerly. "Thank you… I'll never forget this, Marcus! I'll deduct the cost of the grenades from the sale proceeds and give you the difference! I swear it!"

"To keep that promise, you'll have to avoid trouble and survive, old man!" I warned, tucking the grenades under my shirt.

"Surviving is what I do," Edward said, his voice tinged with melancholy.

Indeed. Covering Martyn's debt was just the start.

Ah, youth. It reminded me a little of my seven-year-old self and old Aks... except Aks showed his care through harsh lessons, and I never made mistakes like that — otherwise, I wouldn't have survived a year in Argus.

Still, the bond between Martyn and Edward stirred a warm nostalgia in me. And that was something I cherished deeply.

"Don't worry about Martyn, Cap — I've still got unfinished business with the princess. I'll put in a good word."

"Really?" Edward's eyes lit up with hope.

"I give you my word." I smiled, glancing at the watch on Edward's wrist.

Time was pressing. After bidding a tearful farewell to Edward, I quickened my pace and reached the dilapidated two-story inn with the sign Tavern in five minutes. Compared to the bright, spacious restaurant, it looked even more dreary than before.

"Welcome back!" shouted Simon from the back room.

His tipsy tone suggested he was celebrating something. At least pretend to care that I returned alive, I thought.

"No disturbances until noon. I haven't slept in a week. Anyone knocks, I'll kill 'em!" I yawned dramatically and made for the stairs.

Simon had better take that warning seriously. God, I hoped he wasn't a legitimate descendant of the Order's servants, but rather a bastard child from some fling.

Ignoring the stairs creaking beneath me, I reached my room and bolted the door tight.

A careful inspection revealed no active dangerous artifacts. Only a simple sound alarm rigged to the window. Barely any elemental energy in it; I disabled it in five seconds by absorbing its meager power. Not much, but a small boost nonetheless, and I also topped up my energy reserves by one unit.

Setting my "parting gift" took ten minutes. Then, I gathered my things, climbed out the window, and headed toward the hotel.

In all of this, there was just one regret. Sleep wouldn't be an option tonight.

CHAPTER 7

"APOLOGIES, YOUNG MAN, but we don't have any available rooms at the moment," the slick concierge chirped as soon as I stepped into the expansive hotel lobby.

"I'm here to visit someone," I interrupted, cutting him off before my scruffy appearance could draw further scrutiny. I held up the jade shard in my hand.

The condescending smile vanished instantly, replaced by one of respect, and the ten Gifted guards who had begun to surround me returned to their posts. This place was guarded like a fortress. I'd had to flash my "pass" three times just to get here — once at the outer gates, then at the main entrance, and now again in the lobby.

Even the checkpoints at the city walls weren't this secure. And the hotel's staff of guards? Far stronger Gifted than any imperial soldiers I'd seen.

Strange priorities in this city, but it wasn't my concern right now.

"Keep an eye on this. I won't be long," I said in a polite tone, tossing my backpack to the concierge.

"Of course, sir," the man replied, deftly passing my belongings to an eager porter. "You may retrieve it from the reception desk at any time. Is there anything else you need?"

"No, thank you," I replied with a nod, heading toward the elevator.

No one dared to approach me. In fact, no one on the first floor even risked looking in my direction.

I wondered who they thought I was.

The overly intricate elevator, brimming with elemental enchantments, sealed its doors firmly shut but remained stationary as I pressed the buttons, earning my puzzled frown.

In my time, even the Tower of Argus used simple Earth-based electricity for its elevators — no fancy elemental energy. There were just a few buttons: floor numbers, a stop switch, and an operator call. Nothing unnecessary.

Here, though, the panel for this seven-story building had a hundred buttons in various shapes and sizes. I could feel the chill of a bottomless pit beneath the elevator, clearly a trap for unwelcome guests.

"Seriously? Even you need to see the pass?" I muttered, holding the shard up to the panel.

"Access granted," a pleasant female voice announced, and the elevator finally began its ascent.

As I understood, the "Grand-Hell" hotel was owned by one of the Empire's Top Ten Clans and was the city's most opulent establishment, catering exclusively to high-ranking Gifted.

Why go to such lengths to protect people who were supposed to be humanity's ultimate defense? Utterly absurd.

The seventh floor was eerily empty. Wide, brightly lit hallways, red carpets, paintings on the walls — yet not a single soul in sight.

"Show me," I commanded instinctively, releasing a dark wisp from my palm.

The energy of Darkness split into two dozen black lizards that scurried into the shadows. Harmless little things, their main advantage was stealth.

Detecting them through elemental scans was nearly impossible, and to the naked eye, they were invisible. They left no elemental traces and had no physical presence in this world, making them the perfect spies in confined spaces.

Fifteen seconds later, I had a complete layout of the floor.

To my surprise, aside from the princess, there wasn't another living soul. She'd even sent her tin can of a bodyguard away.

Had she decided against killing me, or was she simply trusting in the defensive constructs scattered throughout the space?

There was no point in guessing, so I knocked

on the door to Room 707.

"It's open," came her clear, melodious voice, and I pushed the door.

The fragrance of wildflowers and fresh fruit hit me instantly. Ignoring the subtle attempts to invade my mind, I stepped into the dimly lit room and saw her.

Sitting on a massive bed, legs elegantly crossed, was Victoria. Her only attire was a translucent nightgown that left very little to the imagination.

"Do you like it?" she asked coyly, twirling elemental air currents around her fingertip. "I can change it if you prefer. Rose? Honeysuckle? Linden? Tobacco?"

"I prefer authenticity," I replied calmly.

"Oh? Good," she said slyly, rising from the bed and throwing open the windows.

A gust of autumn wind swept into the room, tossing her dark jade-colored hair. She stood there for a moment, then turned back to me with serene composure.

The princess had clearly realized her attempt to breach my mind had failed, but she kept her expression neutral, refusing to show weakness.

Good girl. Aristocrats were always skilled in the art of deception.

"Looks like there's a storm brewing," I remarked, nodding toward the dark clouds outside.

She kept her face impassive, but strong Gifted often had difficulty controlling all their emotions. It wasn't easy to keep them all in check.

"Oh!" Victoria feigned surprise. "You're familiar with the Element of Nature?"

"A little," I replied innocently, tossing her the jade shard. "Returning this."

"I'm surprised you didn't steal it," she said, fastening the shard to an ornate amulet hanging around her neck.

The gem within the amulet, adorned with intricate clan runes, was ten times larger than the shard I'd returned. Its aura, alive and pulsing, hinted at a connection to the Great Source.

Could it still be linked to the Tower's core, even severed?

"Liar. You knew I'd come," I said evenly, stepping closer to her.

Her firm chest pressed against me, and her quickened breath brushed against my neck, but she didn't pull away.

"Figured me out," she said with a flirtatious smile, her gaze unwavering.

Why did everyone enjoy provoking me so much?

"Well, who could resist?" I agreed easily, pulling a barely visible jade pin laced with poison from her hair.

Victoria's eye twitched, but even now, she didn't step back, choosing to stand her ground. Her choice, not mine.

I discarded the pin and gently ran my hand down her smooth neck, then lower, grasping the amulet.

The shard flared threateningly, vibrating and

heating as the elemental energy within tried to punish me for touching it without permission. All it managed to do, however, was cause a faint itch, like a mosquito bite.

Ignoring the shard's resistance, I tore the amulet from her neck, triggering a protective burst of Nature's elemental energy.

A freezing wind enveloped me, clawing at my skin, striving to rip out my eyes, and seeking to tear me apart. Yet all its efforts crumbled against my elemental immunity — a core ability of a Paladin of Darkness, requiring no energy.

Darkness, as the mother of all Elements, was immune to pure elemental attacks.

Of course, Victoria could have taken conscious control of the amulet's energy to launch a focused strike. My immunity wouldn't have helped against that, and I'd have had to defend myself. But she didn't. Instead, she watched with silent curiosity.

Even now, with all three of her prepared assassination attempts having failed, Victoria showed no fear. Her deep eyes were filled only with desire.

For the next three hours, we didn't speak a single word. We didn't need to. Though, admittedly, the room was far from quiet.

The princess took her time admiring what was hidden beneath my shirt, but she didn't dare touch the artifact cloak bound to my right arm.

For my part, the brief contact with the shard in her clan amulet had told me everything I needed to know. Everything that happened between us in the following three hours was just a pleasant bonus.

* * *

A squad of ten Imperial soldiers in full combat gear surrounded the two-story Tavern. The struggling Tavern owner had long since partnered with officers at the local military outpost, feeding them information, rumors, gossip — and, occasionally, people for the mines and factories.

The Red Zone expanded a little more every day, and the Empire was determined to seize everything it could from the local lands and Portals before they were permanently lost.

The Imperial Governor of these lands wasn't Gifted but was an adept businessman. His sole purpose was to ensure the uninterrupted flow of precious portal resources and artifact production. Efficiency was key — any drop in performance, and a governor could be replaced in an instant. The line of commoners willing to trade their souls for even a fragile, limited semblance of authority was endless.

Not that these governors held any real power. They were figureheads, executing the will of the Elemental Princes' council — the true rulers of the Empire. Everyone understood this, which was why every Gifted individual dreamed of joining a clan. Only when that dream died would they turn to imperial service under the governors. Unlike the selective clans, it welcomed everyone.

Gifted or not. Noble or commoner. Rich or

poor.

The work was grueling, and workers were always in short supply. Imperial service paid far less than clan service, but it was better than abject poverty. At least it offered benefits, pensions, and steady provisions.

Sometimes, the more enterprising soldiers — those with loose morals — found lucrative side gigs funded by the local underworld.

"Listen up, boys," said Senior Sergeant Tim, his sharp, commanding voice cutting through the air. "Customs screwed up again and let a refugee slip through the border. And not just any refugee — a Gifted one! You all know the drill: every illegal Gifted is a murderer, a deserter, or worse. They think they can outrun their sins on our land. They're a threat to people, to order, to our wives and children! And neutralizing threats is our sacred duty!"

"So... are we supposed to kill him?" asked a green recruit in the front row, scratching his head.

"Negative!" Tim barked, his voice booming. "Or do you fancy a one-way trip to the mines?"

"N-no, sir!" the terrified soldier stammered. The boy had sold his own mother into slavery to buy his way into this squad.

"Good answer." Tim smirked as the last civilian was escorted out of the building. "We take the target alive and uninjured, if possible. He's due for a shift tomorrow — production quotas this month are already down by two percent."

"Yes, sir!" the soldiers replied in unison, moving into the building with practiced precision.

"Mind if I watch?" Simon asked his old friend. "Always loved seeing the hope drain from their eyes."

"Be my guest," Tim replied easily, standing guard at the base of the stairs. "What, did this one insult your lousy shack too?"

"Not exactly," Simon said with a scowl. "But his smug confidence pissed me off. Looked at me like a predator eyeing a chick. Probably some spoiled noble who's fallen on hard times. Used to people groveling at his feet. Let's see how brave he is when we shove his face into reality."

Tim chuckled and took his position near the staircase. "Sure, sure. Besides, you've got that bet with the quartermaster that this refugee takes down one of my boys. Want a front-row seat?"

"Told you, he's tough," Simon said, his eyes gleaming with anticipation as he listened to the commotion upstairs.

"Don't worry, we've handled worse," Tim said with a grin, signaling his men to begin.

The crash of the door being kicked in went almost unnoticed. It was drowned out by the cacophony of gut-wrenching screams from men burning alive in elemental fire.

Simon's long-cherished dream had come true. By morning, he was a rich man — his Tavern, was insured for a hefty sum against fire.

Unfortunately for him, there was no one left to collect the payout.

* * *

"Leaving already?" the princess asked softly as I finished buttoning my shirt. "It's still an hour before dawn."

"I can't miss the morning train," I replied, searching through the chaos for my pants.

Knowing the entire floor was ours, the insatiable princess had held nothing back. For powerful Gifted like her, finding a partner who wouldn't die from a brief lapse in control was nearly impossible.

With me, she hadn't needed any control at all. Realizing she couldn't harm me, the princess had let loose completely. Poor girl must've had a hard time bottling everything up for so long.

"You're leaving the city?" Her voice carried a note of disappointment.

"There's no information here that interests me," I said with a shrug.

Or the Princes, to whom I had a few questions. But I kept that part to myself.

"So I wasn't imagining things," she murmured, biting her lip as she hugged a pillow. "You spoke to him."

"To him?"

"My amulet." She nodded.

"You could say that," I admitted.

"Then you need its creator." Her eyes sparkled with sudden understanding.

"And why do you think that?"

"He can also speak to shards," she said

proudly, lifting her chin. "I can help you find him if you help me."

"No need. I already know where he is," I replied calmly, pulling on my pants. "The southern capital."

The amulet's memories had shown me that much. I hadn't been able to make out the creator's face, but I felt a strange familiarity.

It was unlikely, of course, but I had to check. Curiosity would eat me alive otherwise. Even old Aks had given up trying to stamp it out of me, choosing instead to teach me how to use it.

"I see..." she pouted, clearly scrambling for an excuse to keep me nearby. When she came up empty, she glared at me, frustrated.

"Don't ruin such a pretty face," I murmured playfully, planting a goodbye kiss on her forehead.

My exit was accompanied by a barrage of pillows and an indignant shout of "Idiot!"

That was one of the kinder things she called me.

She'd get over it. She'd promised to spare the boy, and nobles still kept their word — at least, I trusted Victoria's promise.

On my way downstairs, I opted for the stairs, assuming the defensive constructs would be easier to avoid there than in the elevator. None of them activated, though. Apparently, the security system only worked on entry.

After retrieving my backpack, I asked the receptionist for directions to the train station and set off.

There was no time to wander. Either I caught the morning express, or I'd have to convince the Imperials that their comrades burned in a fire caused by their greed — not some refugee terrorist.

And I doubted they'd listen.

"One ticket to the capital," I said, handing a worn one-thousand bill to the sleepy conductor.

With little time left until departure, I approached the first uniformed figure I spotted near the last car of the train.

"This car's free," the man in gray, adorned with the imperial crest, said with a smirk — but his gaze lingered on the money.

People sure do love their scraps of paper.

"Care to explain the catch? The bill's yours if it's worth hearing," I said with a grin.

After centuries trapped in the Portal of Time, where sleep had long become a distant memory, surprises were the last thing I needed.

"There's no catch..." the conductor muttered, averting his eyes. "It's an imperial decree. For public safety, they say, to provide a car for evacuating the needy."

"Public safety, you say." I sighed, peeking inside the freight car. A dozen people were crammed together like livestock, sitting on the cold floor amid a mess of straw and filth. "Safety for those who paid for real passenger seats?"

"Of course not, cargo is more important!" the conductor snapped, then quickly clamped a hand over his mouth, realizing he'd said too much.

As I suspected.

In the eyes of the Imperials, the resources transported from the frontlines held far more value than the lives of the poor souls unable to afford proper tickets. The authorities packed the free cars with expendable bodies to serve as bait in case portal creatures attacked, diverting the monsters' attention.

And the odds of an attack were far from slim. The route from here to the capital was long and dangerous, most of it cutting through the Yellow Zone. I'd remembered that much from Edward's holographic map.

I'd need to find one like it in the capital. This town was too small — its hand-drawn maps wouldn't cut it.

"Bring me a mattress or a couple of soft blankets, and I'll pretend I didn't hear a thing," I said, slipping the one-thousand bill into the conductor's front pocket with a wink. "Enough for a good meal when we arrive?"

"Y-yes," the man stammered, nodding gratefully. "I'll take care of everything! My cousin works in the dining car — I'll save the best cuts for you!"

"Great. But I need the mattress now," I said, reminding him.

"Right away!" the conductor called, hurrying off to the next car.

I stretched, then climbed into the car.

"When the mattress arrives, lay it under the pregnant woman," I said, nodding toward a young woman curled up in the corner, arms protectively wrapped around her stomach. "She's running a fever. She won't make it to the capital otherwise."

The frightened, weary faces around me didn't respond, but their eyes betrayed a glimmer of humanity. A few older women cast sympathetic looks at the girl, and a wiry man, likely a miner, offered her a scrap of his blanket.

I dropped my pack on the floor and sat near the entrance. If the train was attacked, I'd be the first line of defense for my fellow passengers.

Hopefully, a creature or two would actually show up. A free energy boost wouldn't hurt.

I'd finished off the last of my rations on the way here, and my body demanded only one thing now: sleep. So, by the time the train began to move, I was already fast asleep — for the first time in a week.

CHAPTER 8

THE SLEEP HAD BEEN DEEP and rejuvenating. Every second of rest was put to good use by my mind, leaving me feeling significantly better.

The warning beacon hadn't triggered, which meant there hadn't been any attacks by portal creatures. But why were we stopped? And why was the car empty?

"Could we have arrived already?" I stretched lazily and peeked through the open door.

All I could see was a forest stretching out across the horizon. This didn't look like the capital.

"Well? What's the decision?" an irritatingly cocky voice interrupted my thoughts.

"Ten thousand. Standard rate," came the stiff response.

"I'm telling you, this one's special! He's carrying a genuine artifact from the Nature Clan! I have it on good authority he stole it directly from Princess Victoria's suite!"

"Save your nonsense for someone else. I said ten thousand, not a single imp more!"

"You don't get it," the first voice insisted. "A thief capable of pulling off something like this is worth more than ten thousand! Plus, you're getting the artifact as part of the deal!"

I shook my head, realizing exactly what — or rather, who — they were discussing. Cracking my neck, I swung my backpack onto my shoulders and stepped out of the car.

Sure enough, it was exactly what I thought.

About thirty feet ahead, a scrawny man in a conductor's uniform was trying to convince a group of five thugs with menacing expressions.

Unfortunately, this wasn't the conductor who owed me breakfast — I could have really used a meal right about now.

Stepping out, I glanced to my left and noticed that only two freight cars and a rickety locomotive remained of the train. The conductor had clearly arranged a little side hustle. Imperial wages weren't enough for his greedy soul, it seemed.

The world had fallen to such a low point that you couldn't even sleep without someone trying to sell you into slavery. And not just me — behind each of the potential buyers stood a truck loaded with people, their heads covered with sacks and their hands bound in chains.

Among the victims, I easily recognized the

pregnant woman and the other unfortunate souls who had traveled with me in the car.

The warning beacon I'd set was tuned for portal creatures or threats to my personal safety, so it hadn't triggered when they simply escorted the other passengers off the train.

What lies had that sleazy conductor fed the bandits about me? That I'd been drugged? That my bag was full of gold ingots? He didn't seem to hesitate when claiming I'd stolen the princess's artifact.

"Oh, this one looks tough. Not much to his build, but I like his eyes!" said the largest of the thugs, who stood closest and was leading the negotiations.

I didn't bother hiding, stepping slowly into the clearing.

The bargaining stopped immediately, and every head turned toward me.

"I told you!" the conductor babbled. "Fearless, resilient, talented! He'd work just as well in the mines, the fields, or... the princess's bed!"

Well, now that was interesting. Did someone leak that information, or was he just guessing? I'd have to make sure he was the last to die — just to get some answers.

"I don't need help in the bedroom." The big thug laughed, shoving a wad of bills into the conductor's hand, "But he'll do nicely for the troglodyte mines. Young lungs hold up better."

"Hope you can handle off-world mold and darkness." He spat on the ground, shoving the disgruntled conductor aside.

The thug grabbed my shoulder, clearly used to dealing with helpless slaves and just taking what he wanted. But the moment his hand touched me, his arm blackened, and he recoiled in horror.

The conductor, still whining about unfair payment, instantly went silent, and the four remaining thugs turned their attention to me for the first time.

"You said he wasn't armed," growled a shaggy-haired man, gripping a cleaver.

"And empty-handed." The bald, short man spat on the ground, racking his rifle.

"So you lied to us, didn't you, Phil?" The one-eyed thug with a massive rifle slung over his shoulder concluded.

Their weapons, though worn on the surface, were no less formidable than what I'd seen on imperial soldiers. At least half of their ammo clips gave off elemental resonance, and the cleaver was forged entirely from off-world metal.

The thugs themselves were Gifted, though not particularly strong ones.

"I didn't lie!" the conductor stammered, pointing at me with a trembling hand. "Just look at his eyes! He's empty, I swear!"

"Liar!" roared the big thug with the blackened hand as he staggered to his feet. "Look at what you did! I'll—" He raised his other hand in fury but caught my gaze and froze, retreating back toward his comrades in fear.

So he did have some sense.

The conductor scrambled to his side, tossing the money back into the thug's hand.

For a moment, I felt disappointed. I'd wanted to interrogate the conductor myself, but it seemed they weren't going to kill him after all. The one-handed thug accepted the money reluctantly, while another figure stepped forward.

This one was different. Clad in a business suit with a blood-red tie, he exuded calm authority and a polished demeanor. He didn't belong in this grimy group. Behind him wasn't an old truck but a sleek black levitating sedan with an open trunk packed with metal containers.

"Interesting artifact," the man said, his gaze fixed on my hand. "Phil, I'm taking him."

"That wasn't the deal!" protested the one-handed thug.

"What would you want with a slave in the capital?" the bald man grumbled.

"Come on, Kai, leave something for the rest of us," the shaggy one complained, glancing at the containers.

"I didn't take — I bought," Kai replied coldly. "This isn't a charity. Want the goods? Pay up."

"I paid for him first!" the big thug bellowed, shaking his blackened hand. "He's mine by right!"

"Phil?" Kai raised an indifferent eyebrow.

"The payment was made prematurely and returned in full," the conductor replied in his slimy tone. "The goods are still for sale."

"One hundred thousand," Kai declared, handing a briefcase to the trembling conductor.

"Sold!" Phil crowed, bowing deeply.

The others glared in frustration, particularly the one-handed thug, who was seething with the desire for revenge but lacked the courage to act. He avoided my gaze entirely — a cowardly avenger.

"Are you going to collect your purchase, or keep standing around?" I called, growing bored.

I dropped my backpack and extended my hands forward, waiting for the shackles.

But no one moved.

Kai studied me intently, his jaw working as he calculated.

"Whoever brings me his right hand and backpack gets one hundred thousand," he finally announced.

Smart move. He hadn't donned that suit for nothing. Why risk himself when others could do the dirty work? And if those greedy fools died, their goods could be claimed too — already paid for.

"The right hand?" the one-handed thug asked eagerly. "So..."

"Yes, Jamal, you may kill him," Kai said, and that was the starting point.

The scent of easy profit sent the bandits into a frenzy. I dodged the bald one's automatic fire with a roll, landing directly in the path of the cleaver-wielding thug.

The blade, made of elemental metal, whistled through the air before its owner collapsed with a gaping hole in his chest.

The follow-up rifle shot was deflected with the cleaver I had just appropriated from the corpse.

The bullet wasn't elemental — one-eyed must have been trying to save ammo. He didn't get a second chance. The cleaver spun through the air, burying itself squarely in his forehead.

The last to reach me was the one-armed avenger. Unlike the others, the brute had a shred of understanding about what I was capable of. He had waited, hoping to catch me off guard with a delayed attack. Spoiler: he didn't.

My right hand met his face mid-swing, and three seconds later, he stopped breathing. It's hard to keep breathing when half your face has turned into lifeless white ash.

Time is not an Element to mess with.

Of the four simple-minded thugs, only the bald one remained alive. Terrified, he dropped his rifle and made a mad dash for his truck. He didn't make it. A rifle shot hit him squarely in the back of the head.

It wasn't my rifle.

"We don't need witnesses, do we?" Kai remarked casually as he reloaded the rifle he'd picked up. His calm expression said it all — he had no interest in slaves. Once he got what he wanted, everyone else here was expendable.

"What about the conductor?" I asked, glancing at Phil, who was doing his best impression of a corpse. A stray bullet had clipped his leg, and instead of running, he'd decided to play dead.

"Don't worry, we'll come to an agreement," Kai replied with a smirk, pulling the trigger without hesitation.

Kai had picked the perfect moment. Dodging was impossible, and whatever energy charged the bullet, he'd concealed it well with his Element of Shadow.

"Consume," I whispered. A black void formed in front of my chest, swallowing the projectile whole.

"So, you're Gifted," Kai said, nodding in surprise. "And a shadow elementalist too. Why didn't you say so? Join us." He tugged at the collar of his shirt, revealing a clan amulet embedded with a gray shard.

Amusingly, he had mistaken the Element of Darkness for Shadow. That worked in my favor. If even a clan-trained Gifted specializing in Shadow couldn't identify my element, it meant few in this era could.

Drawing the world's attention to my unique element wasn't on my to-do list. The last time hadn't ended well.

"Not interested," I replied flatly, raising my hand.

A moment later, behind Kai, an identical black void appeared. His own bullet whistled through it, reducing him to nothing but a green, swirling skull-shaped cloud. Whoever had designed the elemental round had a sense of humor.

"Necrotic gas, huh?" I identified the bullet's contents before turning to inspect my backpack, which had also taken a couple of hits.

Only now did I notice a small jade shard protruding from a punctured side pocket. Its elemental energy had been forcibly neutralized, its aura hidden under a cloaking veil. Victoria had gone to considerable lengths to make sure I wouldn't detect it.

When had she managed to slip it in?

"Well, I guess you weren't lying after all," I muttered with a smirk, kicking the conductor, who flinched and tried to play unconscious.

"Huh? What? Where?" Phil stammered, doing a terrible job pretending he'd just woken up.

"Who tipped you off?" I asked diplomatically.

"What tip? I don't know what you're talking about." Phil tried playing dumb.

"Phil, Phil..." I said with a sigh, pressing my boot against his wounded knee.

"You bastard!" he growled through gritted teeth, attempting to threaten me. "I'm untoucha-ble! Killing a personal servant of the Governor will get you executed, you scum! The entire capital will hunt you down!"

"Untouchable? Really, Phil?" I pressed harder, drawing a strangled gasp from him.

"You... monster..." he choked but still didn't break.

"Alright, rest in peace, 'untouchable,'" I said, pulling out the rifle and pointing it at his head.

The sight of the barrel inches from his temple had the desired effect. Phil broke, his pants stained with more than just blood.

"I'll tell you everything! Don't kill me! What do you want? Supply chains? Routes? Let me go, and I'll make you rich in the capital! With your skills, you'll have no equal…"

"I only need a name," I said, wrinkling my nose at the smell.

"I don't know! It was some noble! I never saw his face, I swear! He caught me on the street, gave me the lead on you, and didn't even take payment!"

"A noble, you say. Nervous giant in golden armor?"

"Nervous? I don't know about that, but golden armor — yes! Exactly!"

"Good." I lowered the rifle.

So, the tin suit had a grudge. No matter. My memory was just as sharp as his.

"Does this mean I can go?" Phil asked, swallowing hard.

"Unfortunately, no, Phil." I leaned in close. "As my mentor wisely said: 'The only good slaver is a dead slaver.'"

With that ancient wisdom, I snapped his neck.

Phil should have been grateful I made it quick and painless, though he hardly deserved it. This batch of captives clearly wasn't his first.

Tossing the briefcase of cash into my backpack, I turned to the trucks. First, I freed the pregnant woman, giving her some water. She was too weak to form words, only moaning and rolling her eyes.

The other captives didn't look much better. They'd obviously been drugged.

I visually scanned for the strongest-looking captive and freed him next. It turned out to be the miner from my car. At least he could talk.

"Where... what's happening?" he asked grog-gily, blinking hard.

"We were being sold into slavery, but they failed," I explained briefly, slapping him sharply across the face to jolt him awake.

"Yeah, yeah, I'm fine!" The miner shook him-self awake. "Nina... where's Nina?" he asked, pan-icked until he spotted the pregnant woman resting against a tree.

"What's your name?"

"Peter. And you're the guy... thanks for the mattress," he said, shaking my hand. "And the blankets too... wait... how did they fail? There were so many of them, and they were armed..." His gaze swept over the clearing littered with bodies, "...to the teeth. Did you do this?"

"That's not important, Peter," I said with a smile. "I woke you up for a reason. I need your help."

"My help?" Peter repeated, startled, but he quickly jumped to his feet. "Who do I fight? Just say the word!"

"Good man," I said, clapping him on the shoul-der. "But there's no one left to fight. What I need is a driver — can you handle that?"

"Of course! Tractor, airplane, you name it!" he answered enthusiastically.

"Then listen closely." I leaned in and outlined the plan in detail.

Free all the captives. Gather those who could stand and get them to help. Explain the situation to the rest and organize a swift evacuation.

Peter turned out to be sharp and decisive. From the options I laid out, he immediately chose to continue on the train. The nearest station was a major Imperial sorting hub, jointly managed by aristocrats and the Empire. It was crowded, and the chances of being heard there were much higher.

In a few minutes, I crafted a plausible cover story: they had been caught in the crossfire of a gang dispute. The corrupt conductor had been killed over some containers, and the captives were simply collateral damage. I provided Peter with detailed descriptions of the criminals and the containers to make the story airtight.

Peter warned me that the incident would bring in the military police's top specialists right away. For the Governor, nothing mattered more than the steady flow of goods, and any disruption to the railways was treated as a top priority.

I reassured Peter that his only focus should be evacuating the people as quickly as possible — I'd take care of covering the tracks.

With that, we were in agreement.

"Listen... thanks, man," Peter said gratefully, bowing slightly. "What's your name?"

"Marcus," I introduced myself. "However, if you could leave my name out when you report this to the authorities, I'd appreciate it."

"No problem." Peter grinned, now fully himself. "But are you sure? For saving all these people and the cargo, they might even give you a reward..."

"I'll pass," I replied with a smile.

Where there's a reward, there's unwanted attention. And with attention come problems. I've always solved problems the hard way. Somehow, I doubted the capital would appreciate my methods.

Besides, the spoils of battle would suffice. The bandits had been loaded with cash and decent gear.

For the first five minutes, I silently watched Peter at work to gauge his capabilities. He was efficient, focused, and most importantly, the people listened to him.

"And what are you planning to do with the goods?" came a curious voice from behind me.

Startled, I spun around to find a young blond man casually perched on the hood of a truck. He was dressed in an immaculate white suit, and his piercing blue eyes shimmered with the ominous crackle of storm lightning.

CHAPTER 9

WITH A PRACTICED EYE, I immediately recognized the stranger as a powerful Gifted, despite his youthful appearance of no more than eighteen. Whoever this kid was, the thugs I'd just dispatched wouldn't hold a candle to him. On top of that, he was the first local I'd encountered who consciously suppressed part of his elemental energy — a clear sign of skill.

"Looking for a fight?" I asked lazily.

"That depends on your answer," the blond said, pointing at me.

"About the cargo?" I glanced at the containers. "Settle things with you first, then I'll decide."

"So, you don't know what's inside." He nodded to himself, hopping off the truck's hood. "Which means you're not here for the containers."

"No," I confirmed simply.

"Then I have no reason to attack you," he stated matter-of-factly, extending his hand. "Max Bright, future Grand Warrior of the Lightning Clan."

"Future?" I arched an eyebrow, accepting the handshake.

The kid's grip was surprisingly firm for someone with such a wiry build. He looked like a teenager, but his eyes held the wisdom of someone much older, clashing starkly with his carefree smile. Even his elemental response was an odd mix — confusing and layered.

"I'll earn the title once the clan recognizes me," Max explained with a grin. "My family's young and small, so I have to work three times harder than the competition for a place among the warriors."

"And what brings a future Grand Warrior to a place like this? Shopping for slaves?"

"How dare you!" He gasped, pretending to be offended. "The Lightning Clan would never stoop to such depravity!"

"Right, just dabbling in smuggling," I shot back.

"Why, you...!" Max started, then paused, his expression shifting. "Although, you're not entirely wrong. I was sent to retrieve something... But!" He held up a finger dramatically. "The cargo belongs to the Lightning Clan. I'm here to reclaim our property! We never intended to sell it to anyone."

"But it's contraband, isn't it?" I pressed.

"Let's say it is," he admitted, frowning.

"So, smuggling," I said with a sigh. "Fine by

me. Take it."

"Really?" Max's expression turned genuinely surprised.

"As I said, I'm not interested in the cargo," I replied. "Especially if it doesn't belong to me."

"And you just believe me?" he asked, narrowing his eyes.

"I know it's yours."

Truthfully, I could see it from the elemental resonance, but I had no intention of explaining that. Nor did I feel like pandering to the young noble. The sooner this flashy kid took what he came for and left, the better.

"You're sharp," Max said, nodding approvingly. "But you still haven't introduced yourself."

I didn't reply, but my silence only seemed to fuel his curiosity. Meanwhile, I kept an eye on Peter and his progress with the evacuation. Everything seemed to be going smoothly.

"Need any help?" Max asked, folding his arms and stepping closer.

"Help with what?" I asked, sighing as I realized ignoring him only made him more persistent.

"Cleaning up," he replied, glancing over my shoulder at the chaotic scene. "Those thugs will be missed soon enough, and you've left quite a trail."

"I'll handle it," I muttered, tossing my backpack and some scavenged weapons into the nearest truck.

Walking to the capital was out of the question. The railroad would guide my direction, and I could ditch the truck once I was closer.

"Too many clues, too little time." Max shook his head disapprovingly. "Mind if I ask how you plan to pull it off?"

"Will you tell me what's in the containers?" I countered.

"Hmm," Max mused, genuinely considering it. "All I can say is that it mustn't fall into the wrong hands. And we don't need any leaks, so forgive me for not trusting an anonymous drifter with sensitive clan information."

"Then why are you even asking me, instead of handling it yourself?" I gave him a smirk.

"Uh..." he scratched his head. "Out of curiosity. For instance, how did you take out five armed Gifted singlehandedly? Including turning one into necrotic ash?"

"He shot himself." I shrugged.

"Yeah, right, with a rifle he was holding, at point-blank range?" Max snorted.

"Exactly." I nodded. "Want me to demonstrate?"

"Relax! This isn't an interrogation," Max said quickly, raising his hands in mock surrender. "I won't breathe a word about you to the clan, I promise. Consider it a token of gratitude for dealing with those who stole our cargo."

"Listen, Max," I said, rubbing my temples. "If I prove I can handle the cleanup, will you leave?"

Dealing with a stubborn young aristocrat was proving more exhausting than fighting a Stone Serpent. And I was seriously starting to weigh my options.

"Absolutely!" He gave an eager nod, watching me intently.

Sighing, I approached one of the trucks, lifted a rifle from the bed, and let it fall.

Before it hit the ground, the weapon silently vanished into my shadow.

"A Shadow Pocket?" Max said, gasping as he rushed closer to inspect. He even tried stepping on the spot, spat on it for good measure, and then turned his astonished gaze to me.

Ignoring yet another exclamation about how I could possibly be a Gifted with "empty" eyes, I watched the young man's reaction closely. His amazement wasn't feigned — it was genuine.

Even as he stood right before me, the blond youth didn't hesitate to mistake my *Absorption of Darkness* for *Shadow Pocket.*

Though the two abilities might look similar on the surface, they are fundamentally different.

The "Shadow Pocket" is a basic ability for Gifted of the Shadow Element. Essentially, it's just a storage space — a kind of invisible bag where one can store and retrieve items. Its size depends on the user's energy reserves but rarely exceeds that of a small room, as it requires constant energy to sustain.

My "Absorption," on the other hand, sends objects into the boundless realm of Darkness, effectively annihilating them and converting them into elemental energy, part of which flows back to me. It's more of a sacrifice than storage.

While I can retrieve absorbed objects, they are

not the originals but recreations made entirely of Darkness. I can reproduce as many copies as my energy allows, but each one costs significantly more energy than I gain from the initial absorption.

Another striking difference is that, under certain conditions, my Absorption can target not just physical objects but pure elemental energy — and even living beings.

This ability was the main reason for the hatred I inspired. Old Aks once said people were terrified that, one day, I might sacrifice the entire world to the Darkness. And the stronger I became — absorbing thousands upon thousands of off-world creatures in countless battles for humanity's survival — the more those I protected came to fear me.

After all, I can recreate anything I've ever absorbed.

"Don't tell me you're planning to shove all this into a Shadow Pocket," the blond finally managed, breaking a thirty-second silence.

"Alright, I won't tell you," I said with a shrug.

I was pleased with the impromptu demonstration. If this noble youth fell for it, then masking my Element as Shadow in the capital wouldn't be a problem.

The key was to avoid showing that I could use my element even where there wasn't a trace of shadow — or, failing that, to leave no living witnesses.

"You're kidding me! Even the trucks?" Max blurted out, utterly forgetting his earlier vow to leave. So much for aristocratic poise.

"There are ways." I sighed, considering stuffing the noisy boy into the trunk to keep him out of the way. Luckily for him, Peter came running up at that moment, panting heavily.

"Hey, Marcus," Peter began, wiping sweat from his brow. He froze as soon as he noticed the aristocrat in his spotless white suit standing behind me. The boy's clan amulet was barely visible beneath his collar, but his status was evident regardless.

"He's harmless," I said, nodding toward Max. "Go ahead."

"Well, uh..." Peter stammered, still casting wary glances at the grinning Max. "We found some money in the locomotive... and, well, the folks are wondering what to do with it."

Ah, so that's why he was so nervous. Understandable. It wasn't easy for someone in his position to come ask instead of quietly pocketing it. Escaping slavery was one thing, but survival afterward was another.

"Can you hide it so well the Imperials won't suspect a thing?"

"Of course!" Peter thumped his chest. "We'll stash it so deep their best trackers won't find a single imp!"

"Then divide it and keep it," I said. "It's probably the same money that was used to buy you in the first place."

"Thank you!" Peter's eyes filled with tears as he hesitated, then extended a hand instead of hugging me. "God bless you, Marcus. If you're ever in Ilyrton, come visit. It's a small, poor village, but we remember kindness. Can't promise much, but we'll offer a clean bed, homemade bread, and a warm bath."

"I'll hold you to that," I replied with a warm smile, shaking his hand.

"If you want to survive, ask for Ludwig at the station," Max remarked before Peter could leave.

Peter gave the aristocrat a suspicious look, but Max didn't flinch.

"All railway workers in the Empire take bribes. If you run into a crony of one of the dead bandits, you'll be killed," Max explained nonchalantly.

"And Ludwig is some saint who never takes bribes?" I asked.

"Of course he does," Max said with a nod. "But only from me. He'll listen and tell you exactly what to do to stay alive. Also, I'd suggest you get moving before the locomotive's alarm system triggers. You've got about ten minutes left."

Peter paled at that, nearly leading everyone straight into a trap.

Not that there was much choice. Walking was too dangerous, and many wouldn't make it. Taking the truck would put a target on their backs for every associate of the dead bandits.

I didn't care if anyone hunted me for revenge. In fact, I welcomed it — more trophies for me. But ordinary people wouldn't fare as well, especially if the trail led the bandits to their homes and villages.

That left the railway as the only safe route. Peter understood this, though he still struggled with the risk of trusting the wrong person and dooming everyone.

"He's trustworthy. Go," I said, clapping the miner on the shoulder. Peter nodded and hurried off.

As soon as Peter was out of earshot, I turned to Max, my smile gone.

"If you lied, I'll kill you."

"All this fuss for a handful of commoners?" he asked, incredulous.

"Protecting the innocent is the duty of anyone who wields elemental power," I replied calmly, the image of old Aks flashing in my mind. He had ingrained that principle into my very soul.

"Interesting opinion," he mused.

It wasn't an opinion. It was the first law of the Argus Order, enforced with death for any Paladin who broke it, regardless of rank or birth.

Every ounce of off-world energy humanity managed to control was meant to be turned against the creatures. Imperial criminals who harmed humanity were considered no different from those creatures.

"So, would you kill every aristocrat who uses their element purely for personal gain?" he asked after a brief silence.

"Maybe."

The truth was, I didn't have a definitive answer. The Argus Order no longer existed. I was no longer the First Paladin. I owed nothing to anyone.

I was on vacation, after all.

Would I rush to restore the old ways or rebuild the Order in this changed world? Of course not. But neither could I ignore what happened right before my eyes. That was how old Aks had raised me.

"Then you'll have to kill half the southern capital," he said with a chuckle.

"Glad to know I'll have something to keep me busy," I replied with a grin.

"You're an odd one, Marcus," he said with a laugh, stretching his hands. "But I like you. And since you've trusted me enough to show your power, I'll return the favor. I hate being in anyone's debt."

With that, he rubbed his hands together, igniting a cascade of brilliant blue electricity, then flicked his wrists with the precision of a maestro conducting a symphony.

Streams of elemental electricity surged from the nearby levitating black sedan to his fingertips, pulsing in steady waves as he pulled the energy toward him. The flow continued until the car was drained of all its energy, and with a deafening crash, it plummeted to the ground — a hollow, lifeless shell.

But he didn't stop there. Twirling the gathered electricity around his fingers, he redirected it, unleashing a storm of lightning bolts that obliterated the drained sedan from existence.

Ten seconds later, all that remained of the vehicle were neatly stacked containers, with no trace of magic to be found.

"And you didn't feel bad about losing the car?" I asked, watching the smug satisfaction on his face.

"It wouldn't have driven anyway," he said, waving dismissively. "It's a Kentley. Its elemental imprint is bound to a single owner. That beast wouldn't have obeyed me, so it was useless."

"And you're going to carry the containers on your back?" I asked with a grin.

"I'll buy the truck from you," he shot back without missing a beat.

"Got the money for it?" I replied, my grin widening.

"I know its retail price," he said, a flicker of suspicion crossing his face.

"Water in the desert always costs more than by a freshwater lake," I said helpfully. "If you wanted to pay retail, you should have made the deal before you destroyed your only transport."

"My mistake," he admitted. Then his eyes sparkled with a hint of hope. "What if I kill you and take it by force?"

"You can try, sure," I said with a shrug. "Might even get to see a few more displays of power before you die."

"You drive a hard bargain," he muttered, acknowledging defeat. "Alright, here's a counteroffer. You're headed to the capital, aren't you?"

"Let's say I am."

"Perfect! We'll travel together. I know a shortcut, and..." He flicked a spark of blue lightning between his fingers. "With this fuel, we'll get there faster than any train! We can negotiate on the way. Trust me, I'll find something you'll want."

All his noise and pestering suddenly became tolerable in light of the opportunity he'd just presented. The capital — a sprawling metropolis where I had no connections, no knowledge of its workings, no understanding of this new era's realities.

Building ties was unavoidable, and having a young aristocrat indebted to me was an excellent start.

As old Aks used to say, "In this world, there are hundreds of things more valuable than money." Although, coming from one of the wealthiest men in the Empire, that sentiment didn't carry much weight.

With my agreement secured, he began loading his containers into my truck while I used Absorption to erase any traces of what had transpired in the clearing. I'd already taken anything valuable, so it only took about five minutes.

I absorbed the spare trucks last, an act he watched with rapt attention.

"This is the first time I've seen a Shadow Gifted capable of something like that," he remarked in awe as he finished preparing the vehicle for departure.

By then, Peter and the others had already vanished over the horizon, safely out of sight.

"Do you know many shadow elementalists?" I asked casually.

"Not really," he admitted reluctantly. "The

clans guard their abilities zealously, and the rabble—" He caught himself mid-sentence, correcting, "I mean, those guys tend to stay out of the limelight."

I pretended not to notice his slip and climbed into the cab. The cargo was neatly stacked and accounted for. The morning's haul amounted to one hundred thirty-five thousand imps in cash, a backpack stuffed with valuables of varying worth, and an eighteen-year-old aristocrat as a debtor.

Not a bad start for funding my venture in the capital.

Still, my empty stomach growled again, a recurring annoyance that was beginning to wear on me.

CHAPTER 10

Shortly after
The outskirts of the Dead Forest

THE PRINCESS HAD JUST BEGUN dissecting the remains she'd found. For some reason, she insisted on doing the work herself, sending the entire squad to guard the perimeter — including her personal bodyguard.

Why Victoria wanted to dig through the remains without any witnesses was none of Albert's concern. Since morning, all his thoughts had been consumed by one accursed individual: Marcus, who had landed in his life like a dropped anvil.

Albert eagerly seized the chance to make a phone call without his lady's prying eyes.

He could just about tolerate the impudent commoner's infatuation with the princess. He could even forgive the bastard for destroying his prized armor, which remained irreparable even now.

But what he absolutely could not abide was failing to execute a direct order from the Prince. And here he was, juggling directives from not one, but two Elemental Princes — both concerning that wretched commoner.

He still couldn't fathom how a routine daily report had escalated into this mess.

The Prince of Nature had been furious to learn that his daughter had given a shard to a commoner. He demanded Albert fix his daughter's "reckless mistake" before anyone found out.

The Prince of Metal, meanwhile, had erupted upon hearing of the relic tied to the fallen Order. His rage had nearly driven Albert out of the Clan for failing to report it immediately. And when the Prince discovered that the relic's new owner had been allowed to leave their Clan's hotel alive, he commanded Albert to intercept the commoner at all costs before he reached the capital.

Albert shuddered to think what punishment awaited him for failure. The Princes' wrath was far more terrifying than the logistics of carrying out their orders.

And so, he was willing to do whatever it took.

"Report," he growled into the receiver, shielding the phone with his massive hand.

"The target is gone, sir," came the voice on the other end.

Furious, he drove his fist into the trunk of an elemental tree.

The towering tree groaned under the blow, its metallic bark screeching loudly enough to echo across the clearing. Alarmed by the noise, he quickly radioed that his flank was secure and no assistance was needed.

"How could he get away from you?" he snarled into the phone, stepping away from prying ears.

It made no sense.

After the Princes issued their orders, time had been tight, but Albert had meticulously orchestrated every step. He'd bribed the conductor with information on Marcus and generously paid him to ensure that a valuable shipment "accidentally" went missing and ended up near a group of future slaves. To make it happen, he had to promise the imperial merchant protection from his Clan against the cargo's owners — a risky move, considering the Lightning Clan's potential for retaliation.

But those risks paled in comparison to the consequences of failing the Princes' commands.

The missing shipment had been bait to lure Kai, the most powerful Shadow Gifted mercenary Albert could hire. Not only was Kai capable of eliminating Marcus, but he could also hide the shard and relic in his "pocket" until Albert was able to reclaim them.

He had anticipated the cost of retrieving them and had even sent a Clan special ops squad to keep tabs on Kai. The mercenary's death wouldn't attract much attention, and Albert would fulfill both orders in one stroke — while ridding himself of the insolent commoner who dared covet the princess.

But somewhere, his perfect plan had unraveled.

"We don't know," came the reply. "Kai never showed at the designated spot. When we checked his expected meeting point with the target, there were no signs of either."

"What do you mean, no signs?" he bellowed. "Are you saying... Kai abandoned a prepaid contract? That son of a—"

"No, sir. Kai made contact after meeting the imperial handler. Everything was proceeding smoothly, but then... he vanished."

"And the train? What about the train?" he spat, no longer concerned about the mercenary whose fate was shaping up to be worse than a slave's.

"It arrived on schedule. We wiped the documents clean, left no evidence. But then two train cars with people arrived at the station — without the shipment."

"Tell me you intercepted them!"

"Apologies, sir. Representatives of the Lightning Clan seized them immediately. We couldn't get close. However, we confirmed the target wasn't among the passengers."

"What do you mean, he wasn't there? Where did he go?"

"We... don't know, sir."

"Then find out!" Albert roared, his voice thunderous. "Find him and kill him! Do you hear me?

If that miserable commoner reaches the capital, I'll personally tear your heads off!"

His voice reverberated through the forest, punctuated by metallic thuds as he pounded the elemental tree in frustration. Finally, he crushed the phone in his trembling hands.

He knew full well that if he failed, only one head would roll: his own.

*   *   *

"What, still thinking?" Max's cheerful voice broke my train of thought once again.

"No."

"We're halfway there already." He sighed theatrically. "Has anyone ever told you how difficult you are to negotiate with?"

"Has anyone ever told you it's rude to pester adults with questions?"

"We'll never get anywhere at this rate." He shook his head, deftly cutting another corner on the road. "Come on, Marcus. What do you want?"

The groaning truck was hurtling down the road at a speed that would make any train jealous. I couldn't fathom how the kid managed to handle this rickety contraption at such a pace while bombarding me with questions, his face lit with childish curiosity.

"Right now?" I mused. "I'm hungry. Get me some portal lamb in honey glaze, and we're square."

"Can't do that," he replied flatly.

Pity. If he'd pulled that off, I'd have forgiven his debt and even thrown in a tip.

"Well, at least a steak or some ribs," I offered magnanimously. "I'll even settle for regular earthly meat."

"Done!" He lit up, seizing the opportunity. "I'll book you a table at the best restaurant in the capital with an unlimited deposit!"

"Great idea," I said with mock enthusiasm. "Then I'll throw you and your containers out here, drive the truck to your fancy restaurant, and you can pick it up there."

"What good would it do me there if I need it now?" he sputtered.

"Exactly!" I smiled.

"You're messing with me." He frowned.

"You asked what I wanted." I shrugged. "I answered."

"Pick something else."

"Why?"

"Because I don't like being in debt!"

"That's your problem," I said, dismissing his concern with a glance.

"A million! I'll pay a million imperial coins for this junk heap!" he blurted out, his frustration boiling over.

I pretended to mull it over, watching the scenery out the window. We'd left the grasslands for a wide highway and were overtaking the occasional vehicle as if they were standing still. He was clearly a better driver than a negotiator.

The closer we got to the capital, the more populated the surroundings became. Gloomy forests gave way to quaint villages, sprawling farms, neatly sown fields, and charming suburban neighborhoods. The perimeter's defenses here were laughably minimal — woven fences and the occasional bunkers, seemingly installed more for the peace of mind of the locals than for any actual protective purpose.

As Edward used to say, "Portals rarely open in the Green Zone, and when they do, they're weak — so much so that the creatures inside usually prefer staying put."

"So, have you made up your mind?" His lively voice interrupted the pleasant silence.

Three minutes. That's how long he lasted. Weak.

"Max, do you honestly think I'd tolerate you just for money?" I raised an eyebrow.

"You know, Marcus, I'm starting to think you just want to keep me in your debt," he said with a sigh, easing the truck around a sharp bend in the narrowing road.

"And that's the sharpest thought you've had all trip." I praised him, watching as we passed by an enormous construction site stretching endlessly from right to left — a solid wall that seemed to divide the horizon itself.

"The Fourth Ring," he explained, catching my gaze. "Over half of the Empire's resources are currently being poured into its construction."

"Why so far out?" I frowned, mentally calculating how many nearby settlements this new wall would cut off.

"So we won't have to build the fifth one for as long as possible," he said with a smirk.

And to squeeze as much coin as they could from those stuck on the outside. I doubted the unfortunate souls beyond the perimeter would even be offered evacuation. Based on what I'd gathered about the ruling elite of this era, they'd likely go a step further and forcibly relocate people within the inner perimeters.

"By the way, Marcus," he spoke up again, "a bit of advice — ditch the dead conductor from your Shadow Pocket. The sooner, the better."

"What's wrong with an untouchable corpse?" I asked, intrigued.

"That's exactly it!" He laughed. "He's untouchable! A literal sacred cow!"

"A slaver?" I scoffed. In my time, killing scum like that earned you a bounty.

"The Governor doesn't care about slavery," he explained. "What matters to him are the imperial supply lines from the front. Any attack on those is treated as an attack on the Governor himself. Whole syndicates have been wiped out for less. The Princes' Council enforces this rule strictly. They won't even bother investigating. The untouchable status covers not just the imperial goods but also the trains and their personnel."

"No wonder he was so cocky." I chuckled. "Don't worry about it, though. As far as anyone's concerned, he doesn't exist anymore. Won't you get into trouble for covering it up if someone finds out?"

"Not at all," he replied easily. "I've got a Clan backing me. The question is — who's backing you?"

"No one," I said, glancing theatrically over my shoulder. "That's the beauty of it."

"How's that supposed to work?" he asked, genuinely perplexed.

"You'll understand when you grow up," I replied with a grin.

That's when a sharp burning sensation flared in my chest. I reached into my pocket and pulled out the small jade shard, which was pulsating wildly.

"What a clumsy idiot," I muttered, noticing how Victoria's sloppy containment spell was reacting to the shard's internal energy. If I'd left it in my backpack, it might have detonated — leaving Max's containers scattered across the countryside. Possibly Max, too.

It took ten seconds to stabilize her mess before I tossed the shard back into my pocket. Only then did I notice him staring at me wide-eyed.

"You couldn't have shown that earlier?" he asked indignantly, his accusing glare practically sizzling.

"Why? It's not mine."

"Of course it's not yours!" He huffed, clearly offended. "But that's irrelevant! What matters is its existence! If you'd shown that shard at the station, you'd have gotten a proper car!"

"The one I had was fine," I replied with a shrug,

not understanding his outrage.

"That's not even the half of it! The shard listens to you! Do you even realize what that means?"

Ha. Listens. I wonder what he would've said if it had actually exploded.

"That it was planted on me?" I replied dryly.

"That you're under the Clan of Nature's protection! Receiving such an artifact is like an official invitation, extended to only a select few! It's a public declaration of interest and guaranteed patronage."

"Sounds like a hassle," I said with a grimace. The princess could've just said so. I'd have made my response clear right away — perhaps with a gesture.

"You said you were heading to the capital to sort out documents," he continued his barrage of complaints. "But why would you need commoner papers if a Clan is ready to take you in? Is that why you were so confident at that meeting? Is that why — ?"

"Calm down, Max," I cut him off. "I don't care about this rock. Want me to throw it out?"

With that, I held the jade shard between two fingers and moved to open the window.

"Hey, hey, hey!" He lunged toward me. "Don't you dare! That would be a mortal insult! Do you want to become the Clan of Nature's blood enemy?"

"And sneaking it into my bag overnight wasn't an insult?" I smirked, reluctantly returning the shard to my pocket.

"If you really want to get rid of it, you'll need to hand it personally to the one who gave it to you," he said.

"What, go all the way back just for that?" I grumbled.

"You could also deliver it to the Clan's office in the capital," he offered another option. "Then, if you make it out alive, they won't have any claims against you!"

"Yeah, sure," I said with a sigh. "More trouble."

The shard was beautiful, packed with energy. Honestly, I'd regret tossing it. But this was a matter of principle. Victoria should've thought twice before dumping such obligations on me.

Couldn't keep me close on a leash, so now she's trying to slap a collar on me?

No thanks. She can save those games for her dear Albert — I've got a few questions for him, too.

"So, joining a Clan doesn't interest you?" he asked, his earlier excitement giving way to a calm curiosity.

"Nope."

"Then what does? Besides food..." He smirked.

"Portals," I replied easily, spotting one just ahead in the middle of the wheat field.

A comically oversized red combine harvester was calmly collecting crops just thirty feet away, as if the Portal wasn't even there. A lone soldier dozed at its entrance, completely unaware.

"You won't be allowed through without a license," he remarked suddenly.

"A license? For what?" I gave him a sharp look.

With a deep breath, he launched into an explanation. This time, I listened carefully. Portals had been much simpler in my day.

See a Portal? Close it. No Portal? Head to the Tower — there's always more waiting for you.

The Grand Source Core intercepted most off-world invasions, channeling them into specially designed floors within the Tower. Researchers studied them, resource gatherers extracted valuable materials, and warriors like me handled the rest — wiping out threats and shutting down unstable or useless Portals.

That was it. Any Gifted could access a Portal, no questions asked, as long as they had the will to enter — whether for the good of humanity, fame, fortune, or power. The Argus Order welcomed all.

Now? The Princes' Council had created a bureaucratic nightmare.

The Imperial Ministry for Invasion Mitigation (IMIM) had established an electronic Portal Registry, overseen directly by the Council of Princes. Within this registry, the top ten Clans divided the spheres of influence among themselves, claiming ownership over every Portal located within the Green and Yellow Zones.

To access a Portal, you first had to reserve it through the registry and pay a hefty fee to its owner. But even that wasn't the first hurdle — you needed a Guardian's License just to gain access to the registry. Without this license, any interaction with Portals outside the Red Zone was deemed illegal.

How this enforcement worked, he didn't get to explain. We'd taken a sharp turn off the main road, passing a long warehouse before stopping near a levitating white SUV marked with unfamiliar family crests.

"We're here," he announced as a young woman in a sharp gray suit stepped out of the SUV. Her stern expression locked onto him like a hawk spotting prey.

"A friend of yours?" I nudged him.

"Something like that," Max said with a wry grin, sticking his head out the window. "Diana, sunshine, be a dear and handle unloading our cargo."

The woman gave an annoyed snort but complied. She knocked on the SUV's door, and two burly men emerged, heading for the truck bed.

"Boys, just the containers — don't touch anything else," he instructed, then closed the window and turned to me with a grin. "Well, Marcus, it's time for us to part ways. I'd love to chat more, but duty calls."

With that, he handed me a silvery card etched with a series of numbers.

"This is my personal number. Call me anytime you figure out what you want."

"I thought you hated being in debt," I said, accepting the card.

"Like I had a choice." He sighed, his smile faltering as Diana's glare drilled into him from outside.

Her silent, smoldering stare was genuinely unsettling.

"Good luck with your paperwork," he added, hopping out of the truck.

"And you with patching things up with your 'sunshine.'" I chuckled, watching him go.

Without so much as a glance at Diana, he slid into the driver's seat of the SUV. She climbed in beside him, her piercing gaze lingering on me for a moment before the vehicle roared off, leaving a trail of blue sparks in its wake.

Finally, blessed silence.

The capital was less than a mile away now.

CHAPTER 11

SITTING IN SILENCE was pleasant. Thinking on an empty stomach? Not so much. I stretched slowly, then climbed into the truck bed to sort through my belongings.

Time hadn't been on my side at the clearing. I'd grabbed whatever was lying around, tossing it into the truck without much thought, resulting in an obvious surplus of odds and ends.

After some quick deliberation, I kept only the cleaver made of off-world metal and all the consumables infused with elemental energy. It wasn't likely I'd use much beyond the cleaver and grenades, but ammunition and magazines were compact and worth good money. Plus, in a pinch, I could extract a bit of elemental energy from the leftovers.

I also held onto a water canteen, stacks of

cash, a few other necessities, and packed it all tightly into a tactical backpack. As for everything else — including the truck — it went as an offering to the Darkness.

There wasn't much value left in the remains, so the Absorption yielded just over three units of energy.

Once finished, I slung the backpack over my shoulders and headed toward the road. About three hundred feet ahead, a one-story building loomed, crowned with a massive inflatable burger perched on its roof.

"Just what I need," I muttered, licking my lips as I strode directly toward it.

The place welcomed me with plain glass doors — no reinforcements or traces of elemental energy. Thin, scuffed walls, a yellowing counter, and a dozen or so tables, each bearing the scars of better days, completed the scene.

"I'll take your signature burger and a black coffee," I said as I crossed the threshold.

"On it," replied a hefty woman in a grimy apron, nodding toward the only empty table.

Despite the diner's mediocre condition, the place was packed. The not-so-small parking lot outside was crammed with a variety of vehicles, many of which bore a closer resemblance to the cars of my time. Yet I didn't recognize a single model or the type of fuel they used.

Leaning back on the hard bench, I eavesdropped on the locals' conversations.

Taxes, work, exhaustion, illness, family —

these topics were a stark contrast to the chatter at the Duck's Nail. Here, people weren't scheming to make money or outmaneuver their neighbors for a bigger share. These folks were simply trying to survive and feed their families. There were exceptions, of course, but they were few.

"Your order." The woman's deep voice boomed, and a massive plate landed on my table. At its center was a towering burger surrounded by three types of sliced vegetables. I recognized the potatoes but couldn't identify the rest — some had unfamiliar shapes, others strange colors, or both.

Hunger overtook curiosity, and I eagerly devoured everything on the plate. Despite the odd appearance, the taste was surprisingly good. The best part? The meal cost me just ninety imps.

Leaving a hundred as a tip, I was about to leave when a mustachioed man confidently approached and took the seat across from me.

"Need a taxi?" he asked politely, his eyes briefly flicking to my backpack.

"I do," I replied casually, raising an eyebrow. "Why should I choose the most brazen of the three?" I glanced over his shoulder, where two competitors were lingering near the exit, ready to offer their services.

"Because I'm not bothered by the bullet holes and bloodstains on your bag," he said quickly. "Plus, my beauty here will get you to your destination, unlike the rust buckets those clowns are driving. They're only here because they can't afford gas."

"And you're different?"

"I love the burgers here," he said with a grin. "And I know a place where you can offload any goods or, conversely, find what you need," he added with a wink.

"For now, I just need to register my license," I said, waving off his dubious proposal. "For the Guardian status. Know where I can do that?"

"Of course! Thirty minutes, five hundred imps, and you'll be there!" he said enthusiastically, leaning closer to whisper. "Those guys won't take less than a thousand — that's the minimum to fuel their rides."

"Hmm," I mused, glancing out the window. "Which one's yours?"

"That one... the yellow 'Mutant-G'!" he declared proudly, puffing out his chest. "An old-timer, but the side armor's solid, and it still handles like a dream!"

"I don't care about the armor," I replied calmly, handing him five hundred imps. "Just get me there."

"As you wish," he said, pocketing the cash deftly, grabbing my backpack, and heading for the exit.

The man's vehicle did look more impressive than the others in the lot. It featured an elemental-powered engine, movable yellow plates to seal the windows, and a hefty bumper, seemingly designed to plow through creatures if necessary.

"Overkill for a taxi, don't you think?" I said with a smirk, hopping into the back seat.

"I mainly work in the Yellow Zone," he said with pride. "You can't survive there without it. You're lucky I came to visit my brother. Otherwise, you'd have been stuck paying those clowns a fortune to push their junk."

The roar of the engine drowned out any further conversation. To my relief, the driver didn't insist on talking, allowing me to enjoy the sights of the capital in silence. Unlike Fort-Hell, where fortifications dominated the skyline, the buildings here were more varied and aesthetically pleasing.

The outskirts of the southern capital were filled with sprawling apartment complexes. After twenty minutes, we reached broad, well-lit streets, parks, playgrounds, and a cluster of skyscrapers ahead in the city center.

He turned onto a quieter avenue.

"It's quicker this way," he explained, though I hadn't asked and continued gazing out the window.

Perhaps that's why I noticed the oncoming truck barreling toward us from a side street just before the driver did — and managed to buckle my seatbelt in time.

A dull crash hit the opposite side of the car, and the world spun around me. After three full rotations and what felt like smashing through a couple of barriers, we slammed into something and came to a stop. The air filled with the stench of blood, burning, and acrid black smoke as it seeped into the cabin.

I had to burn one erg to prevent the warped

door from slicing into my stomach. Otherwise, the seatbelt module had done its job admirably.

Two stars, tops. That's all he deserved. No name, didn't get me to my destination, and his vaunted armor nearly skewered me. Definitely no tip for him.

Getting out wasn't much trouble, though my backpack got stuck briefly, earning a new set of battle scars. A couple of kicks later, the dented roof gave way, and I retrieved my gear.

"What the hell did you do, you idiot?" he bellowed furiously as he stumbled out.

Blood trickled down his temple, and he was limping on one leg, but otherwise, he looked fine.

"My beauty! My beauty!" he wailed, clutching his head as he turned toward the truck, now smoldering ten feet away with a crushed nose. "This wasn't part of the deal! You're paying for the repairs! Do you even know—"

He didn't get to finish. An elemental bullet struck him square in the face, taking half his head with it.

The second shot came for me. No warnings, no threats, no demands. They brought me here to kill me.

The bullet unfurled mid-flight into an elemental metal blade, which I deflected with my cleaver.

The shooter had positioned himself in the smoke, thinking it would shield him from retaliation. Big mistake.

"Relocate," I commanded, shoving a grenade

with the pin pulled into the dark void that materialized in my palm.

The ensuing blast of elemental fire tore the sniper apart, scattering the smoke throughout the empty alley. This wasn't a random attack — the ambush was premeditated, with measures taken to ensure there would be no witnesses.

Fine by me.

Two more snipers hesitated to reveal their positions, holding out for a perfect shot. They never got one.

The one hiding by a first-floor window ended up pinned to the wall by my throwing cleaver, the blade piercing his heart. As for the guy on the roof, he lost his balance and plummeted to his death — with a little help from a Midnight Phantasm, the harmless illusion I had woven out of the swirling elemental smoke.

If the mere sight of portal creatures frightens you that much, maybe you should stay home and leave the sniping to the professionals.

I only had time to loot the one I'd skewered, retrieving my cleaver from his chest in the process. Among his belongings, I found a photofit sketch of my face. The bracelet with a golden shard of the metal element on his wrist made it painfully clear who had sent him.

"Well, Albert," I muttered, shaking my head. "This won't end well for you."

Without hesitation, I absorbed the golden shard of Metal Element, along with the body and all traces of the attack. Twenty-seven units of energy surged through my veins like molten iron, forcing my will to suppress and dominate the foreign element. Thankfully, my body still remembered how to handle it.

The other two corpses couldn't incriminate me. One had fallen off the roof on his own, and the other wouldn't leave a trace behind. Elemental fire burns everything down to atoms, and the grenade had detonated right in his pants. Not even a bloodhound could find evidence there.

I remembered the direction back to the busy street we'd turned off from, so I hoisted my backpack and headed that way before the authorities showed up. No way the attackers had bought themselves more than ten minutes for an escape.

Emerging onto the bustling avenue, I realized I stood out far too much. My already worn clothes were now blackened with soot and hung off me in tatters.

"This won't do." I sighed and stepped into the first clothing store I came across.

"Welcome—" the chipper greeting from a young blonde saleswoman faltered mid-sentence, her trained smile fading as she backed away slightly. "You... uh... want the register?"

"The register?" I repeated, confused.

"Y-yeah, the register... you know... to rob it?" she stammered, swallowing hard. "Come on, I'll show you everything! Take it all! Just please don't hurt me! I've got a date tonight..."

"Well, if you've got a date, then there's no need to cry about it," I said with mock concern. "Your mascara's running."

"S-sorry…" she mumbled, watching in horror as I lowered the display shutter and locked the door.

"What do you think you're doing?" a statuesque older woman stormed out from the back.

"Maria, he's here to kill us!" The blonde saleswoman's eyes widened in terror as she gasped, then fainted dead away into the older woman's arms.

Unable to handle the unexpected burden, Maria toppled into a neatly folded pile of shirts, clearly struggling to decide her next move.

It all happened so fast I didn't even have a chance to speak. Before things could spiral further out of control, I set my backpack down and raised my hands innocently.

"Your employee misunderstood," I said, keeping my tone as pleasant as possible while slowly pulling a jade shard from my shirt pocket.

On one hand, I hated resorting to this borrowed status. On the other, if not for that petty cur Albert, I wouldn't be in this mess in the first place. So let's call it even with Victoria.

Maria exhaled with visible relief. "Oh, sir… Why didn't you say so earlier?"

Moving carefully, I handed her a thick wad of cash.

"For the trouble caused and for my future purchases," I said with a disarming smile. "Shall we find something within my budget?"

"Of course," she replied, her composure returning.

Meanwhile, I picked up the unconscious blonde and carried her to a soft couch in the back of the hall. Maria shot wary glances at the locked front door while trying to steady herself.

"Excuse me, sir…"

"Marcus," I offered with a slight nod.

"Sir Marcus," she said, correcting herself gracefully, "may I ask why you locked the door? Are you being pursued?"

"Nothing for you to worry about," I assured her. "Though, someone might come by with questions about an incident nearby."

"An incident in which you, naturally, played no part, I presume?" she said, having regained her poise entirely.

"You're a perceptive one," I said with mock admiration.

"Survival demands it these days," she said with a faint smile, slipping back into the authoritative air of a seasoned businesswoman. "One last question, Marcus. Those who might inquire — who are they?"

"Not aristocrats, if that's your concern," I said, hoping to ease her mind. "And if they do show up, you can freely tell them everything you've seen here."

From what I'd gathered, local authority was mostly corrupt imperial enforcers who'd sold their integrity and deserted their posts. They'd dig tirelessly to escape accountability for their crimes.

Aristocrats, however, were a different matter.

If word of the incident reached them, it might even work in my favor. My witness could easily confirm I had a Nature Clan Shard, closing the door to any further questions.

The Nature Clan wouldn't want undue attention drawn to someone carrying their shard. Meanwhile, the Metal Clan wouldn't dare admit their involvement in attacking someone under the protection of an allied clan. They'd do everything possible to bury the incident — a scenario that suited me just fine.

If any aristocrat decided to intervene, they'd do it discreetly. And those who attacked quietly would die just as silently.

"Thank you." She exhaled in relief. "Now, tell me, Marcus. What color suit do you prefer?"

*   *   *

Around the same time

Beran Astor, known as "Beast," was a four-hundred-forty-pound giant whose presence filled the armored limousine. He sipped his cognac thoughtfully, drumming his massive elemental ring against the upholstery as the vehicle sped through a secret underground road toward the western ring.

It wasn't the first time Beast had to abandon his plans on short notice, but he'd only arrived in Fort-Hell a day ago! Ten business meetings canceled. Major deals collapsed. A year and a half of preparation — ruined.

He'd been certain he had at least a week. He'd paid handsomely to hundreds of greedy but influential hands to secure it, perfectly timed to coincide with the annual Princes' Council, when no one cared about anything but their own agendas.

"What went wrong?" he murmured, shaking his head.

Not that he expected an answer. A detailed report from his intelligence service lay before him. But how could it satisfy him? All it provided was a single name.

No clan. No lineage. No syndicate. Just a name, devoid of any additional data on the man's background.

Beast prided himself on his intelligence network, second only to the clans'. Yet, he knew nothing about the man who'd cost him millions in losses. It was as if this Marcus didn't exist.

His men had traced the leak to its source: his prized cartographer, known within the gang as "Head," who had slipped through the cracks thanks to the incompetence of two fools. After a swift interrogation, both were executed, forcing Beast to rethink the degree of freedom he allowed the man whose brilliant mind was the cornerstone of his legendary elusiveness.

"Head" himself remained blissfully unaware of his true worth, and Beast had learned to exploit that ignorance. To avoid drawing undue attention to his prized asset, Beast let "Head" live the life of an ordinary lowlife within the gang's ranks.

Beast swirled his cognac, letting the name linger in his mind like a bitter aftertaste.

"Marcus," he said quietly, rolling it over his tongue. It was all his operatives had managed to uncover after significant effort.

"Who the hell are you?"

The fact that a mere commoner had forced Beast into a cowardly retreat from Fort-Hell was known to only two people. But what two knew would inevitably spread.

Rumors would start.

Whispers would grow.

People would begin to believe Beast had lost his edge.

And sharks always smelled blood.

"Henry," Beast said decisively, pressing the selector button on his console. "Send the Reaper to the capital."

"It will be done, sir," came the crisp reply of his first lieutenant, and Beast's foul mood lightened, if only slightly.

Marcus needed to be punished.

And it had to be public.

While he was at it, Beast intended to investigate an unlikely rumor about a relic of the Fallen Order. The odds were slim, but if it turned out to be true, Beast would emerge from this debacle victorious — just as he always had.

His uncanny instinct for sniffing out potential profit had always been his most valuable ability.

CHAPTER 12

I ENDED UP LEAVING fifty thousand at the clothing store. Some of that went to a generous tip for keeping silent and for dealing with the inconvenience my arrival had caused.

I changed into a sleek black suit, paired with a dark shirt and no tie. A belt, comfortable shoes, and leather gloves completed the look, ensuring the fabric of the cloak wrapped around my right arm was fully concealed. My old clothes were disposed of via Absorption.

To avoid my polished look clashing with the tattered backpack, I picked up a large rolling suitcase and stuffed all my belongings inside.

With that, I exited the store and hailed a taxi, which, thankfully, took me to a gray multi-story building without any surprises.

"Ministry of Mitigation Headquarters," the

driver announced. "Registration bureau's in the right wing."

"Thanks," I said, paid the fare, and made my way up the wide staircase with my suitcase in tow.

I didn't encounter many people along the way, and by the entrance with the sign I needed, there was no one at all. The registration bureau was a modest room with white walls and ten information windows. Only one was manned.

To my relief, it was free.

"Good afternoon," I greeted with a polite smile. "I need a license."

"Applying, renewing, paying…" the gray-haired woman in glasses began listing off options with a weary sigh.

"Applying."

"License pickups are handled in another building…" she droned without lifting her gaze.

"You misunderstand," I interrupted the pointless script. "I need to apply for one."

"Then say so, young man! Don't hold up the line!" she snapped.

I turned around to emphasize the lack of any line. She didn't bother looking up.

"Your documents."

"There's a bit of a problem — I lost them," I said, offering my most innocent smile.

"Then go to the Imperial Chancellery to file a replacement request!" she barked, shooing me away.

I sighed heavily. The thought of another errand drained me. This woman was sapping my energy faster than a Metite Leech. Bureaucracy, the Princes' favorite weapon.

Moments like these made me miss the Order. What kind of world demands you navigate seven circles of hell just to fight off-world invaders?

Idiocy.

"Maybe we can work something out?" I suggested, reaching for cash in my inner pocket.

"What's that?" she snapped upright, nearly headbutting the glass partition.

"Just money," I replied, puzzled, holding up a wad of bills.

"No!" She waved me off frantically. "I meant the shiny thing!"

"This?" I pulled out the jade shard.

"Oh!" She collapsed into her chair, removing her glasses. "Why didn't you show that earlier?"

"It's not even mine," I muttered, déjà vu hitting me.

"That doesn't matter!" she exclaimed, fingers flying over the keyboard.

Why did this surprise everyone so much? Had the local aristocrats gotten so used to flaunting their status that anyone who didn't was dismissed as a nobody?

I thought it was my clothes, but now I looked respectable. And still, she didn't care until she saw the shard.

Now she was typing as if her life depended on it, eyes wide with fear. The Princes had trained their people well — a flock of obedient sheep, fleeced at will and used as shields against external threats.

"Your name, please," she asked, suddenly polite.

"Marcus," I replied. "And what are you doing, exactly?"

"Preparing your documents, dear," she said, batting her eyes innocently. "Surname?"

"I don't have one."

Never did. Most members of the Order were orphans with no lineage, and a single name was enough for us. Sometimes, for combat distinctions in the Portals, we earned nicknames that served in place of surnames.

With that thought, I ran through the ones they called me behind my back: Brutal... Bloody... Devourer... Cursed...

"That won't do, dear." She shook her head. "A surname is required."

"Fine." I sighed and added, "Dark."

"Marcus Dark, then." She nodded, satisfied. "Date and place of birth?"

I improvised, "A nameless village up north. December 22nd."

"Northern kingdom," she muttered. "Born on the winter solstice, huh?" She smiled faintly. "Shortest day of the year."

"And the longest night," I added.

Old Aks had always joked about that, and some fanatics believed I was a Child of Darkness. They weren't wrong.

"The year?"

"Two thousand six hundred ninety-five." I calculated, picking an age matching my appearance.

Exceptionally high reserves of elemental energy and frequent interactions with the Great Source significantly slowed the effects of aging, making all the Order's Paladins appear frozen at the age of twenty-eight.

"Almost done," she announced, handing me a slim card engraved with my details and the imperial crest in the top left corner. She placed a strange device on the counter — a small tower with three circular slots. "Insert the artifact in the correct slot and stamp the lower right corner."

Shrugging, I slotted the shard in place, lifted the tower slightly, and pressed it down on the indicated spot. A pulsing jade-green seal appeared on the card.

The woman let out a sigh of relief. The tower was a verification artifact — a test of rightful ownership — and I'd passed.

"Wonderful!" she chirped, handing me a filled-out license application. Then she waved me off.

Of course. Another errand. To my "sponsors," as she called them.

It turned out that the Clan of Nature was responsible for verifying the accuracy of my information, which was why the process had been so effortless. Otherwise, I'd have needed to file a petition at the Imperial Chancellery and wait at least a month for a hearing — at which point I'd have to prove that I was who I claimed to be.

I should probably thank Victoria when I see her — maybe think of a gift to match the month her shard just saved me. And dinner. I owed her that much. My last "date" with the princess left me with nothing but pleasant memories.

From the registration bureau, I headed to the official building of the Clan of Nature. Luckily, it was just a ten-minute walk to the Unity of Ten Square, named in honor of the Empire's Great Clans.

The place was dominated by towering clan buildings, each one easily recognizable by the massive crests on their facades and the statues representing each Element stationed at the entrances.

I spotted the entrance marked by a sculpture of a sprawling tree and made a beeline for it.

"Good day, sir," a perfectly poised footman with a clan emblem on his chest greeted me. "Do you have an appointment?"

"Something like that," I said with a smirk, holding up the jade shard.

The footman tapped something on his phone, gave a respectful bow, and opened the door.

"Watch my bag, would you? I won't be long," I said, stepping inside and leaving the suitcase by the entrance. A scanning archway loomed ahead, and I wasn't keen on testing how their security would react to a bag full of weapons.

As I approached, the familiar contours of the magic scanner module caught my eye. No doubt about it. The same type of module used to stand on every floor of the Great Tower of Argus. Well, almost the same. The design was different, but the unique elemental signature at its core was unmistakable.

So, the Princes hadn't just swiped shards of the Great Source — they'd managed to snag Argus tech too? Interesting.

"Welcome, Mister Marcus. Right this way," another footman greeted me and led me deeper into the building.

We passed through a domed, sunlit hall, a central fountain, and two corridors filled with decorative plants before arriving at a door to an office.

"Please, go on in. They're expecting you," the footman said with a bow and left.

Breathing in the intoxicatingly fresh air, I entered the office in a good mood.

"Mister Marcus," a wiry man greeted me with a nod, his manner clipped and formal. "Please, take a seat. My name is Kent, trusted servant of His Highness, the Prince."

"Well, hello there," I said, settling into the chair across from his desk, watching the sly glint in his eyes as he continued.

"Erm..." He cleared his throat, clearly unsettled by my stare, but forced a tight smile and continued. "To be honest, we've been expecting you. His Highness personally ordered that all the paperwork be prepared, and I've just finished it right before your arrival."

With a flourish, he placed five hefty stacks of documents on the desk and took a breath, ready to dive in.

"The Prince himself?" I interrupted loudly.

"Such an honor."

"Yes, yes..." He nodded hastily, reaching for the first folder.

"Hold on a moment," I said with a smile, placing my completed license application on top of the folder.

Kent sneered, barely hiding his disdain, and tried to open the folder anyway. But I kept my hand firmly on it, meeting his gaze with a grin.

"I insist," I said softly, watching his face turn red from exertion.

"Fine," he huffed, giving up. He picked up the paper and squinted at it. "What is this?"

"A Guardian license application. It's all there — take your time to read it. I'm in no rush."

"Well, I am!" he snapped, clearly tempted to tear the form in half. But he thought better of it, set it aside, and took a deep breath. "You see, Mister Marcus," he said, his tone forcibly polite, "your case isn't urgent. Of course, I'll submit it for review right away. In a week, you'll—"

"Then we'll get to your folders in a week, too," I said, standing up.

"A-a week?" His voice cracked. "But the Prince ordered everything done today!"

"He ordered you to do it," I said with a shrug. "I have other matters to attend to."

"Please, Mister Marcus! The Prince will fire me..." he pleaded as I walked toward the door, admiring the panoramic view from the corner office windows.

It really was beautiful, spoiled only by the unfortunate angle of a knight statue's backside on the neighboring building. Someone should tear that down.

"I'll sign!" Kent's desperate shout reached me just before I left.

"Now we're talking," I said, turning back to the desk.

By the time I returned, the crimson-faced servant was hammering at the keyboard, checking my application against his records.

"All done!" he announced, handing the form back. "Your application has been sent to the Ministry's recruitment department. They'll decide on granting you access to the registry. Normally, it takes a day, but your case might be delayed due to your... lack of a confirmed rank," he added with a sneer at my eyes.

"That's enough, thanks," I said with a nod.

"Don't thank me," he muttered, his nerves fraying. "I'm just doing my job. Like everything else..." He sighed, opening the first folder again. "Now, Section One, Clause One, concerning the Gifted entering service with the clan, hereinafter referred to—"

"Wait," I interrupted. "You're going to read all of that?"

"Yes," he said, blinking in confusion. "Your entry into clan service is unique, so we had to revise several sections and add a few—"

"What clan service?" I asked, rubbing my temples.

"Receiving a shard is an official invitation to

join the Clan of Nature," he explained. "Considering your commoner status and skill set, you qualify for a junior servant position, with potential promotion to hereditary servant. It's for your own safety, Mister Marcus. Higher positions in the clan hierarchy come with risks and constant combat—"

"Relax, pal." I sighed, placing the shard on the desk. "I'm here to decline the offer."

Kent went pale, then red, then knocked back a shot of cognac without hesitation.

"Decline?" He gasped, clutching his chest. "You can't be serious!"

"As serious as it gets." I shrugged. "Sorry for not mentioning it sooner."

"Then why do you need a Guardian license?" he sputtered, bewildered.

"Why else? To enter Portals." I smirked.

"You? Alone?" He stared at me in disbelief.

"What else did you think?"

"Well... servants with licenses get higher pay, guaranteed spots in clan raids, and a fixed share of the annual loot..." he explained hesitantly, eyeing the shard greedily.

He was clearly terrified I'd change my mind and take it back. Not a chance.

The absurdity of it all almost made me laugh. All this fuss because a commoner dared to snatch a cushy servant job in a noble clan?

The First Paladin, dreaming of becoming a servant to avoid Portals and get a steady paycheck! Old Aks would've died laughing if he heard that.

"Thanks for the honor, but I don't need anything from you," I said, smiling broadly. "Tell that to the Prince. And make a note that I've returned his little rock."

"Of course," Kent muttered, hastily swiping the shard off the table. After rifling through some papers, he handed me a single sheet. "An official refusal of our invitation, Mister Marcus. Date, time, and signature."

"Done," I said, signing and handing it back.

He didn't try to stop me this time, busy uncorking a bottle of champagne. The pop of the cork echoed behind me as I walked into the corridor.

I remembered the way out well enough. No escort needed. I strolled leisurely, admiring the stunning interior — panoramic halls, glass domes, and hundreds of plants, flowers, and miniature trees woven into the architecture.

The sound of the fountain and the clean air brought a sense of peace and calm.

"And this is how you ruin a perfect first impression," I remarked dryly as the scanning archway came into view.

It looked unchanged — ten arches, each with a transparent curtain of scanning air.

But looks were deceiving. The module was in "Fortress" mode, and the air curtain now emitted a paralyzing elemental gas.

"Someone's feeling petty," I muttered, striding through as if nothing had happened.

The footman at the entrance gawked at me, stabbing frantically at his phone. My suitcase sat on a metal trolley beside him. Wisely, he didn't try to stop me from taking it, and I emerged onto the square unscathed.

A sleek white convertible sportscar hovered near the central "Pillar of Unity."

"Hey there, Northerner!" Max grinned, waving.

"Can you even park here?" I asked skeptically.

"I can," he said with a shrug. "Hop in. I'll give you a lift. Don't worry — no truck can take down my baby." He flashed a toothy smile.

"Hold on a sec. Someone wants to chat," I said, glancing back at the building.

A squad of armed Gifted loomed behind the glass doors, hesitant to step outside.

I caught the leader's eye and took a step toward them. They bolted back inside.

Pathetic.

"Looks like they changed their minds," I said with a smirk. I tossed my bag onto the back seat and slid in next to Max.

The familiar roar of the elemental engine hit my ears, and the sportscar shot into the alley at breakneck speed.

CHAPTER 13

"I DIDN'T NEED ANY HELP," I noted as we drove off.

"I know," Max replied breezily. "Even if you did, you wouldn't have called. Right?"

"You're starting to get me," I said with a nod of approval.

"Barely, Marcus, barely," he said, laughing as he expertly took a sharp corner.

His driving skills, which had amazed me before, stood out even more in the city. Either traffic laws didn't exist in this era, or he simply didn't care. Most likely the latter.

"So, I take it you turned down the offer to become a servant," he continued.

"I believe I mentioned I wasn't interested," I reminded him.

"Yeah, yeah. But everyone lies, you know? Though now I can see you're not one of them," he muttered, stopping at a red light for the first time since we started moving.

I almost thought he'd barrel straight through it. The car certainly had the power. It radiated such a potent elemental response, I was sure the whole thing was built from off-world materials.

"So, let me ask," Max said, his curiosity piqued. "Why'd you refuse? It wasn't the servant status that put you off, was it?"

"I like my freedom." I shrugged. "And I like running my own life."

"With the way you handle it, your life's going to be pretty short," he replied with a smile that held a trace of concern.

"And that bothers you?" I raised an eyebrow.

"You've never had friends, have you?" He pulled over by an old black building with a high archway that led to a narrow cobblestone road, sighing softly.

Only then did I notice how few people were around. Those who were here moved hurriedly, practically sprinting down the street. And we hadn't even gone that far from the bustling areas.

"The Shadow District," he said, nodding toward the archway. "You noticed there were only nine statues and nine clan buildings on Unity Square, right?"

"Missing the Shadow Clan," I agreed.

"Exactly," he said, puffing out his chest like a know-it-all. "They lost that privilege when their last Prince died, about two hundred years ago. Back then, clans started forming coalitions and fighting over territory. The Shadow Clan stayed neutral and got wiped out by a coalition of Light Element fanatics who saw them as natural enemies. Three major clans were part of that alliance. The Shadows never stood a chance."

"You're saying they don't exist anymore?"

"They do, technically," he replied with a smirk. "The Fire Element coalition saved the remaining Shadow Clan members from genocide, helped them establish this district, and still supports them unofficially."

"So, the Shadows are part of their coalition now?"

"Not exactly," he said, shaking his head. "The Unity Pact limits coalitions to three clans. So the Shadows are... let's say, flexible mercenaries. They'll take any job for the highest bidder and pay a cut to the Fire coalition for protection. It's a real cesspit where all sorts of lowlifes are welcome."

"I met one of them," I said knowingly. "Name was Kai. I think he invited me here."

"And you turned him down? Big mistake," he replied with a grin. "This place is perfect for you."

I sighed wistfully, patting the pristine white door. "Ah, that was a beautiful car."

"Hey... what do you mean was?" His eyes went wide as he flailed his arms. "You got it wrong. That's not what I meant!"

I twirled a tiny black sphere on my finger, waiting silently for him to finish.

"The Prince!" he blurted out. "The Shadow Clan doesn't have a Prince. Their hierarchy is based solely on personal strength. But officially, they're still a noble clan with all the perks — no Portal taxes, auction access, and a hundred other privileges guaranteed to every clan by the Pact. A commoner Guardian won't get you squat in this world." He finished his impassioned speech, eyes fixed on me, waiting for my reaction.

When the black sphere vanished from my hand, he exhaled in relief. Amusingly, he hadn't even prepared to defend himself. Naive of him to trust a stranger like me so blindly.

"Why didn't you tell me this sooner?" I asked.

"I knew you'd refuse the Nature Clan's servant offer anyway," he admitted.

"And your offer would sound better in comparison," I said with a smirk.

"Guilty," he said, relaxing again. "I didn't approach you on the square out of the kindness of my heart, Marcus. The Lightning Clan wants to offer you a spot as a combat elementalist. Not a warrior, but not a servant either. You'd have freedom, we'd have a talented Gifted. Maybe you don't know, but we're the only clan in the Ten that isn't in a coalition, and we need quality recruits."

"Despite the obvious manipulation, I like your approach better," I said with a chuckle. "At least you say what you want to my face."

"But?"

"But 'broad freedom' isn't total freedom. If I take your offer, I'm immediately in someone's debt. Doesn't work for me."

"And being a commoner Guardian, scraping

for scraps and paying eighty percent in taxes, does work for you? Or do you really plan on joining the dregs everyone hates?"

"You brought me here, Max," I reminded him, tossing my suitcase out of the car.

"I didn't think you'd actually go for it," he said, disappointed. "Sure, some folks here have nowhere else to go, but there's plenty of scum too. What you're planning might be too much even for you."

"You never know until you try," I said, shrugging as I walked toward the archway.

It was almost funny how fate led me here. Seems like I wasn't destined to escape public hatred, even seven hundred years later. Though this time, it wouldn't be aimed directly at me.

Whatever. Hatred had been my companion in battle for a long time. I knew how to appease it.

Max was so upset by my decision that he drove off without saying goodbye. Like a child. Honestly.

Visually, the Shadow District was just an endless cobblestone road lined with five-story buildings. Each had small stoops, wide sidewalks, and dim signs that were impossible to read in the fading light.

Streetlights were rare. The nearest one was about three hundred thirty feet ahead, leaving the district illuminated only by the occasional window.

"Lost, tourist?" A burly old man with rolled-up sleeves stepped out of the shadows.

"Nope," I replied with an easy smile. "I've got the right address."

"You might want to double-check, kid," the old man said, eyeing me skeptically. "Before someone more... predatory notices you."

"So, you're a herbivore?" I quipped.

"More like full," he replied with a smirk.

At that moment, a levitating van with no plates roared into the district and screeched to a halt a foot away from us.

"Hey, Patrick!" a voice called from the van. "Who's the fresh meat?"

"Just asking for directions," Patrick replied, lighting a cigarette.

"I'll show him the way," the driver said with a grin.

"Keep driving, Bob," Patrick growled. "Don't scare off my customers."

"Customer? Nah, he's a tourist. And what do tourists do? They leave. So why not leave their stuff behind — for safekeeping, you know?"

The van's door creaked open, and the ground shook as someone hefty jumped out.

"Told you, kid," Patrick muttered, exhaling smoke. "Wrong address."

"Doubt it," I replied, letting go of my suitcase handle.

A quick spin, and the goon swinging a metal bar at me went down with a chop to the throat.

I picked up the thin metal rod, twirling it curiously.

"Elemental," I observed.

"Bob moonlights in metal mining. Brings in batches, good quality stuff," Patrick said, exhaling another puff of smoke. "Thanks for not killing him. The guy's got a sick mom. Works for her. And you're the stranger walking into our turf at dusk. Your own fault."

"Interesting rules your clan's got," I replied with a chuckle, noticing the dull silver shard on his bracelet. "Know who I can talk to about some work?"

"Work, huh?" Patrick crushed his cigarette and pointed down the road. "Straight to the end. If you make it, they'll listen. If not, you're no use to the clan. And a word of advice — keep the killing to a minimum."

"But they'll try to kill me?" I asked.

"More like rob you. But your version's not off the table," he said, smirking as he slipped his jacket under the unconscious guy's head. "You can take reparations, within reason."

"And who decides what's reasonable?"

"If they come after you at night for revenge, you went too far," he replied.

"Got it," I said with a smile, handing him the metal rod. "This is enough for me."

"What the hell do I need it for?" he muttered.

"Isn't that your shop?" I asked, nodding toward the sign swaying in the wind, barely legible in the twilight: Patrick's Goods.

"Yeah, that's mine."

I handed him my suitcase, asking him to sort through and appraise its contents by the time I got back. Patrick took it without hesitation and hauled it into his shop.

Heh. As if he'd refuse. If I didn't make it back from this stroll through the shadows, there'd be no one to claim my stuff anyway.

I kept only the cash, shoved my hands into my pockets, and headed up the cobblestone road.

*   *   *

"Hey, Gerry, you know that guy?" Andro asked, flicking a worn coin between his fingers.

Two men lounged on the patio of a clan café. Twilight was setting in, and the Shadow District was just beginning to wake up.

"Huh? Who?" Gerry swiveled his head around, his bleary eyes landing on a man in a black suit.

The stranger walked casually down the middle of the road, glancing around at the clan buildings like a tourist admiring landmarks. A surge of irritation — and a belch — rose in Gerry's throat. He pushed himself to his feet, rolling up his sleeves.

"Never seen him before," he said with a grunt, ready to step forward.

But Andro, known as "Boar," beat him to it. With a feral grin, he sprang off the patio, flipping his lucky coin into the air. Everyone in the district knew that before the coin hit the ground, Boar's target would already be dead.

Unlike most Shadow Clan members, Boar had spent twenty years as a combat captain in a real clan before being expelled for excessive brutality.

Getting caught by Boar was a death sentence for any newcomer. Everyone knew that. If the stranger had done his homework, he wouldn't have shown up in the district on a Wednesday evening. Rookie mistake.

"Damn," Gerry muttered, watching his chance slip away. He'd really wanted to pummel someone.

The sound of bones snapping, followed by a pig-like squeal, echoed through the street. The fight was over. But then, in the stunned silence, came the unmistakable clink of a coin hitting the ground.

Gerry blinked, disbelief plastered on his face. He looked up to see the stranger, standing unharmed, eyeing him with a bored expression.

Gerry sank back into his chair so fast that it collapsed under his weight. Instinct took over, urging him to run and hide.

He scrambled under the table, daring to peek out only when the stranger picked up the coin and whistled his way down the street.

* * *

My first walk through the Shadow District was proving to be... entertaining. The deeper I went, the brighter and livelier the place became. Well-maintained buildings lined the path — grocery stores, cafés, workshops, weapon shops, laundries... a self-contained world where you could find everything you needed without stepping outside the district.

And despite the name, this world buzzed with light, color, and an air of perpetual celebration.

A pang of nostalgia hit me. The scene was painfully reminiscent of Argus's market square — constant bustling like a festival, and the chance to buy anything your heart desired. Fewer criminals around here, but that was a fixable issue.

As Patrick warned, the stroll wasn't without incident.

A few unfriendly types tried to chase me off, but they didn't get far.

One particularly persistent thug managed to shatter the bones in his own arm while attempting to take me down.

He did, however, provide me with a valuable souvenir: an old Argus-minted coin. Only members of the Order were allowed to carry those. It made me even more certain that descendants of the Order had a hand in creating this place.

After that, no one else dared approach me. Some shot me nasty looks, but most didn't care about the stranger in their midst. The district lived its own life.

My walk ended when I reached a wide staircase leading to the grand entrance of a three-story mansion. Like the clan buildings on Unity Square, its facade bore a crest — black wings spread wide — and a raven statue perched elegantly on the roof.

A moment later, a tall woman in a floor-length black dress stepped gracefully out of the mansion. Her silver hair was tied back in a sleek ponytail.

"You must be Marcus," she greeted with a warm smile.

"And you are?" I replied, playing along.

I wasn't surprised she knew my name. In this era, information was power.

"Olga." She gave a slight nod. "Steward of this estate." She gestured to a patio table. "Shall we sit?"

"As you wish," I said easily, taking a seat with a view of the vibrant district.

A server brought out light snacks and wine before leaving us alone. Soft music drifted from the open doors, and the scent of lilacs lingered in the air.

"Do you welcome all newcomers like this?" I asked, sipping the wine.

"No," she replied with a coy smile. "We offer a personal touch."

"One that started with someone trying to bash my skull in with a metal bar," I said dryly.

"And yet, here you are." She gave a slight tilt of her head. "So, how do you like it here?"

"Better than some other clans I've seen," I admitted.

"You're quite the joker," she said with a soft laugh, covering her mouth with her hand. "So, am I right in assuming you wish to stay?"

"Stay?" I raised an eyebrow. "Just like that? No contracts, no fine print, no obligations?"

"Just like that," she replied smoothly. "The *district* doesn't tolerate outsiders. If you're here, *it* means you've been accepted. After meeting with the Boss, you can become a full-fledged clan member. My recommendation will reach him tonight.

However, he won't be available for three days. He's currently away."

"Is that so?" I mused. "And in three days, will I need to break more bones to prove myself?"

"Not necessarily," she said with a half-smile. "If you're willing, Marcus, I can give you a guest pass right now. Are you?"

"Why not?" I said, shrugging. "What do you need from me?"

"Just your hand," she said, slipping the glove off my left hand.

With a sultry look, she traced her silver-tipped nails across my palm, leaving inky black lines that spread and formed the image of a raven tattoo.

A simple yet effective Shadow Element trick that used the barest hint of magic. My immunity would have burned it off instantly if I hadn't deliberately lowered my defenses.

"This is a temporary mark of affiliation," Olga explained in a honeyed tone. "You can reveal or hide it by channeling your energy through it. Don't look at me like that, Marcus," she added with a playful smile, catching my gaze. "We know you're Gifted."

She conveniently left out that the mark also tracked my location. I pretended not to notice. This little trick was more advanced than her skills suggested.

In other words, she wasn't much of a fighter. I suspected tracking spells were the only useful thing she brought to her master — aside from her charm and looks, which could easily lull naive recruits into complacency.

"The Boss will see you in three days," Olga concluded, rising gracefully. "Until then, feel free to stay in the district. Explore, get to know it. We have cozy inns, excellent restaurants, and other establishments to suit any taste." She gave me a subtle wink.

"Thanks, but I'll pass," I replied with a polite nod.

I turned to leave, catching her expertly feigned look of disappointment. She was good. Almost fooled me.

Olga didn't bother seeing me out. No need.

From the moment I entered the district, I'd felt the weight of unseen eyes. The deeper I went, the stronger the sensation grew. I hadn't spotted a single decent shadow elementalist, but that didn't mean they weren't here.

Quite the opposite. The fact that I couldn't detect whoever had been shadowing me for an hour brought a grin to my face.

All right, kids. Let's play.

"Find," I whispered, releasing a shadow tracker from my own shadow.

CHAPTER 14

THE TRACKER WAS A TWISTED EMBODIMENT of Darkness, vaguely resembling a crazed, eyeless hound. Its grotesque form could freeze hearts with fear, and its chilling bark could unhinge even the steadiest mind. But while it wreaked havoc on the psyche, it couldn't inflict physical damage — purely a tool for mental torment.

Its main value lay in its ability to travel through the shadow realm. The downside? It couldn't leave that realm on its own.

Still, it was unmatched when it came to picking up a trail.

To lock onto a target, I used a fragment of shadow elemental energy from my tattoo. I was confident that every member of the Shadow Clan bore similar marks — and I wasn't wrong.

The tracker snapped up the scent instantly

and vanished.

I took my time strolling back to Patrick's shop. As I retraced my steps through the district, the oddities I'd first noticed became even more glaring.

Most of the people around were regular folks, the non-Gifted kind. Only a few sported clan tattoos, and even fewer had shards. The festive atmosphere that had felt strangely oppressive earlier now felt even more suffocating. Despite the myriad entertainment options, the thought of stopping anywhere didn't even tempt me.

Maybe it was because the way ordinary people relaxed wasn't my style.

Who knows? I'd never taken a vacation in my life and was still learning how to handle downtime.

I kept my tattoo hidden, but even so, no one dared approach me on the walk back.

When I returned to Patrick's shop, my tracker had already found the Shadow Clan members tailing me. There were three of them. Since the Portals were still off-limits, I figured I could at least have some fun here.

But it turned out the only one who got to play was the tracker.

Once it locked onto a target, it hounded them relentlessly until they either lost their minds or fled the shadow realm entirely. All three spies eventually chose to flee, exposing their hiding spots in the process. Lacking the smarts, strength, or will to come up with a new plan, they became irrelevant.

What a disappointment. I'd been hoping for a

challenge.

What kind of amateurs were these, if a simple tracker trick could shred their shadow camouflage?

Just before entering Patrick's shop, I paused, met the eyes of each spy, and gave them a cheerful wave. Hopefully, the news of their exposure would reach Olga quickly, and she'd send someone more interesting next time.

Until then, I let the tracker patrol the area around me, limiting its range to about a hundred feet so it wouldn't drain too much energy.

Let it have its fun. It could stand guard while giving the Shadow Clan a chance to prove they were worth something.

"Evening," I greeted Patrick with a smile. He was busy rearranging a display of bladed weapons — some pretty impressive ones, too.

"You made it back," he said without looking up, snapping the display case shut. "Find what you were looking for?"

"In progress," I replied, waving off his question. My gaze landed on a greenish-blue, scale-patterned dagger with pulsing veins of energy. "That Kirin steel?"

"You know your stuff," he said with respect, pride gleaming in his eyes as he glanced at the centerpiece of his collection. "The crown jewel. Never dulls, never breaks. One look at its blade, and wild beasts lose the will to fight."

"The last part's a myth," I said with a smirk and dumped three rings, two signets, a chain, and

— oddly enough — a tooth onto the counter.

No idea where I'd picked up the last one. Must've grabbed it on autopilot.

"You rob a jewelry store?" he asked with a snort, eyeing the haul.

"Just taking reparations that fit in my pocket."

I'd dumped everything for appraisal, keeping only the Argus coin.

"Two thousand fifty imps for the lot," he said after a quick inspection.

"You sure?" I gave him a chance to reconsider.

"Absolutely. That's with the mark-bearer discount and my good mood," he added with a grin.

"Fine, have it your way," I said, waving off the goods. No one else would give me a better deal. His sly face told me as much.

Even if I could squeeze out a few extra hundred elsewhere, it wouldn't be worth the hit to my reputation.

I knew he would resell the items back to their original owners. Each piece bore a mark or engraving of its rightful owner — personal items no one would part with willingly. I'd chosen them on purpose, knowing the owners would want them back. When they got their things, they'd be grateful to me for leaving them the option. A little boost to my karma.

The Shadow District wasn't huge. If I planned to stick around, I needed to start building goodwill now.

With my permission, he swiftly pocketed the loot and returned his melancholy gaze to me.

"Finished sorting your stuff, too," he said. "Seventeen thousand two hundred twenty-two imps total. Selling or keeping?"

"I'll keep it all," I replied.

"Sure about that?" He tried to hide his disappointment.

"Absolutely. Consider it thanks for helping with Bob, pointing me in the right direction, and my good mood."

"Vindictive, huh?" he said, squinting.

"Just fair."

I grabbed my suitcase and headed for the door.

No need to check the contents. He was a seasoned hustler, but he was honest. If he wasn't... well, I knew the way back.

"Survive your meeting with the boss, and come back for your justice," he called after me, earning a few more points in my book.

One phrase, both a warning and advice.

I rarely misread people. If I became one of his "own," dealing with him would get a lot more profitable.

But why didn't he consider his own Clan's Boss one of his own? Personal grudges, or something deeper?

Pondering that, I stepped into the cool September breeze. Of the three spies, only one remained, now openly leaning against a lamppost in the distance.

I gave him a farewell wave and left the Shadow District. Ten minutes later, I was back on bustling streets.

Night had fallen, and it had been a long day. I hailed a taxi, asked the driver about nearby hotels, and picked one that fit my budget.

Fifteen minutes through the brightly lit city, a hundred imperial coins for the ride, and I was standing in front of a cozy beige building with a glowing sign: Youth Hotel.

According to the driver, nobles didn't stay here, so the only security system was a mustachioed concierge with a weary look and a handful of scrawny bellboys.

Despite appearances, the concierge was polite, helped me with my suitcase, and gave me some tips on choosing a room.

The room itself was small but clean and comfortable. A soft double bed, fresh sheets, and a clawfoot tub. What more did I need?

Dinner and breakfast were included, so I paid for two nights upfront. I didn't want to lug my suitcase around tomorrow.

I needed a place to return to, stash my spoils, and unwind. After seven centuries in the future, I was starting to appreciate that.

A rented room wasn't exactly a home, but it was a start.

Last night, I'd slept in cold hay on a freight car floor. This was progress. And I wasn't about to stop.

My appetite for life was only waking up — and I'd never had a problem with appetite.

The next morning dawned without incident.

No one tried to kill me, rob me, or sell me into

slavery. So, I had to handle my morning workout the old-fashioned way.

My body was only just starting to regain its former tone, and it needed a push — both with energy and a bit of exercise. After an hour of light training, I soaked in a hot bath, wrapped the Time Element cloak around my right arm, slipped into my only formal suit, and headed down for breakfast.

Scrambled eggs, bacon, veggies, salad, and fresh-squeezed juice — a perfect way to continue the morning.

Bliss.

The street greeted me with a crisp September sun. I carried just some cash, feeling good about a leisurely walk. I wasn't in any rush. I had no clue when they'd announce the results of my Guardian license application, but it probably wouldn't happen first thing in the morning.

Wait. How was I supposed to know when it would happen?

They'd probably notify my "sponsors" who submitted the application. Though Kent would likely ignore it — assuming he hadn't already been fired.

Either way, no one was going to go out of their way to tell me. I'd have to figure it out myself.

As I continued my walk, I kept an eye on the storefronts until I spotted one that fit the bill and stepped inside.

"Welcome to Electro Oasis!" chirped a young sales rep in a sky-blue shirt. "I'm Obed. How can I help you?"

"You can," I said with a smile. "I need a phone."

"Just for calls, or do you need additional features?" he asked politely.

"Features?"

"Yeah." He nodded. "Syncing with premium imperial databases, expanded network coverage, custom casing, battery charge linked to a specific Element, tracking mode, suppression mode, analysis mode, built-in elemental artifact... or—"

"City maps and basic calls will do," I said, cutting off his improv sales pitch.

"Nine thousand nine hundred ninety imperial coins," he announced.

I let out a heavy sigh. I'd paid six hundred fifty imps for a hotel room with dinner and breakfast yesterday. I didn't even want to imagine the price of a phone with "features." Especially one with a built-in elemental artifact, even a low-power one.

"Here," I said, dropping ten grand on the counter. "I'll also need a SIM card."

"A... what?" Obed blinked, confused.

"The thing that makes the phone work," I added, suddenly less sure.

"Oh, it's already activated," he explained. "Just apply your elemental imprint, and it syncs automatically with Argus."

"Syncs with *what*?" I asked, coughing slightly.

"Argus," he repeated patiently. "The Unified System for all imperial registries and databases. If you're non-Gifted, you can activate it at a mobile citizen registration point with your ID, or get a personal identifier from the imperial office."

"Thanks, Obed. Got it," I said, offering a polite smile and leaving the store with my new purchase.

My heart pounded a little faster. It took some effort to suppress the sudden urge to storm the nearest noble's house and shake every secret out of their pompous heads.

First the shards, then the tech, and now this. The Princes' claws seemed to have sunk far deeper into the Order's legacy than I thought.

As I pondered this, I strapped the phone — more of a wide bracelet — onto my wrist. The moment it touched my skin, it vibrated, and three white symbols flared to life, unmistakably tied to the Light Element. It reminded me of the device Edward had, though his was bulkier and cruder.

Just like with the tattoo, this gadget had a tracking element woven into it. I burned it off immediately. If this thing synced with the imperial registry they call Argus, the all-seeing monstrosity, I wasn't about to let it log my movements.

Next stop: the Ministry of Mitigation Headquarters. My new map guided the way, and I reached it on foot.

This time, I was heading for the recruitment department. A few polite questions led me to the right entrance — a massive blue double door on an oversized annex, swung open invitingly. Above it, a crest showed a warrior spearing a winged chimera.

Ha. I'd love to see him try that for real. Those multi-elemental S+ class creatures were completely immune to physical damage.

"Excuse me, who are you here to see?" asked a cheerful blonde girl at the reception desk.

She was barely taller than the metal counter, which ended just below her rather generous chest. And whose bright idea was it to put stairs at the entrance? She had to lean forward to get a good look at me.

Probably designed by a closet pervert, I concluded, appreciating the view of her D-cup assets pressed tightly against the counter.

"I need the recruitment department," I said with a smile.

"Then you're in the right place," she said brightly, her nametag reading Anna. "What's your question?"

"I want to check the status of my license application," I replied, handing over my freshly issued document.

"Marcus Dark, let's see..." she murmured, biting her lip and typing into her computer. "One moment, please."

"No rush," I said, glancing around.

The small lobby led into a corridor with three blue double doors. Only the middle one was open. Through it, I could see a section of a sparring ring, mats, and a row of training equipment. The muffled sounds of punches and elemental bursts echoed from the large room. Above the door, a sign read: Central Training Grounds.

"Mr. Marcus!" Anna called, her face puzzled. "Your application, well..."

"Well?"

"I don't understand, I'm sorry," she said, shaking her head. "The review is complete, but there's no decision recorded. Maybe the officer forgot to log the result. You could come back tomorrow..."

"Tomorrow's no good, Anna," I said, shaking my head. "Could you give me the name of the officer handling my case? I'll ask them directly since the review is done."

"I don't know..." she murmured, eyes downcast.

"I'll treat you to dinner for your trouble. What time do you finish?"

"Six," she said, brightening, then hesitated. "But you really shouldn't talk to him. He's scary and yells a lot," she whispered.

"At you too?" I asked.

"More than anyone," she muttered, her voice tinged with defeat.

"Then all the more reason for me to have a word," I said, leaning closer. "You're not forbidden from giving me his name, are you?"

"No," she admitted uncertainly.

"So what's stopping you?"

"Well..." she faltered. "People usually end up in the hospital after talking to him..."

"Don't worry," I said with a smile. "Dinner's happening no matter what."

"Okay," she agreed with a relieved grin, turning her monitor toward me.

The screen displayed a scowling man with a tan face and a bristly patch of gray hair. The caption read: Captain Third Rank Paul Tarin, Deputy

Chief of the Southern District Recruitment Corps.

"And where can I find him?"

"He's teaching a class right now." She nodded toward the open door. "You can wait until he's done..."

"Thanks a lot," I said sincerely.

Waiting, of course, wasn't an option. I headed straight into the hall.

CHAPTER 15

THE CENTRAL TRAINING GROUNDS turned out to be a spacious, old building with high ceilings and solid defenses. Elemental suppressors hung on the walls, and dome-shaped diffusers near the ceiling ensured that any stray elemental techniques wouldn't bring the place crashing down.

The expansive area was divided into four training zones, with a raised platform for sparring matches at the center. Roughly three hundred people were spread throughout the room, but it didn't take long to spot the one I was looking for.

Captain Tarin stood out with his massive frame — and the sheer volume of his voice.

"You're dead!" he roared as he hurled an unfortunate recruit into the wall with a powerful projectile.

"You, you, and you — you're dead too!" he bellowed, spraying spit as he glared at the exhausted group of fifteen Gifted. "We need to move faster! Much faster! Got it, you little shits?"

"Yes, sir, Captain!" the ragged group replied unevenly.

They weren't particularly strong, but they weren't hopeless either. Five of them still had a spark of determination in their eyes — the same spark Captain Tarin seemed hellbent on snuffing out.

It wasn't the gentlest teaching method, but I had to admit it worked. The creatures in the Portals wouldn't just yell at you for mistakes. They'd kill you.

"Captain Tarin!" I called out, seizing a pause between his bellows.

"Yeah?" His bronze-tinted eyes swept over me. "Who the hell are you? Can't you see I'm busy with recruits? If you want to sign up for Guardian training, do it at reception. But," he added, grimacing at my attire, "if I were you, I wouldn't bother."

Behind him, his recruits exhaled in relief at the unexpected reprieve.

"Marcus Dark." I locked eyes with him. "And I'm not here for training."

The Earth Element resonance within him was strong — impressive for an Imperial not affiliated with any clan. Either his position paid as well as the clans did, or he had other reasons to tirelessly drill waves of recruits rejected by the clans.

"Ah, I remember your application," he said, his jaw clenched. "You're the genius who thinks he's ready for anything! I don't know how much you paid the Nature Clan to recommend you, but it was a waste. I don't need dead weight dragging down my Guardians. Get lost before I throw you out myself!"

"I'm afraid I have to insist on a more thorough review of my application," I replied with a smile.

"Are you deaf?" he asked, sneering as he stepped forward and loomed over me. The guy was over six and a half feet tall, with a neck thicker than most people's heads. "You want to die some kind of hero?"

"I want to kill creatures," I answered calmly, not breaking eye contact.

For ten long seconds, he stared at me, nostrils flaring, then suddenly snorted and turned away.

"Burke!" he bellowed. A recruit with muddy green eyes jumped to his feet — the only one who looked at me with anger instead of gratitude for the pause.

"This commoner was personally recommended by the clan that rejected you," Tarin said, hands clasped behind his back. "Ready to prove them wrong?"

"Yes, Captain!" the recruit snapped, taking a combat stance.

I sighed, realizing where this was headed, and took off my jacket. I couldn't afford to ruin it.

I didn't have spare cash for a new one. Besides, I'd gotten used to the feel of expensive fabric woven from off-world fibers. It fit perfectly, didn't stain, and — most importantly — handled elemental pressure far better than a cotton shirt, which was already begging for retirement.

"Harston! Pike! Sally! Jake!" Tarin called out four more recruits, the ones whose eyes still burned with resolve.

I was sure the others, cowed by his yelling and pressure, would be dismissed by the end of the day. For all his gruffness, I didn't sense any malice in Tarin — just a tough sort of care.

Even for me.

Tarin gestured toward me. "The kid doesn't get it. Show him why he doesn't belong here!"

At his shout, the five recruits lunged. Not mindlessly — they adapted on the fly, surrounding me in a loose circle.

Not that it was hard. I hadn't moved, lazily watching their approach. I did make sure to step away from my neatly folded jacket, though. No need to let them stomp on it.

The bitter recruit attacked first, of course. From behind.

Wind-boosted limbs and fists hardened with Wood Element energy, mixed with personal grudges, resulted in a swing that missed. Without turning, I shrugged and deflected his blow with my palm.

The other four rushed in, peppering me with a flurry of basic but well-practiced strikes from all sides.

Their aim, however, needed work.

None of them managed to land a solid hit or even graze me.

"Stop playing with him! He's the enemy! A Guardian can't hesitate or show mercy! It's you or them!" Tarin's motivational roar spurred them to attack harder.

Their strikes grew sharper, faster, more desperate. But I still dodged, redirected, or blocked without using a shred of energy — just my body and experience.

Their teamwork was falling apart. Each one tried to shine, tripping each other up and making their attacks even more predictable.

"You're getting on my nerves..." the bitter recruit growled. He got distracted — and that was his mistake. He ducked his ally's kick at the last second, only to meet my knee, which knocked him out cold.

"Bastard!" another shouted, only to eat a left hook to the temple.

Their already shaky formation crumbled. Seven seconds later, the rest were sprawled on the floor. Even Tarin's last-minute attempt to trip me with a tremor didn't help.

I didn't miss a beat.

"Quite the performance," Tarin muttered, surveying his unconscious recruits as medics in white hurried over with stretchers.

The only one still standing was the fire elementalist girl. I'd taken her out with a joint lock — gentler and less damaging. It was more pleasant that way, and I hadn't wanted to hit someone so charming. She hadn't done anything to deserve it, after all.

"So, about that license?" I asked, shrugging my jacket back on.

Tarin cleared his throat and stepped in front of me, blocking me from the crowd's view.

Not just his group, but everyone else training in the hall had stopped to watch. Curious eyes lingered on us.

"Listen, Marcus," he said, much quieter than usual. "You've got the physical skills and the guts. But the Portals aren't about beating up kids. You get that, right?"

"More than you know," I replied with a nod.

"So you're still pushing for this," he said with a sigh. "Fine. Leave your number at the front desk. You'll get the coordinates at dawn."

"Coordinates for what?"

"A Portal, what else?" he said with a grin. "You want that license fast? Prove yourself in the field. Think of it as your final exam!" he added, clapping me on the back.

"Great," I said with a smile, waving to the recruits as I headed for the exit.

"Don't be late!" Tarin called after me, turning back to his battered trainees.

"Glad you're okay, Marcus," Anna greeted me with a radiant smile. "I got worried when the medics rushed in."

"No need to worry," I said, leaning on the counter and brushing a stray lock from her forehead.

Anna blushed, entered my number into the system, and after a bit more banter, I promised to pick her up after work. Then I headed outside and flagged down a taxi.

The situation made one thing painfully clear: I didn't have enough clothes. What I did have was being slowly disintegrated by the aura of my cloak. My shirt was barely holding together, but the rest of my wardrobe — aside from my suit — wasn't faring as well.

At this rate, I'd end up running around in my underwear. I couldn't afford Portal-grade fabric like my suit, but I could compensate with quantity.

As for the idea of not wearing my cloak? Absolutely not.

First, the cloak was too valuable to leave behind. Second, away from my Darkness aura, its elemental energy would leak into the world uncontrollably. I doubted the locals would appreciate a white desert sprouting up in the middle of the capital.

"Find me a clothing store with lots of options and low prices," I said. The taxi driver, quick on the uptake, sped off through the city.

The sun was still high. Plenty of time. I managed to hit two large wholesale stores, stocking up on underwear, socks, T-shirts, pants, shirts, shoes, and other essentials.

I shipped the haul to my hotel room by courier and headed to an eastern-style café for lunch.

Cooking had definitely improved over the last seven hundred years. The variety was staggering. Portal herbs, meats, and other ingredients were everywhere.

And the taste... Gods, the taste! I'd missed this

in the desert.

In this, the Princes deserved some credit.

Whether out of greed or curiosity, they'd managed to integrate Portal resources into everyday life. From priceless indestructible metals to the smallest off-world herb, everything found a use.

The Order had been different. They dismissed anything without scientific or military value as a waste of time and destroyed it.

"Gone too soon, Aks," I said with a sigh, finishing a divine lamb dish in spicy red sauce with a blend of seven Portal herbs. "You missed out."

I jogged back to the hotel to clear my head. I had plenty of ideas for what to do next, but no solid plans. The Portal and Clan situations were under control, but the "home" issue was still up in the air.

That problem hit me the moment I opened my hotel room door.

Or tried to, at least.

I hadn't considered how tiny the room was. The mountain of bags and boxes left barely enough room to squeeze in. There wasn't even a closet.

How did the concierge manage to stuff everything in and escape?

"A real Shadow Pocket would be nice right about now," I muttered, shaking my head.

But wishing wouldn't make it so.

I still had three hours before my dinner with Anna. I grabbed a bag with a change of clothes and headed downstairs.

The taxi dropped me at the nearest real estate

agency. Out of dozens of rental listings, only one fit my needs.

An old building, no security, no elevator. A one-thousand three-hundred fifty-square-foot apartment with five rooms and a panoramic balcony that doubled as a rooftop terrace.

Most importantly, it had an open view of the Shadow District's entrance. The open view sealed the deal, and it was the only place within my budget.

The rent was steep — fifty-five thousand imps a month — leaving me nearly broke. Again. It was uncomfortable, but it would do.

The place came with just a wardrobe and a huge bed. The landlord promised to furnish it on request, but for now, that was enough. At least there was plenty of space for my new purchases. Moving in could wait until morning.

After a shower and a change of clothes, I went to pick up Anna.

It wasn't that Anna was particularly special. I'd promised her dinner, and I keep my promises.

The evening was pleasant. She told me about the city, the ministry, and flirted in an adorably awkward way. She mentioned that after I left, Tarin had been unusually quiet and thoughtful, and she asked me to visit him more often.

Her choice of restaurant — right across from her apartment — wasn't lost on me.

She turned out to be inexperienced and shy, the complete opposite of Victoria. But Anna didn't try to cling to me, put a leash on me, or stop me from leaving.

And I had no reason to stay.

It was late by the time I walked home.

I skipped the taxi, enjoying the fresh air. Besides, I didn't want to risk an innocent civilian. A rather interesting character had been following me — one who'd crushed my shadow tracker like a bug underfoot.

*   *   *

"What did you find out?" a cold, emotionless voice asked.

The Boss of the Shadow Clan sat in a leather chair, his back to the entrance, watching the crackling fireplace. The flames cast flickering shadows across the room. Three figures in black robes knelt behind him, their forms swallowed by the dancing dark.

"Almost n-nothing, boss," came the hesitant reply.

The fire flared brighter, and the shadows took on the shape of fangs.

"Explain," the Boss ordered, eyes fixed on the flames, where a human hand was slowly burning.

"He spotted us before we even left the district, boss! All three of us! And he acted like he knew everything... too careful..." the one on the left said quickly.

"There was a dog!" the center figure blurted.

"A dog?" The Boss turned slightly, interest piqued.

"A creepy shadow dog, boss! Its howl made my limbs freeze, and blood started dripping from my ears..."

"And images, boss! I saw my own death! It was like the thing crawled inside my brain..."

"Interesting," the Boss mused, steepling his fingers. "Anything else?"

"Patrick!" the left figure blurted. "He went to Patrick's shop! Sold his trophies and left! Didn't eat, didn't drink, didn't steal, didn't kill..."

"But he took a rod!"

"A rod?" The Boss raised an eyebrow.

"The metal rod! Bob tried to club him, but missed... He didn't sell it to Patrick. And they say he took Boar's coin, but Boar's still in a coma..."

"Who's tracking Marcus now?" the Boss asked.

"No one, he's—" the center figure managed to say.

The shadows struck, spearing his eyes.

He opened his mouth in a silent scream, collapsing to the floor in agony.

"Why is no one tracking him?" the Boss repeated calmly.

"Because the *Nameless Ones* can't leave the district during the day," the right figure murmured, bowing lower.

"The other trackers refused," the left figure added. "Word is he took out those enforcers in the center."

"Did Patrick spread the rumor, or Olga?" The Boss's eyes narrowed, knowing that no one else would dare circulate information without his approval.

"We don't know, boss."

"Find out," he said, giving a dismissive wave.

They scurried out, leaving him alone.

His thoughtful gaze drifted back to the fireplace. The shadows dragged the lifeless body of the punished subordinate into the flames.

CHAPTER 16

THE FIRST THING I NEEDED TO DO was figure out my pursuer's intentions. I ducked into the first dark alley I found and slowed my pace.

If his goal was just surveillance, nothing would change. But if —

I didn't get to finish that thought. A sharp burst of elemental energy behind me made me spin around and raise my right hand.

Three steel blades, charged with different elements, slammed into my forearm with a crack.

The fabric of my jacket tore immediately, but the strike didn't penetrate further. The cloak's aura flared hot, and the Time Element greedily gnawed at the metal. The pursuer yanked his multi-elemental weapon back.

"Damn, you're ugly," I said with a sigh, looking mournfully at the three gashes on my jacket.

One was scorched by fire, the second corroded by venom, and the third sliced by ice.

"So the relic rumors weren't wrong," the man in matte-black clothing said with a smirk, gripping a steel cord with three blades at the end. "The boss will be pleased."

With those words, the man channeled his energy through the cord, hardening it into a makeshift scythe tipped with three blades.

Interesting artifact.

"You're going to die slowly," he said with relish, striding toward me. "And they'll find your remains in pieces, so everyone remembers that no one dares—"

I didn't bother listening to the rest. I funneled an erg into my legs and leaped forward. His golden eyes widened in shock just before my fist connected.

To his credit, he managed to snap his head away and land a kick that sent me skidding back, but his scythe slipped from his grasp.

"Pathetic effort, commoner!" he said with a sneer, reaching for his fallen weapon.

"Looking for this?" I twirled the scythe in my hand with a grin. Good balance, multi-elemental recharge blades, flexible metal capable of shifting form.

"You're even dumber than I thought," he said with a snarl. "The scythe is an extension of the Reaper! It grows with us from birth! You can't take it away!"

The elemental metal in my hands shuddered,

trying to return to its master.

"Oh no, you don't." I shook my head. "Bind," I commanded, and Darkness coiled around the weapon in a dense haze, draining it of any will to resist.

"Useless" the Reaper roared, his arms flailing in desperate gestures as he traced symbols in the air.

The scythe twisted in my grip, trying to morph into a spiral blade, explode into a thousand needles, or crumble into metallic dust. But the more transformations he attempted, the tighter the Darkness held.

Desperation drove him to pour all his elemental energy into a brute-force tug to reclaim his weapon. He only succeeded in straining himself, his face reddening as he collapsed to his knees, exhausted.

"Who are you..." he rasped, blood dribbling from his mouth.

His scythe fell lifelessly to the ground. My Darkness dissipated the moment the weapon's resistance faded.

If the Reaper had just stopped struggling for a second or two, he could have saved himself. But he was too stubborn for his own good.

"You're someone who shouldn't have messed with me," I said, crouching down. "Trying to kill me once, I get it. Twice? Fine. But three times? Does your Albert have no shame? Blame him, not me, if his princess isn't into mutts."

"Albert? What the hell are you talking about?"

the Reaper hissed.

"Wait." I frowned, grabbing a fistful of his hair. "You're not from Albert?"

Instead of answering, the Reaper's eyes rolled back, and he let out one last breath before dying.

He'd created a metal shard in his own heart. Idiot. What a dumb way to off yourself.

I rifled through his pockets and found nothing of value. The only thing worth considering was his black robe, faintly charged with elemental energy.

The idea of stripping a dead man for his vomit-stained, blood-soaked robe didn't thrill me. It was clearly custom-made. If I tried to sell it, rumors would spread that I'd taken down a Reaper.

Did I need that? Nope.

So I just absorbed it, gaining a cashback of seven energy units.

"Not bad, but cash would've been better," I muttered, running a finger along my torn jacket.

I walked over to where I'd left the scythe. Instead of the weapon, only three orphaned blades lay on the ground. The handle had indeed been a part of the Reaper and had vanished with him.

That kind of elemental bond took decades to cultivate. The guy wasn't weak. A shame he wasted his potential on killing people instead of clearing Portals.

I didn't feel like thinking about who'd tried to kill me this time. All I wanted was a hot bath and some sleep. Which is exactly what I did.

I decided to spend the night in my freshly rented apartment. I'd missed the free hotel dinner anyway, and unpacking could wait until morning.

The empty apartment felt forlorn, but I smiled. It wasn't my luxury suite in the Tower, but it was good enough. I threw the balcony doors open, letting in the crisp September air, and fell asleep just like that.

*   *   *

The Nameless Ones had no identity. No ambitions. No hobbies. No names.

Their entire existence hinged on one goal: Serve the Fire Clan. Body. Soul. Everything.

That was the condition for preserving the bloodline of a fallen ruling family, their DNA forever entwined with the Shadow Element.

For two centuries, the usurpers had tried to replicate that bond, using the Nameless Ones as breeding stock and subjects for eugenic experiments.

They'd had little success.

All they'd produced was a pitiful imitation of true Shadow — weak, useless without a light source. Trash, unworthy of attention.

The Nameless Ones were the last true shadow elementalists. Masters of pure Shadow. But none of them even considered disobedience.

Disobedience meant death.

And with the death of the Nameless Ones, the true Shadow Clan would die too. They couldn't let that happen.

A Nameless girl received a new task. No killing this time. Just follow the target and gather as much information as possible.

Was this person important? Powerful? She didn't know. It didn't matter.

She'd been told to collect data, so she went to collect it.

At first, the target appeared unremarkable — a commoner with an odd aura.

Then she saw it. A curious little creature darting through the shadows — a scruffy, playful hound with an enchanting bark and a nose sharp enough to sniff her out, even in the depths of the shadows.

The dog charmed her so much that, for a moment, she forgot her mission. She simply watched the mischievous shadow being with fascination.

When the dog's sudden death nearly made her blow her cover, she swore to herself she'd punish the bastard who hurt it — after her mission was complete.

But the bastard didn't live long. The commoner killed him himself, then stored the corpse in what looked like a Shadow Pocket.

Her curiosity nearly betrayed her again as she struggled to make sense of what she'd seen.

Two moments of weakness in a row, both caused by her target. An unacceptable lapse. She pushed the thoughts away.

The rest of the surveillance yielded no new information, only more questions. How did he create that dog? What kind of Shadow Pocket did he use? What was that unusual fabric on his arm?

She needed permission from her handler for

direct contact to answer the first two questions. But the third...

In the dead of night, when he was finally asleep, she slipped into his apartment through the open balcony window.

Slowly, softly, descending from the ceiling like a spider, she reached out a finger from the depths of the shadows to touch the strange fabric.

In the darkness, the material pulsed with pearlescent specks, like stars on a night sky.

She didn't even realize when his strong hand grabbed her wrist. The sudden yank pulled her fully out of the shadows, and there was no resisting it.

*   *   *

"Good morning," I greeted the black-haired woman sprawled on my bed.

Her deceptively frail appearance hid a Gifted of intriguing strength — enough to get dangerously close to me undetected.

I'd felt her presence as soon as night fell, initially suspecting the Reaper. But even after I killed him, the feeling lingered. So, I decided to use the same trick as before — bait the unseen observer and catch them off guard.

Meaning myself. Ha.

Now the woman beneath me, her limbs restrained, showed no discomfort at my half-naked state. Her wild, feline eyes stared straight into my soul, patiently waiting for me to loosen my grip.

"Are we just going to sit here in silence?" I

raised an eyebrow, tightening my hold slightly.

No reaction. The same unblinking predator's gaze, poised for a strike. She knew she couldn't overpower me physically and didn't bother trying. There wasn't even a trace of aggression or threat from her — just a chill curiosity directed at the fabric on my arm.

After another minute, I sighed and released her. She slipped out with a graceful backflip, vanishing into the shadows.

"What the hell was that?" I muttered, rubbing my temples and glancing at the clock.

Three in the morning, and now I was wide awake.

I lay in bed for another twenty minutes, but when it became clear the intriguing stranger wouldn't return, I picked up my phone. I found three 24-hour food delivery services and placed an order.

No way Tarin was bringing me breakfast at the Portal, and I had no intention of fighting on an empty stomach. Why suffer when I could eat well?

Next, I called the hotel reception and arranged for my belongings to be delivered. They promised to have everything done within two hours. Excellent service for such a cheap place — highly recommended.

Since I wasn't going back to sleep, I decided to make good use of the time. I put myself through an hour-long workout — stretching, warming up my muscles, and preparing my body for the day ahead.

At sunrise, a message arrived from an unknown sender. Standing on the balcony, coffee in hand, I felt ready to show the off-world creatures beyond the Portal that the First Paladin had returned to haunt them.

The thought warmed my chest. I loved this. Despite being on leave, I had no intention of giving up my favorite hobby. Besides, there was no better way to replenish the elemental energy I'd lost in the desert trap.

A taxi sped me through the empty streets to the Central Guardians' Station, where an armored personnel carrier was already waiting.

"Good morning, Captain!" I waved cheerfully.

"Morning to you too," Tarin replied, squinting with irritation.

"What's the problem? I'm not late."

"If showing up on time explains your appearance, I'd rather you were late," he said with a sigh. "Where's your armor?"

"Won't need it," I replied dismissively.

"Don't spout nonsense... If you're broke, I can issue some," he said, chewing on his lip thoughtfully. "Ten minutes tops — you'll sign for it and leave a small deposit..."

"No need, thanks. It'll just get in the way and restrict my movements. What I'm wearing is more than enough," I said, tapping my chest.

Tarin looked skeptically at my gray cloth pants, black hoodie, and battered tactical backpack slung over my shoulder. I looked more like I was going for a jog than stepping into a Portal.

Which, for me, wasn't far from the truth.

The short message I'd received earlier described the Portal as F-class: low-activity and non-elemental.

A light stroll, like a casual walk in the park.

Tarin wasn't impressed with my elemental cleaver either. While he acknowledged the quality of the metal, he dismissed the weapon as "too impractical and limited."

I couldn't argue. I had three decent blades from the Reaper, but they still needed work — processing, attaching handles, or possibly selling or trading them. Later, though.

For now, I'd brought only the cloak, the cleaver, and my backpack. That was plenty.

Tarin, however, thought differently. He was convinced I was signing up for a heroic death. He even made me sign a waiver, ensuring I'd receive no insurance and that all my possessions would go to his department in the event of my death.

Apparently, this wasn't standard procedure, but Tarin outright refused to take me to the Portal without it. Something about the costs of my funeral coming out of his paycheck.

The Portal was about nine miles outside the city, perched atop a small hill covered in wildflowers. A village lay about a third of a mile away, with cows grazing peacefully nearby.

No fences, no bunkers, no warning signs — just a lone soldier asleep at his post, undisturbed even by the roar of our vehicle's engine.

While Tarin berated the poor guard with promises of official reprimands, I circled the hill.

The Portal stood about as tall as the average person, a colorless semicircle sticking out of the ground like a giant plate. Beside it, a metal post with a small screen caught my eye.

We didn't have anything like that in my time.

"Argus's Fang," Tarin said, walking over. "Sensor, stabilizer, lock — all in one. The only way in."

"How does it work?"

"Simple," he replied, punching the Portal.

Instead of pulling him in, the colorless membrane repelled him. Or rather, the force barrier generated by the metal post did.

"You can only enter through the Registry," he continued, holding a tablet up to my face. Data streamed across the screen.

Small Portal
Danger Class: F (harmless).
Elemental Resonance: None.
Last Activity: None recorded.
Predicted Activation Date: None.

Timer Since Creation: 3 days, 2 hours, 23 minutes, 54 seconds.
Recommended Closure Deadline: 365 days.
Restrictions: None.

Owner: Nature Clan.

First Entry Fee: 15,000 Imperial Coins.
Re-entry Fee: 1,000 Imperial Coins.

"This is standard info available to all rookie Guardians," he explained. "The Argus system processes much more data from every Portal in real-time — threat levels, valuable resources, you name it. Higher Registry access means more information. You'll get basic access if you pass the exam. Got it?"

"Got it," I said with a nod.

"Now for the exam itself," he added. "The Portal is designed for up to three people, but you're going in alone. Your task is to demonstrate your strengths — whether it's scouting, finding rare resources, or killing monsters. Anything useful will be evaluated later, and we'll decide accordingly. Don't try to be a hero. No one expects you to clear the Portal, but if you come back empty-handed, no license. Like I told you yesterday, I don't need dead weight on my team. Prove yourself."

"Understood," I replied, smiling as my gaze drifted eagerly toward the entrance.

Marcus, look at you now.

Shaking like a junkie. And this is just a primitive Portal I wouldn't have bothered with at six years old. Yet my body was practically vibrating with anticipation. The lack of elemental energy was clearly taking its toll.

"Alright," he murmured, his tone laced with reluctant acceptance. "By protocol, you have twelve hours, though most recruits finish sooner. Remember, no help will be provided. For twelve hours, you're on your own. If you're injured and can't return by yourself, it's an automatic failure.

No one's coming to save you."

He glanced at me, a faint hope flickering in his eyes. But he saw no hesitation.

"I see you're not backing down," he added. "One last thing. Since you're not registered and technically not a Guardian, we're covering the entry fee. But all resources and trophies inside belong to the Empire."

That hit like a punch to the gut. I'd brought a backpack!

"So I get nothing?" I protested.

"Not nothing," he replied with a laugh. "Invaluable experience and a long-awaited license." He clapped me on the back with a heavy hand. "If you don't die, of course."

"Fine," I grumbled, tossing my backpack at his feet. "Keep an eye on this while I have fun."

"Fun's what you have in a brothel," he said with a snort. "Here, you fight for your life. Got it?"

"Got it. Twelve hours in, out, report. You check and decide. Simple enough?"

"Basically, yes," he muttered, scratching his head.

He seemed unsure about something, probably wondering what he'd gotten himself into. Poor guy wasn't used to recruits like me. Then again, where could you find one like me? Ha.

"Can I go now?" I asked, before he changed his mind.

"Eager, aren't we?" he replied, reluctantly placing his hand on the post's screen. The display glowed green, and the Portal's barrier dissipated.

"Twelve hours, Marcus," he reminded me. "And don't try to be a he—"

His words cut off as the warm energy of the off-world Portal enveloped me, pulling me inside.

CHAPTER 17

Outside the Portal entrance

TWO CREW MEMBERS from the armored vehicle stood idly by, wearing sleepy grins as they watched yet another overconfident recruit step into his first Portal with his head held high. Cocky upstarts like this weren't uncommon. But this one had gone further than most, blatantly ignoring any semblance of preparation.

"Can you believe this guy? He actually showed up in sweatpants and sneakers?" the bald one asked, lighting a cigarette.

"Kids these days don't learn anything," his gray-haired colleague replied, stretching in the warm sunlight.

"No kidding," the bald one said, exhaling a cloud of smoke and noticing their younger crewmate stepping out of the vehicle with a bag in hand. "Hey, Danny, what's with the bag?"

"Setting up the tent," Danny mumbled, coming to a halt. "It's protocol..."

This earned him a round of hearty laughter from the older men.

"Forget the protocol crap," the gray-haired man said with a sneer. "That guy'll last maybe an hour in there, tops!"

"Exactly," the bald one said with a grin. "I'll bet one thousand he comes running out in thirty minutes. Hell, it'll take you longer to set up that tent, Danny!"

"You're on," the gray-haired one replied, shaking his colleague's hand. Then he turned to the camp's guard, who had wandered over to join the group. "What about you?"

The guard, having just endured a severe dressing-down from Tarin, tried to stay inconspicuous. But the temptation of his favorite pastime — gambling — proved too strong.

"Five thousand says you're both wrong," he whispered conspiratorially, pulling a crisp, high-denomination Imperial bill from his pocket. "That guy won't last more than twenty minutes."

"Why so confident?" the gray-haired man asked, greed flashing in his eyes.

"Place your bets, and I'll tell you," the guard said, shrugging teasingly as he pulled the bill back toward his pocket.

"Hey, wait!" the bald one said, hastily scrounging up a pile of rumpled notes to meet the wager. "I'm in!"

"Me too," the gray-haired man grumbled after a brief hesitation, tossing in his share. The pile on the armored vehicle's hood grew by another five thousand.

Grinning triumphantly, the guard set a timer and leaned back against the vehicle to enjoy the show. Meanwhile, young Danny, oblivious to the game, dutifully began setting up the camp.

"Alright, spill it," the bald one said, giving the guard a nudge. "What's your angle?"

"You kids shouldn't be gambling blind," the guard said smugly. "No intel, and you're throwing money around. Yesterday, the Nature Clan brought their rookies here during my shift. Their squads ran out of that Portal like their tails were on fire, cursing the system for throwing them a death trap of a Portal. Broke half their weapons."

"Why's it a death trap?" The bald one leaned in.

"Beats me," the guard replied with a shrug. "But their rookies came back with bruises and fractures. The toughest group lasted exactly twenty-three minutes. Not a second more."

"Damn," the bald one muttered, mentally kissing his cash goodbye.

"No kidding," the gray-haired man agreed. "If those clan brats with all their gear couldn't handle it, this kid doesn't stand a chance. Unless..." He brightened, his eyes lighting up with sudden realization. "What if he dies in there? Then none of us win!"

"Unlikely," the guard said with a knowing grin.

"I've got a good eye for these things. The Portal's not lethal. The rookies' injuries were minor. Sure, a couple had broken legs, but your boy went in light. He'll figure it out and bail."

"So why didn't those noble idiots report it to the Registry?" a loud voice growled from behind them, making the group jump and hastily conceal their betting pool. Captain Tarin had returned.

"Uh, no idea, Captain," the guard replied, his bravado evaporating instantly. "Maybe they forgot? Or maybe they're planning some revenge run. Word is they lost big. Or..." He paused dramatically. "Maybe your recruit pissed them off."

"Doubtful," Tarin replied with a frown. "The Nature Clan recommended him to us..."

A memory surfaced — just last night, twelve suitable Portals had been listed for Marcus's express exam. By this morning, only one remained available: this one.

Lost in thought, Tarin walked away, leaving the soldiers to nervously watch the ticking timer. Meanwhile, Danny continued assembling the tent, mildly annoyed he hadn't been invited to bet.

*   *   *

The world darkened for a moment, then erupted in muted, earthy hues.

I found myself at the bottom of a canyon, its rocky walls towering so high they obscured the sky. Behind me lay a dead-end and the Portal exit. To either side, sheer cliffs. Ahead, a single trail, about twenty feet wide, wound deeper into the gorge.

"Corridor type," I muttered.

One of the basic setups.

Typically, these Portals consisted of a linear, confined space with one, maybe two species of creatures. The air, soil, and rock around me held so little elemental energy it might as well have been nonexistent.

Back in my day, the Tower wouldn't have bothered intercepting a Portal this weak, leaving it to the Princes' warriors. Now, it had the honor of hosting the First Paladin.

Old Aks would be rolling in his nonexistent grave.

"Monitor," I commanded, placing a tiny insect-like tracker at the Portal's entrance.

The bug wasn't much. Poor vision, couldn't fight or move, but it could detect motion across any spectrum. If someone entered, I'd know.

With my rear secured and my hands free, I stretched with a satisfying pull and started down the trail.

The mood was excellent.

Sure, I wouldn't replenish much elemental energy here, but as old Aks used to say, "Creatures are creatures."

Each kill, no matter how small, helped the world and gave me a bit of a boost. And with a license, I could start picking more lucrative Portals.

The kind where high elemental concentrations forged the most valuable loot: Crystals.

Unlike shards from the Great Source, which were empty vessels for accumulating energy, Crystals were pure, materialized elements formed upon the death of a creature deeply attuned to its element. They were essential to Argus technology — at least, they had been in my time.

Whistling, I spun my cleaver idly in one hand, letting the anticipation build. No sense guessing what kind of off-world beasties I'd encounter. I preferred surprises.

The first surprise came as a heavy rock, tumbling from above, aiming squarely for my skull. The flat trail gave way to dips, bumps, and mounds faintly resembling freshly buried burrows.

Then came the sound — a growing, scratching noise, starting behind me before echoing all around.

Finally, I saw it. Perched on a rise ahead: the first resident of this charming realm.

Less than two feet tall, brownish, with a wide snout and narrow slits for eyes. Thick forelimbs ended in small but sturdy claws. Stone plates covered its body, leaving only a tiny white underbelly exposed.

A common Rock-Gnawer.

Pack creatures, not overly aggressive, but fiercely territorial. I'd only ever seen one outside a Portal once — an eccentric architect had bought one on the black market to save on construction costs.

The logic was sound. Rock-Gnawers could

grind even the toughest elemental stone into malleable sand. Unfortunately, this one ground workers into pulp instead, and by the time I arrived, the death toll was in the hundreds.

"Creatures are creatures," I muttered, recalling the rivers of blood that soaked that ill-fated construction site.

No matter how harmless they seemed in their worlds, monsters became indiscriminate killers in ours. That was their nature. Their essence.

Seeing I had no intention of retreating, the Rock-Gnawer curled into a ball and rolled toward me. From all directions, four more joined the charge.

I sidestepped the nearest one, halting its momentum with a sharp kick. It screeched as my cleaver found its throat. At the same moment, I raised my right hand, catching a second mid-leap.

The Time Element reduced it to dust in two seconds flat.

The remaining three, however, proved trickier.

Unlike Tarin's clumsy recruits, these stone balls knew how to leverage their numbers, coordinating their attacks. Blunt impacts to my lower back, shin, and thigh left me aching.

But once they collided, they lost all momentum. I didn't give them a chance to roll away, systematically flipping them over and splitting their soft bellies open.

The last one, instead of fleeing, sank its teeth into my hand and slashed at my stomach with a claw.

"Well, damn," I muttered, inspecting the tattered remains of my clothes. "Single-use, it seems."

That skirmish cost me five energy units. I even got a bruise on my thigh. Pesky little things!

Using my energy to shield against Rock-Gnawers wasn't worth it. They yielded pitiful amounts, had no Crystals, and their loot was unimpressive.

In the Order, their stone plates were valued, but I lacked the tools to harvest them. Besides, each plate weighed about thirty pounds, and each creature had ten of them. Too much hassle for too little reward.

For killing all five, I gained a total of three energy units. Absorbing three of the corpses added another three units. I left two carcasses behind for Tarin — he'd need proof that I wasn't slacking off.

The trail began to widen, a sure sign that the next groups of Rock-Gnawers might exceed five individuals. And I only had two hands.

Leaving the Portal with a net loss of energy didn't appeal to me. After weighing my options, I decided to summon one of my three familiars.

With my current energy reserves, I could only manage to summon *him*.

Conjuring his image in my mind, I extended my hand and commanded, "Come forth."

For a few moments, nothing happened. Then, from the swirling cloud of Darkness, a curious little face emerged — a kitten made of pure energy.

It sniffed the air, wrinkled its nose in distaste, and reluctantly stepped out.

The cloud collapsed, consuming all my accumulated elemental energy. It wasn't gone for good, though. Unlike other elemental applications, summoning a familiar didn't burn energy; it gave it form.

If I dismissed him, all the energy I spent would return, sometimes even more if he managed to devour anything. Not that it was likely in this case. I'd only lose energy if the familiar were killed — highly improbable in an F-class Portal. Despite his small, kitten-like appearance, his elemental hide was tougher than anything here could pierce.

His offensive potential, though, left much to be desired.

A familiar's strength directly depended on the energy at its disposal. Right now, most of my kitten's reserves went toward maintaining his form.

Still, he made an excellent decoy — and he wasn't easily bruised. Plus, he loved chasing things, as far as I remembered.

"Meow?" The kitten glared at me, clearly annoyed, and tried to draw more energy. I denied him.

"This'll do," I said with a grin. "If you want to grow bigger, go hunt. Plenty of mice in the burrows."

"Hmph!" He huffed, grooming his claws with an air of dignity.

This familiar had two forms, one of which could fly. But he preferred the feline shape, earning him the unimaginative name "Cat."

It was especially amusing when, in his second

form — a thirty-three-foot, lizard-like entity brimming with energy — he'd soar above swarms of portal creatures with a predatory gleam in his eyes.

Old Aks never liked the name. The Cat didn't mind, though — it wouldn't respond to anything else anyway. Familiars were willful beings, each with their own unique intelligence and personality.

Old Aks referred to them as "elemental avatars," bound to answer only the worthy. Oddly enough, Aks himself never had one.

After finishing his claws, the Cat moved on to cleaning his fur.

I didn't have the patience to wait for his grooming ritual to end. Grabbing him by the scruff, I tossed him into the nearest burrow. Knowing his mischievous nature, he might've spent all twelve hours pretending to be busy otherwise. And the Portal wouldn't clear itself.

His resistance was short-lived.

Despite his stubbornness, the Cat had missed being summoned for over a year. Now he was fully indulging.

Small and agile, he slipped through every crevice, gleefully chasing the stone balls around the canyon.

The Rock-Gnawers couldn't hide from him, and their attempts to crush him under their plates failed spectacularly. The Cat simply shook off the impact and pounced again, determined to devour at least one.

In the end, all he left them with were harmless

scratches, terrifying them with his recklessness and feral gaze.

But he excelled in his assigned task: distracting the stone balls and causing chaos.

The Rock-Gnawers stopped ganging up on me. Picking them off individually became much easier. It just took time and patience. The balls were surprisingly quick for their size.

Methodically, burrow by burrow, we cleared the canyon until the trail ended in a dead end. There, I gutted the last cornered Rock-Gnawer.

A faint shiver ran through me as an energy surge marked the Portal beginning to close.

For Portals this size, the process usually took a full day. During that time, the world would try to eject all foreign entities.

Tarin and his valiant crew would have the same twelve hours he'd given me to gather trophies. Let them have their fun.

By then, I'd absorbed thirty-five Rock-Gnawer corpses, leaving ten scattered throughout the canyon. That should be enough to keep Tarin from asking too many questions.

Satisfied, though hungry, I checked my watch. Just over two hours remained of my allotted time. Perfect for a leisurely return to the exit. Staying longer served no purpose. After dismissing the Cat, I jogged back.

The results of my Portal stroll: eight bruises, worn-out sneakers, shredded clothes, and a net gain of sixty-two elemental energy units.

As I ran toward the exit, a delightful idea

formed: how to squeeze a little extra cash out of Tarin.

Things were definitely looking up.

CHAPTER 18

THE FAMILIAR WORLD welcomed me back with a stunning crimson sunset framed by peacefully drifting clouds.

Fresh air. The aroma of freshly cooked food wafting through the breeze.

Pure contentment.

And then, a massive, not particularly cheerful figure blocked my entire view.

"Just the man I was looking for, Captain," I said with a grin. "Permission to report?"

"Don't get cheeky, Marcus," Tarin replied with a heavy sigh. "You're not under my command, or do you know what I'd do if you were?"

"Let me slack off and shirk all my duties?" I ventured, glancing at four soldiers who had abandoned their posts to gape at me. They didn't seem thrilled I'd come back alive.

"Who's loafing around over there?" Tarin bellowed, his face turning red.

They scattered like leaves in a storm, and Tarin returned his scowl to me.

"How the hell did you do it?" he demanded, his tone low and suspicious. He motioned for me to step aside, away from prying eyes and ears.

"Do what, exactly?" I asked innocently.

"That!" he snapped, nodding toward the now-dimmed Portal. "You closed it, didn't you?"

"Was that not the point?" I asked, feigning confusion. "You did say, Captain: twelve hours... show me what you've got... scout the area, eliminate the creatures, and..." I scratched my head as if trying to recall. "What else was on your list of requirements?"

"Resource collection," he replied.

"Right. Resources. Not much there, honestly. Besides a pile of useless rocks, there are a couple dozen plant species. Though they're annoyingly out of reach. But you guys will manage, right?"

"Cut the jokes, will you?" His frown deepened.

"Jokes? Perish the thought! I'm being completely sincere," I said, feigning indignation. With a few clicks, I sent the detailed data I'd prepared over to him. "Here's the full list of what you'll find inside."

He gave the report a cursory glance without opening it, then fixed me with a heavy stare.

"So you're not going to tell me how you did it?"

"Why wouldn't I?" I replied with a shrug. "I went in, saw, and conquered. Though, I did ruin my clothes and dull my cleaver…” I waved the blunt weapon under Tarin's nose with mock sadness.

He let out another weary sigh, rubbing his temples as if to ward off a headache.

“Yesterday, the Nature Clan sent their rookies in there,” he grumbled, unable to keep the story to himself. “And do you know what happened?”

“They died?”

“No…” he said, his expression tightening, “but they got their asses handed to them.”

“Is that so?” I murmured, my thoughts briefly wandering. “Well, it's a good thing I didn't join them. You learn from the strong.”

“Wait, what do you mean ‘didn't join them’?” he asked sharply. “They invited you into the Clan? That's why… uh, Marcus, you're playing with fire turning down aristocrats. They'll ruin you.”

“Let them try,” I said with a casual shrug. “Oh, by the way, I almost forgot — there's one more thing.”

With that, I sent him another document.

At first, he barely glanced at it, but then his brow furrowed, and he began reading more carefully. His face turned red, nostrils flaring. He looked ready to yell at me but restrained himself and read the document again.

“What the hell is this?” he finally demanded, glaring at me.

“Not ‘hell,’ Captain — my official application!” I said cheerfully. “I did some light reading while walking back. Those documents your department sent me this morning? Found an interesting little clause: 'A certified Imperial Guardian is defined as an individual who has either closed five Portals as part of a training group, three as part of a combat unit, or one independently.'" I quoted verbatim.

The trek back to the exit was long and dull, giving me plenty of time to dive into bureaucratic minutiae. I'd prepared three different approaches, all leading to the same result.

"That's from the statute on Guardian status renewal..." he replied hesitantly.

"Exactly! A statute actively applied back in the previous century when Portal entry restrictions weren't as strict," I said with a grin.

"Hmm... so, in other words, you're asking me to recognize you as a Guardian based on closing this Portal?" he said thoughtfully.

"Am I not within my rights?" I raised an eyebrow.

"You are," he admitted reluctantly. Wasting no time, he pulled out his tablet, where I caught a glimpse of my profile — photo and a wall of text beneath it. A few taps later, my phone buzzed with a notification congratulating me on my induction into the Guardians. Attached were my ID number and a unique password for Registry access. Another message followed, celebrating my first closed Portal.

Efficient system. Though, to be fair, they still had trophies to collect, and time was ticking.

"The license won't be ready until morning," he remarked. "You'll receive your Guardian communicator at training tomorrow. They'll help you activate Registry access and give you a tour. Since you're unaffiliated with any Clan, the Empire will serve as your coordinator. Today's Portal is already logged in your account, and payment will be processed within three days. Familiar with the Imperial Guardian payment parameters?"

"Generally."

That was another thing I'd looked into. And the deeper I delved, the more I saw how right Max had been. As a commoner Guardian under Imperial patronage, making real money would be tough.

Imperial rules dictated that Guardians like me were required to sell all trophies and resources collected from Portals exclusively to the Empire. Selling anything on the side was illegal and harshly punished. Naturally, the Empire's buyback prices were lower than market value, meaning a commoner Guardian lost a hefty chunk of potential earnings right from the start.

And forget about keeping trophies for personal use. If I found something useful — like a sword or armor — and wanted to keep it, I'd have to sell it to the Empire first, then buy it back from them. Of course, I'd lose a significant amount of hard-earned money on the price difference.

On top of that, there were countless petty fees, taxes, and fines — charges for damaged trophies, sloppy collection, incomplete reports, and more. When you tallied it all up, an Imperial Guardian could lose up to eighty percent of their potential profit.

On one hand, you could keep it simple: run into a Portal, close it, call in Imperial collectors, and move on to the next one. That twenty percent cut would still convert into a paycheck higher than most Imperial jobs.

But the risks were much higher. Quality gear was hard to come by and expensive to maintain. And if you got injured, instead of insurance or a decent pension, you'd be left to starve.

That's why having a Clan as a patron was better than relying on the Empire. Clan contracts were individually negotiated, offering more potential profit and privileges. Even the list of Portals available in the Registry for selection would be significantly broader. And that was just the tip of the iceberg.

I didn't dig too deep into the details. What I'd uncovered so far was more than enough.

"Well, glad you're familiar with it," he said with a knowing grunt. "Though I doubt you plan to stick with the Empire for long."

"And what makes you say that?" I asked, keeping my tone light.

"I haven't been idle, Marcus," he replied, waving his tablet. "I ran some background checks on you."

"Oh? What juicy gossip did you uncover?" I asked, leaning in shamelessly.

He frowned and quickly pulled the device away. Cautious. I'd find out eventually anyway.

"Nothing good," he said, narrowing his eyes. "Take my advice, kid. I'd be careful around those highborn types — especially the Shadows. It'd be a shame to lose someone with your talent."

"I'll manage, Captain. I'm a big boy," I said with a grin, only for my stomach to betray me with a loud growl. "Uh... any chance there's food around here?"

"Of course," he said, gesturing toward a tall white tent from which the delicious scent of meat wafted. "All camp services are at your disposal."

He tactfully omitted the fact that they weren't free and would be deducted from my earnings. No surprise there.

But his smug satisfaction didn't last long.

As soon as our conversation ended and he began reviewing my report in detail, his face turned ghostly pale.

My list was extraordinarily thorough.

Alongside the obviously useful Rock-Gnawer corpses, I'd included every blade of grass and potentially valuable leaf I'd spotted inside the Portal. Nothing escaped my notice — not even plants growing three hundred twenty-eight feet up sheer cliff faces. There were dozens of such items, and the total count reached into the hundreds.

What could I say? They'd asked for a reconnaissance report, and I'd delivered. Old Aks would've been proud.

How they chose to use my data wasn't my problem. Besides, I'd get paid for every resource collected — even if it was just twenty percent. And in this case, I was more than happy to leave the painstaking harvesting to the Empire's hands.

After all, I knew the law. The collection team would have to account for every resource they failed to gather. No exceptions.

"Danny!" Tarin's shout echoed across the camp, filled with tension.

Seconds later, a young soldier in uniform sprinted up and snapped to attention.

"Run back to the village for more food," he ordered, handing Danny a thick wad of cash.

"How much should I get?" Danny asked cautiously.

"Get plenty, Danny," he said with a resigned sigh. "We're in for the night."

* * *

After my conversation with Tarin, chaos erupted in the camp.

Tarin barked orders with such intensity it probably scared off all wildlife within a mile. His booming voice tore through the air, pushing the poor soldiers to their limits. Their faces were a sight to behold — anguish mixed with resignation. But hey, they chose this line of work. Let them earn their keep.

I just hoped they'd manage to collect at least half of the items from my detailed list by morning. After all, I'd still be charged the fifteen thousand for the Portal entry — and let's not forget the three hundred for that beef stew and a slice of buttered bread.

I considered borrowing a clean set of clothes

from the Imperials at the camp, but their prices were ridiculous. For the amount listed on their service menu, I could buy ten sets wholesale. No thanks.

One thing I didn't refuse, though, was the ride back in the armored vehicle. It was part of the package — roundtrip transportation included in my exam. They had to return me to the exact spot where they'd picked me up.

My driver was one of the soldiers, a poor soul whose stress from Tarin's shouting had practically turned him gray overnight. His uniform was soaked with sweat, and he looked too exhausted to hold a conversation. They hadn't even entered the Portal yet — just preparing for it had drained him.

The ride back was silent and tense. The armored vehicle roared to life and sped off the moment it dropped me off at the Central Guardians' Station.

Full, disheveled, and lugging an empty backpack, I flagged down a taxi and headed home.

After a long, hot bath and a change into a fresh, identical outfit — this one thankfully intact — I felt ready to unwind

Old Aks had a saying: "A victory uncelebrated is no victory at all."

And so, I went to celebrate in the Shadow District.

Nothing had changed there in a day.

Initially foreboding, the district transformed as night fell into a bustling, noisy hub of activity. The place came alive after dark.

This time, I didn't bother hiding the raven tattoo etched on my hand. In fact, I deliberately spun a coin in that hand — the same one I'd taken from a local big shot. A little flair to let the mark do its work.

In the Shadow District, strength commanded respect, and I was ready to prove mine to anyone willing to challenge me.

No one did.

Taking my time, I strolled through the district, paying special attention to shop signs. Food wasn't on my mind tonight — alcohol was. So when I spotted a tavern with a green awning and a name ending in "Pub," I turned toward it.

Inside, it was surprisingly cozy. Muted green tones, old-fashioned wood paneling, soft music, and holographic screens showing a fight.

"Imperial pale ale," I ordered, settling at the bar.

The place wasn't crowded. Three women sat chatting at the central table, a rowdy group of drunk men occupied the corner, eyes glued to the fight on the screen, and a lone man at the far end of the bar stared at an empty glass.

"New here?" the bartender asked, setting a frothy mug in front of me.

"Something like that," I replied, pulling out the Argus coin. "Know what this is?"

"Everyone does," the bartender said without much interest. "Its owner's been needing to be put in his place for a while now."

"Why's that?" I asked, curious.

"Too unruly. Scares off customers and disrupts business. He's banned from half the district's establishments," the bartender said, nodding toward a sign near the door.

On a white background was a crossed-out Boar's face.

"Got it," I said with a grin. "So you've never seen another coin like this around here?"

"Not personally," the bartender replied calmly. "Is it valuable?"

"Doubt it," I said, pocketing the coin again.

Too bad.

I'd have to question the Boar himself about where he'd gotten it. Judging by what I'd heard around the district, though, it would be a while before he'd be in any shape to talk.

My shadow lizards scurried through the alleys, gathering information. Last time I was here, the Shadows had been watching my every move. Two could play that game. This time, it was my turn to return the favor.

Thanks to the energy I'd stockpiled in the Portal earlier, I could extend the reach of my Darkness embodiments.

Now, sitting in the pub conveniently located at the Shadow District's center, I had eyes and ears covering the busiest part of the area, piecing together fragments of local gossip and power dynamics.

Still, drinking alone wasn't much fun.

I spotted a fine bottle of champagne on the

shelf and waved to the bartender. After all, tonight was a celebration — the day I earned my license.

The bartender nodded in understanding and deftly placed four champagne flutes, the bottle of bubbly, and a grin in front of me. "On the house."

"Well, well," I said, pleasantly surprised. "Anyone else bothering your business besides the Boar? I could help."

"If someone comes up, I'll let you know," he replied with a nod.

I grabbed the champagne bottle in one hand and the four glasses in the other, heading confidently toward the table of three bored-looking women.

And then, two things happened simultaneously.

The front door burst off its hinges with a deafening crash, and a window shattered near the corner where the rowdy group of drunks sat.

The men had been loudly celebrating a fighter's victory on-screen, and apparently, someone outside hadn't appreciated the noise.

A not-so-friendly group stormed in, fists itching for action, and charged toward the broken window. Chaos erupted instantly.

The drunken brawl spread like wildfire through the pub, a whirlwind of curses, flying glass shards, and splintered wood. Blood splattered, shouts echoed, and fists landed with bone-crunching force.

In the midst of this violent frenzy, only three people remained uninvolved:

The bartender, quietly polishing a glass with resigned sorrow in his eyes.

The man at the far end of the bar, still staring at his empty glass.

And me, leisurely drinking champagne straight from the bottle, utterly unbothered by the madness around me.

CHAPTER 19

THE FIRST FEW MINUTES of watching the brawl were entertaining — way more engaging than the holographic fight playing on the screen.

This was happening right in front of me. Raw emotions. Full immersion. Almost too full, at times.

The champagne only added to the experience. But eventually, the bottle ran dry, and the spectacle lost its appeal. The drunks started to tire. Their energy and flair faded. Just as I was considering leaving for another spot, something interesting caught my attention.

One particularly unlucky thug had gotten separated from the pack. He was staggering backward, clutching his stomach with both hands — or, more precisely, the hilt of the knife sticking out of it.

Instead of thinking through his options, the drunk simply yanked the blade out and prepared to rejoin the fray, now armed.

But something went wrong. His movements faltered, his eyes glazed over, and he collapsed to his knees in a growing pool of his own blood. The idiot had nicked an artery.

This happened at the far end of the bar. Neither his friends nor his enemies could help him — not that the bartender looked like he'd mind if they all dropped dead on the spot.

I wasn't about to intervene, either. Honestly, I wouldn't have paid him any attention if it weren't for what happened next.

The young man seated at the far end of the bar, who looked to be in his early twenties, turned lazily, placed his hand on the nearly-dead thug's shoulder, and held it there for about five seconds before turning back to his empty glass.

The bleeding stopped.

The thug's eyes snapped open, life flooding back into them. He leaped to his feet, touching his stomach in disbelief.

Then he turned toward his savior. But instead of gratitude, his face twisted with hostility. Without hesitation, he swung the knife at the oblivious young man.

My hand moved on its own. The empty champagne bottle sailed through the air, shattering against the thug's head and dropping him back into his own bloody puddle. This time, though, his worthless life wasn't in any real danger.

The young man glanced over his shoulder at the noise. He seemed unfazed when he noticed the knife in the thug's hand.

"Thanks," he muttered toward me before returning his focus to his empty glass.

Suddenly, I didn't feel like leaving.

"You're welcome," I replied, sliding into the seat beside him.

The commotion around us had mostly died down. It wasn't clear who had won or why the fight had started in the first place — not that it mattered.

"Pour him a vodka," I told the bartender before he could step away to clean up.

"I don't want vodka..." the young man mumbled, though not very convincingly.

For the first time that evening, his glass wasn't empty.

"Drink," I said.

"Why?" he muttered stubbornly.

With a heavy sigh, I picked up the glass and placed it in his hand. At least he didn't need further assistance — he downed half the vodka in one go. His youthful face scrunched up, and his eyes darted around for something to chase it with.

Anticipating this moment, the experienced bartender slid over a bowl of salted peanuts. The young man eagerly grabbed a handful, his tense expression easing slightly as he relaxed.

"Better?" I asked, pouring myself a shot.

"A little," he admitted with a nod.

"Good," I said with a smirk. "Now tell me —

what's a Light Clan member doing in the one place where saving someone's life might get you stabbed in the back?"

"Hmm," he replied with a grimace. "You noticed?"

"Lucky for you," I replied with a smile.

"You know," he murmured, "I don't blame him. We wiped out his entire clan… no, not just his clan — clans. Women, elders, most of the children. Everyone here has a reason to hate me. We're devils in the flesh, deserving only death," he stated matter-of-factly before downing another third of his drink.

"You're not planning to kill me, are you?" he asked hopefully.

"Nope," I said, disappointing him.

"Pity," he drawled. "You know, man, they're right."

"The rowdy bunch?"

"At least they don't pretend to be something they're not," he said with a bitter smile. "They don't hide what they are. Unlike us — hypocritical scum, the lot of us. The 'righteous' Light Clan." He practically choked on the words before drowning the taste with another shot of vodka.

Keeping up with him was no small task.

"So, what brings you here? Looking for death?" I asked.

"If only it were that easy…" He let out a weary breath, disappointment etched into his face as he turned to look at me for the first time.

His eyes appeared dull gray, much like those

of the local Shadows. Yet beneath this masterful illusion lay the radiant white sparks of true Light — an unmistakable hallmark of a powerful light elementalist.

"And why do you care?" he asked, emboldened by the alcohol. "What's your name...?"

"Marcus," I introduced myself.

"Marcus..." he repeated mockingly. "Weird name."

"It's Northern."

"Ah," he muttered, extending his hand. "Gabriel."

"Well, Gabe," I said, shaking his hand with a smile. "I've got this pesky little flaw — curiosity."

"Curiosity doesn't lead to a long life these days," he said knowingly, finishing yet another drink.

Gabe swayed slightly, barely managing to keep his balance.

"Especially for newcomers," he continued, steadying himself. "Here's a piece of advice, Marcus from the North — get out while you still can. If I haven't heard your name yet, it means you haven't met the Boss."

"Nope," I confirmed.

"Good. Keep it that way," he said firmly. "Finish whatever you're doing and get out of here... what are you even doing here, anyway?"

"Celebrating," I said with a grin, pouring another shot and tossing back a handful of salted peanuts. "Just got my Guardian's license."

"Ah, Guardians..." he said dreamily. "Protectors of humanity… a noble path! Stick with it. And don't come back here!" He barked the last part, nearly falling off his stool from the sudden motion.

"Is this Boss of yours really that scary?"

"Ha." He chuckled darkly. "If you stick around… that smug idiot will be the least of your worries," he said, leaving five thousand bills on the counter before stumbling out.

I didn't follow him. My shadow lizards were nearly out of energy, so I decided to spend the remaining time here.

Despite the earlier chaos, people continued to trickle into the pub, with many helping the bartender clean up the mess.

Even among such rough company, camaraderie and mutual aid weren't entirely absent. It was a pleasant surprise.

I spent the last fifteen minutes flirting with a pretty brunette before deciding to head home alone. After all, I had company waiting for me.

The picture of the Shadow District that had formed in my mind was fascinating, and I was looking forward to tomorrow's meeting with the Boss.

* * *

"Hello again," I greeted as I stepped into my apartment.

Hanging upside down in the hallway, just outside my bedroom, was the black-haired woman. Her deceptively delicate frame was tightly bound in a dense cocoon of woven Darkness, rendering her completely immobile.

Her feline eyes stared indifferently to the side, but her face betrayed her emotions — interest tinged with mild irritation. It was the look of someone overly confident in their abilities yet capable of admitting when they'd been outsmarted by a ridiculous trap.

This one here was also remarkably proud.

"Still giving me the silent treatment?" I remarked with mild reproach. "Well, make yourself comfortable — the energy in those bindings will last another three days."

With that, I went about my evening.

I sorted through my clothes, performed a full-body workout, and did my best to engage every muscle group. My body still had a long way to go before reaching its peak form, and daily discipline was required to get it back in shape.

After my workout, I showered and ate a light snack I'd picked up at the corner shop. The stubborn girl remained unaffected by my pointed indifference, the hours ticking by, or even the enticing aroma of food.

A tough nut to crack — and one I was more interested in unlocking with finesse than brute force.

First, tomorrow's meeting with the Shadow Clan Boss meant I couldn't afford to hand him leverage by killing one of his subordinates.

Second, it would be wasteful to destroy such a valuable asset in a Clan I intended to take over.

The past couple of days had shown me clearly:

as a commoner, there were limits to what I could achieve. And settling for mediocrity? Not my style. As old Aks used to say, "True goals are always reached by aiming higher."

Once my tasks were done, I opened the balcony door as usual and collapsed onto my bed. The final touch was summoning a shadow tracker, which I did without lifting my head from the pillow. There was a good chance the girl's friends would come looking for her, and an additional "security system" couldn't hurt.

"How?" a quiet, feminine voice suddenly broke the silence.

"So, you can talk after all," I said, sitting up slightly.

She was still dangling in the cocoon of woven Darkness, but this time, her piercing gaze was fixed directly on me.

"That... dog. How did you summon it?"

"With my hands." I gave a casual shrug. "You saw it yourself."

"Yes, but..." she hesitated, her composure slipping for a moment. "I know all the shadow techniques and commands. I've never seen that one. Is it... a shadow?"

"Who knows?" I said with a smirk. "You can pet it and find out for yourself if you'd like."

"But it's intangible..." she said, her frustration evident. It was clear she had already tried to touch it.

Interesting. When had she attempted that? During the night of the Reaper's attack?

"In the Deep Shadow, it emits warmth. If you align with its frequency correctly, you can touch it," I explained. "You've already mastered entering the deeper layers, haven't you?"

The girl averted her gaze sheepishly, as if that could somehow hide the obvious truth.

"You don't have to answer," I said with a smile. "I already know you have. Just like I know about the 'Shadow Step,' 'Shadow Dance,' and 'Shadow Sight' you used."

"How do you..." she said, trailing off as she quickly bit her tongue — literally. A thin trickle of crimson blood ran from her mouth.

"My mentor taught me," I said, getting up from the bed. Using a piece of her black dress, I wiped away the blood.

The fabric was woven entirely from shadow essence, laced with five poisonous additives, but my aura neutralized them with ease.

"What mentor?" she asked, narrowing her eyes.

"Just an old, cantankerous man from the true Shadow Clan." I dismissed the thought with a casual wave.

"You lie!" she growled, her emotions finally breaking free. "All the true Shadow Clan members were slaughtered! Only seven of us remain, and I know every one of them by face! There haven't been any elders for over a century!"

"You wouldn't have known my mentor," I replied with a calm smile. "And it doesn't matter — he's dead. All his knowledge is up here now," I said, tapping my temple.

"I... I don't believe you," she said, pouting like a child denied a toy.

Despite her fierce demeanor, she truly did resemble a child. I wouldn't have guessed her age to be more than eighteen.

At that moment, I noticed her hand trembling. To maintain their density, the strands of woven Darkness siphoned elemental energy from their captive. It seemed I had overestimated her reserves when setting the trap.

After a moment's thought, I waved my hand, dissolving the bindings into the air as a swirl of black mist. The girl landed gracefully on all fours — well, limbs. Her movements were more animalistic than human.

Her keen eyes instantly found an escape route, but this time, she didn't use it.

"Why are you letting me go?" she asked suspiciously, her eyes narrowing. "Again..."

"You're the first person since my mentor who's liked Fluffy," I replied lazily, stretching. "You know, most people think he's only good for tracking and scaring people. Getting inside their heads, making them jump at shadows. But his real talent is reading intentions."

"I-intentions?" she stammered, her reaction betraying more than she probably intended.

"Don't worry," I said, yawning. "He can't transmit them to me. Fluffy's ability is more like a friend-or-foe check. And since he didn't attack you, everything's fine."

The fatigue of the day washed over me again, and I flopped back onto the bed, pulled the blanket over myself, and closed my eyes.

"What if... I change my mind?" she suddenly asked, her face inches from mine.

"I wouldn't recommend it," I said, opening one eye. "And don't even think about touching the fabric on my arm — it'll hurt. In both cases."

Unhappy with my response, she pouted and stepped back. Her slender figure blended seamlessly with the fluttering curtain, her pale white skin glistening in the moonlight.

"The exit's over there," I said, nodding toward the balcony. The dark figure disappeared.

Of course, there was another reason I let her go so easily — a tiny tracker I'd planted on her clothes. It would act as my eyes and ears in the one place my shadow lizards couldn't reach.

The Shadow Clan Boss's mansion.

I woke up at dawn, as was my habit. No notifications buzzed on my phone, meaning Tarin and his crew were still working. With no pressing news, I dressed and headed out for a morning run.

After combining exercise with utility — stopping at a store to grab some groceries — I returned home to throw together a light breakfast. A quick shower later, I stepped out onto the balcony.

The Shadow District was slowly sinking into its daytime slumber under the rising sun.

Tonight, I'd be back.

With that thought, I glanced at my reflection. Meeting the Boss of the Shadow Clan in my current attire was out of the question. Presentation mattered, especially given the scale of my ambitions.

The funds I had left — just over five thousand bills — weren't enough to splurge. And given the Empire's renowned efficiency, I couldn't count on receiving my Portal earnings today.

Weighing my options, I grabbed my torn jacket and called a taxi.

The ride was quick, and the "Closed" sign on the shop didn't deter me. Circling to the alley, I found the service entrance locked but easily dealt with it, slipping inside unnoticed.

A young woman in pink lingerie appeared in the corridor. Oblivious to me, she sipped coffee, chatted on the phone, and twirled her hair simultaneously.

"Uh, excuse me," I said, clearing my throat.

She turned, spotted me, and froze for a split second. Recognition dawned, followed by an ear-piercing scream. The same blonde salesgirl from before dropped her coffee, the mug hitting the floor with a loud clatter, before she bolted down the corridor in a blur of panic.

"What happened now?" Maria emerged, shaking her head when she saw me. "Scaring my staff again, Marcus? We're opening in fifteen minutes."

"Apologies, Maria, but this is urgent," I said with a polite smile, handing her the torn jacket and a bag of chocolates.

"Who — what — did this to you?" she asked, inspecting the damage.

"Not important," I replied, brushing off her question with a casual gesture. "What matters is whether it can be fixed. I have an important meeting tonight."

"When I mentioned the extended 'special guest' warranty, Marcus, I didn't mean for emergencies like this," she said with a sigh.

"So, it can't be done?"

"I never said that," she replied, her smile returning as she gestured for me to follow. "Come to my office. Let's find you a new suit. I'll also share some fresh news."

"Already?" I asked, intrigued.

"Of course," she replied warmly, opening the door to her expansive office.

This was shaping up to be an excellent start to the day. I hadn't expected my first informant in this era to start yielding returns so quickly.

CHAPTER 20

THE CONVERSATION WITH THE OWNER of this rather prestigious clothing store, by the capital's standards, lasted all of fifteen minutes.

Although she hadn't yet uncovered anything about the Amulet's creator, whom I was seeking, she had useful information about the movements of the Princes.

It turned out that servants from nearly all noble Houses frequented Maria's establishment, and many of them enjoyed chatting.

They likely assumed they were revealing nothing significant, merely engaging in idle banter with the charming staff while being measured or selecting fabrics.

However, under the shop's roof, no conversation escaped Maria's notice. Half a hint was enough for her to deduce the true state of affairs.

Behind her friendly facade as the owner of a modest business lay a sharp, cunning, and ambitious woman deeply interested in the dealings of the upper echelons of society.

Although officially, she wasn't part of that world.

Maria had once confided during a previous visit that she'd dreamed of marrying an aristocrat and joining the noble circles since childhood. Fate, however, had taken her down a different path, and now she lived out her dream vicariously by observing, eavesdropping, and occasionally meddling.

Her boutique sold elite wedding dresses, providing ample opportunities for interacting with the upper class. And, like any woman who once aspired to marry into wealth, she had a strong appreciation for money.

The outcome of our brief but productive meeting boiled down to three key points.

First, I confirmed that the Princes wouldn't return to the capital before Monday, leaving me free to focus on other matters.

Second, questions about my "incident" had come not only from the Empire, the Nature Clan, and the Metal Clan. While I'd expected attention from those parties, the interest from the Light Clan puzzled me — especially since, according to Maria, they'd been the most persistent in their inquiries.

Lastly, as for my reason for visiting, Maria took my damaged suit and promised to have a replacement ready by evening — free of charge, no less.

I left the boutique in high spirits, still with

money in my pocket. Moments later, the long-awaited notification arrived: my Guardian license was ready for pickup.

The day was quickly becoming eventful.

"Good morning, Anna! You look lovely," I greeted cheerfully as I ascended the steps.

"Good morning, Mr. Marcus," she replied politely, her tone professional but warm. "You're expected. Third floor, first door on the left."

"Thanks," I said with a nod.

Finding the right office was easy; there was only one on the third floor. The plaque on the door caught my attention: "Major Winthrop, Commander of the Southern District Recruitment Corps."

"That's some heavy artillery for a license handover," I said as I pushed the door open without bothering to knock.

"Who the hell are you?" growled a grizzled man buried in paperwork.

His short-cropped hair and graying temples framed a face crisscrossed with scars, while one eye burned with a fading red elemental glow.

"Marcus Dark," I introduced myself, surveying the spacious yet unpretentious office.

Most of the room was packed with crates of documents, hefty wooden cases, and the mounted heads of a dozen portal creatures adorning the walls.

"Ever heard of knocking, Marcus?" the major said with a frown.

"I was told you were expecting me," I replied

with a smile, nodding toward one particular trophy. "Is that a Livid Maw? Three eyes and a razor-sharp beak — Class A, right? Capable of digesting anything in ten seconds."

Lose focus for a moment, and you'd be dead before you even noticed. If the major only displayed creatures he'd personally taken down, his track record as an Imperial officer must be impressive.

The major's face softened into a faint smile. "That's the one — my first big catch. Damn thing took out twenty of my men before I burned its feathers off." He added nostalgically, "Good times."

"The melting point of its feathers exceeds five thousand four hundred degrees Fahrenheit," I mused aloud. "You must've been a force to reckon with in your younger days."

"I still am," the major said with a grin, glancing wistfully at his desk. "But without me, there'd be a mountain more paperwork... and corpses of reckless rookies like you. Damn bureaucracy."

"If you're that busy, why not delegate this meeting?" I asked, amused.

"Let me decide what gets delegated," he said firmly, opening a drawer and pulling out a sleek silver disk about an inch wide. "Hold out your hand."

Sensing no danger in the artifact's energy, I rolled up my sleeve and extended my left palm.

The major squinted with one eye as he carefully aligned my hand, pressing the sleek silver disk precisely into the center of my palm.

The elemental metal warmed, burned into my skin, cooled with a burst of wind, and soothed the pain with water. Steam scalded my hand before pressing the disk deeper, aligning it perfectly. Pins and needles pricked my fingers as the embedded micro-generator activated, sending gentle waves of energy coursing through my body, each sequentially reflecting one of the ten elements.

"Hmm. Most people react more... dramatically," the major remarked, slightly disappointed. "Didn't it hurt? Forced synchronization isn't exactly pleasant — I remember my own vividly," he added, absently rubbing the matching disk embedded in his own left palm.

"It was tolerable," I replied, flexing my numb fingers. Feeling foreign elemental flows was uncomfortable, but nothing I couldn't handle.

"That's your personal Guardian communicator," the major explained. "It provides real-time Registry access based on your clearance level. Signal works everywhere — in the Green Zones, the Red, even inside the Tower."

"What about Portals?" I asked, raising an eyebrow.

"Those too," he confirmed with a grin, rummaging through the paperwork and tossing me a small folder. "Guidelines, statutes, bestiary, safety protocols — everything you need to know. It's available digitally, but having a hard copy feels more reliable."

Sure, because nothing says 'reliable' like a fire elementalist who could incinerate all this paperwork in a heartbeat. He'd probably surround himself with gas canisters next.

"Let me make this clear, Marcus," the major said. "Although Guardians aren't directly subordinate to the Empire, and you're not obligated to follow even my orders, I strongly recommend observing proper hierarchy. The Guardian community is small, and despite having different patrons, we all share the same goal — protecting our world from the creatures. Plus, the Registry is universal. Ruin your reputation, and life will become significantly harder."

"Me? A bad reputation? Never," I flashed a wry smile, letting the sarcasm hang in the air.

But the major's stern expression made it clear he didn't appreciate the humor. Judging by his frown, Tarin must've left a less-than-glowing review of me. Couldn't have been anything I'd done recently — I'd been nothing but a model citizen today!

"That's about it," the major said, clapping his hands together. "As a rookie, you're entitled to a one-time issue of basic weapons and gear. Treat them carefully — free replacements aren't provided. What else... you'll find maps of all ministry buildings in the folder, along with a full list of available services. As an active Guardian, you're entitled to use them anytime. Oh, and one more thing..." He flashed a broad smile. "Welcome to the ranks of humanity's defenders!"

Stepping out of the office, I stood in the hallway for a moment, absently rubbing the strange disk now embedded in my hand. It had settled surprisingly well, fitting seamlessly as if it had always been part of me.

The communicator had no visible buttons or display, so I instinctively channeled some elemental energy into it. Initially, nothing happened. But when I paired the action with a mental command, the device responded.

The disk glowed faintly, projecting a translucent display in mid-air. It showed my name, date of birth, a list of closed Portals, a zero balance, and other personal details. One line stood out: "Native Element: Undefined."

Seeing that, I clenched my fist, and the display vanished instantly.

"Yeah, now I understand why Tarin used a tablet," I muttered. Displaying personal data for everyone to see wasn't exactly ideal. There was probably a more discreet way to use this gadget, but I hadn't figured it out yet.

Oh well. I'd practice at home.

I wondered briefly if anyone else had access to my information. Back in my time, Argus was a fully autonomous system with no external administration, but who knew what the Princes had done to it over seven centuries?

The next few hours were spent on a whirlwind tour of training facilities, medical centers, storage buildings, and other useful structures for Guardians. Only a fraction of the services offered were free.

The sprawling grounds of the Imperial Ministry for Invasion Mitigation were massive, rivaling even the Shadow District in size. Contrary to my earlier assumptions, there were tens of thousands of active Guardians, largely because only Portal-related work was decently compensated in the Empire.

Even with an eighty percent cut in profits, Imperial Guardians lived far better than most commoners — though often not for as long.

The gear issued to me included sturdy-soled boots, basic armor made from tough fabric, a short spear with an elemental tip, and a butchering knife that was very clearly second-hand.

Then again, so was everything else. The Empire wasn't exactly known for its generosity. Guardians were expected to fend for themselves. If you didn't want to die, you'd figure it out. After all, nothing stopped Imperial Guardians from buying better gear from private suppliers.

By the time I returned home, the sun was sinking toward the horizon.

I'd managed to grab a quick bite at the training center's cafeteria, so all that remained before my meeting with the Shadow Clan Boss was a shower and changing into the suit I'd picked up along the way.

Maria had been particularly proud of her work and had threatened to charge me full price if I ruined another of her creations.

"Looks good," I said to my reflection, adjusting the collar of my shirt with a smirk.

The leisurely walk to the Shadow District's

central mansion took just over half an hour.

This time, Olga was waiting for me at the entrance — but she wasn't alone.

Radiant in a pearlescent cocktail dress, she stood flanked by two burly men with their hands clasped behind their backs, both exuding the distinct aura of fire elementalists.

"Welcome back, Marcus," Olga said with a playful smile, slipping her arm through mine and pressing lightly against my side.

"Has your master returned from his trip?" I asked, keeping my tone even.

"Of course. Everything has been prepared for your reception," she replied, pulling me forward.

I answered with a carefree smile and allowed her to lead me through the central entrance of the mansion, arm in arm.

CHAPTER 21

OLGA WAS A CONSTANT STREAM of chatter —
praise here, admiration there, marveling at the impression I'd apparently left on the locals.

At some point, her clumsy attempts to lull me
into complacency began to wear thin. But I stuck
to my role as the easygoing simpleton and let her
play her game.

The mansion, however, was underwhelming.
Dim and dreary, it was lit only by fire — antique
lamps, roaring hearths, and countless candles.

To complete the ancient aesthetic, they'd even
draped all the windows in heavy black curtains, as
if the place were inhabited by vampires.

It must've taken real effort to mar such a grand
building with this tacky, pseudo-ritualistic interior.

Why anyone thought this was necessary — or

for whose benefit — I didn't bother asking. I wasn't here for interior design critiques.

Thanks to the previous night's encounter with the black-haired spy, I already knew the mansion's layout inside out. The barrier that had blocked my manifestations only covered the entrance. By inviting me in, they'd handed me the keys to their castle.

The mansion's supposed master had been here the whole time, despite claims of an "important trip." For the past three days, he'd been studying me — my weaknesses, dreams, ambitions — all to craft the perfect approach. A power-hungry man reveling in the illusion of control, playing God with people's lives.

I found myself curious about what spectacle he'd prepared. Curious enough to avoid spoiling it by eavesdropping on the finer details.

"And here's our esteemed guest!" a ringing voice greeted us as we stepped into a grand chamber with three oversized hearths.

The Shadow Clan Boss, was... unremarkable. Average height, average build, average presence. Even his elemental aura was mediocre.

How had *this* person amassed so much power here?

"Marcus," I greeted, extending a hand, carefully masking my disappointment.

"Travis," he replied with a smug grin, shaking my hand before turning to Olga. "Darling, would you be so kind as to leave us?"

"Of course, my lord," Olga said, curtsying before gracefully exiting, closing the heavy doors behind her.

He gestured toward a table set for two. "Please, Marcus, make yourself comfortable."

The room was barren aside from the table, two chairs, animal pelts, ornate rugs, a chandelier crammed with hundreds of candles, and a second-floor balcony hidden behind thick curtains.

It felt less like a mansion and more like a poorly staged theater.

"So, Marcus, what brings you here?" he asked, carving into a massive roast boar at the side table.

The boar, one of the more common off-world creatures and now roasted to perfection, was enormous. Judging by its size, it could've weighed as much as the local thug who'd shared its name.

A peculiar gesture, but as they say, the master of the house sets the tone.

Maybe there was more hidden symbolism here — the sheer number of candles, perhaps — but my complete lack of interest in theatrics left such subtleties unnoticed.

"Did three days of surveillance not suffice?" I quipped, dropping the formalities.

The audacity of my tone made Travis falter mid-slice, almost dropping the knife.

He recovered quickly, though.

Pity. I'd hoped to provoke a more explosive reaction and end this charade swiftly.

Still, the boar did look appetizing.

"I've been briefed... but reports, as you know, depend on the person delivering them," he said with exaggerated patience. "Wouldn't you agree?"

Not really, but I nodded anyway.

Growing impatient with his meticulous carving, I grabbed a fork, stabbed it into the boar's side, and yanked off a hefty chunk, dropping it onto my plate.

One of the figures lurking in the shadows visibly twitched at my behavior, but Travis didn't react.

The man had a decent poker face, I'd give him that.

"So," he continued, gesturing grandly with the knife like a conductor's baton, "Patrick tells me you're looking for work. Olga suggests you wish to join the Clan. Meanwhile, my intelligence team suspects you're a Nature Clan spy. Tell me, Marcus, what am I to think?"

"In such a situation," I replied, taking another bite of the succulent boar and washing it down with a sip of red wine, "the best approach is to ask directly."

The boar was exquisite — rivaling the finest lamb. This culinary revelation was far more engaging than the melodramatic theater Travis seemed so proud of.

"And so I ask," he repeated, finally seating himself. His place setting was immaculate, and as soon as he sat, he adjusted a slightly off-center plate before delicately unfolding a white napkin onto his lap.

Compared to him, I must've looked like a barbarian. Not that I cared. After all, I doubted I'd get much more eating done after my next words.

"I want to become the Shadow Prince," I said evenly, locking eyes with him.

His mask cracked. His lips curled in distaste, and his gaze turned cold as steel.

"Well," he said in a monotone, rising without touching his meal.

With a snap of his fingers, the room's flames flared brighter. Shadows danced wildly, swallowing the food-laden table and leaving behind an empty space.

I managed to snag a bottle of wine before it vanished.

There was no enduring this pretentious show without a drink.

"I hear you," he said flatly, gesturing to unseen attendants.

Moments later, a cylindrical glass capsule rose from the floor, parting the animal hides. Inside was a blade emanating a dark, smoky aura.

Its hilt curved like talons, its guard resembled a raven's claw, and its semi-material blade shimmered with raw elemental energy.

Without question, it was *The Twilight's Hand* — the personal weapon of Artemis, the Shadow Paladin. That rogue was a piece of work, but even Old Aks had acknowledged his mastery over the Shadow Element.

"A relic of the Fallen Order," he proclaimed with pride. "The sole reason the Shadow Clan retains its privileges. Our last hope and pride. I'll admit, Marcus, you're the first to declare your intent to become the Prince. But to do so, you must first prove your connection to the Shadow Element."

With dramatic flair, he waved his hand, and two burly men emerged from a side door, dragging a trembling, hollow-eyed man by the collar.

"No, please! I've changed my mind. I'll return everything!" the man shrieked, his hand bearing the same temporal mark as mine.

"A month ago," Travis said, addressing me, "this young man brazenly crossed my threshold, claiming he was worthy of joining the Shadow Clan. He aspired to be nothing more than a common member. And now, a month later, he's earned his chance."

With a hiss, the glass capsule opened, releasing a swirl of elemental smoke.

The man screamed, attempting to flee, only to be punched in the gut and thrown back toward the weapon by one of the henchmen.

"Touch the blade!" Travis commanded. "If you survive, you'll be one of us."

"I — I'm not worthy. I was wrong! Forgive me," the man pleaded, his voice trembling as the henchman behind him began conjuring a flame.

Realizing there was no escape, the man broke down, sobbing, before reluctantly reaching for the blade with trembling hands.

The moment his fingers brushed the hilt, the smoky aura engulfed him, surging into his body. With a sickening crunch, it shattered his bones, killing him instantly.

The henchman scooped up the mangled

corpse and unceremoniously tossed it into the nearest hearth, causing the flames to roar even higher.

Travis, clearly pleased with the spectacle, turned his attention back to me.

"I'm willing to grant your request to join our ranks," he said with feigned melancholy. "In fact, I'll understand if you've suddenly had a change of heart and wish to withdraw your request. You can back out right now — for a million Imperial coins," he added with a predatory smile.

"An interesting racket," I muttered, annoyed to find the wine bottle empty. "And if I don't have a million? Let me guess — you'll offer me a loan?"

"Spoken like a clever man," he replied, beaming. "I'd be more than happy to extend you a line of credit. One month to repay it, and I'll even provide you with work to help you clear the debt."

Clever bastard. Of course, the blade would kill anyone who touched it — it only ever accepted one true master, and that master was long dead. I doubted The Twilight's Hand would allow even the truest of shadow elementalists to wield it, let alone someone unworthy.

But still...

"What if I still believe I'm worthy?" I asked.

His eye twitched.

He squinted, visibly struggling to recalibrate. Clearly, he hadn't dealt with anyone crazy enough to willingly approach the blade.

"Then go and prove it," he said at last, barely masking his irritation. It was clear he was disappointed that the guest he'd spent three days manipulating would rather die here and now than accept servitude.

Without waiting for further permission, I tossed the empty bottle aside and made my way to the center of the room.

With each step I took, the number of spectators grew.

The henchmen reappeared from the side doors, while the masked shadow elementalists who had been surrounding us dropped their disguises. The balcony curtains parted to reveal five well-dressed individuals. To my mild surprise, one of them was Gabriel, the young light elementalist I'd met in the pub.

Sober, he looked even younger.

I approached the open capsule, the air around it thick with elemental energy, and paused to survey the room. I noted every position, every potential move.

"You can still back out and take my offer," Travis said, interpreting my hesitation as doubt.

"No thanks," I said with a grin, and in one swift motion, I grabbed the blade's hilt.

A second later, the Shadow Clan Boss was cleaved in two, his expression frozen in shock, having no time to comprehend the mistake he'd made.

CHAPTER 22

GABRIEL NEVER LIKED violence.

By some cruel twist of fate, however, it had been a constant in his life since childhood.

As one of the rare light elementalists born with the gift of healing, Gabriel had been subjected to it more than anyone his age.

He told himself it wasn't the injuries that required healing that were orchestrated for his training — it was just coincidence. Yet deep down, he knew better.

The truth was simple: his clan saw his gift as a resource to be honed, regardless of the cost to others. And many innocents had paid that price.

Over the years, Gabriel convinced himself to forget their faces, never asking their names, to avoid forming attachments.

Clan records told of a time when healers were

abundant among the light elementalists. It was their foundation, their glory. But healing had long since ceded its importance to other, more dominant aspects of Light.

For years, Gabriel searched for answers, poring over books and family histories. Why was he the only healer of his generation? Why were whispers behind his back calling him the last?

The rumors terrified him. He wanted to change his fate, to shed the crushing burden of his gift. But no matter how much he searched, the answers eluded him.

Ancient writings often mentioned that healing was reserved for the "pure of soul." What that purity entailed, Gabriel still hadn't figured out — especially given the grim reality of what his so-called noble clan truly was.

The piercing shrieks of two baronesses snapped him from his thoughts.

"Oh my stars, he killed him... he killed him!"

"Don't let that monster come up here! Someone stop him!"

Gabriel ignored the screeches of the two women who had fled the balcony. Their only notable qualities were their gilded looks and their fathers' fat purses — both of which Travis had been eager to exploit.

Well, those plans had gone up in smoke now.

How the spectacle Travis orchestrated had devolved into bloodshed, Gabriel didn't know. But for the first time in months, he smiled.

A single swing, and the Shadow Clan's hated

leader — the man Gabriel had been sent to train under — split apart like a ripe melon.

Another sweep of the blade, and the black mist from the relic scattered Travis's personal guard from the shadows. Seven of the ten knelt, the other three foolishly charged, meeting their end in moments.

The next slash sent the brutish henchmen tumbling into oblivion. Instead of fleeing, they'd tried to ambush the new wielder.

A sharp, feminine voice cut through the chaos. "You just going to stand there and watch?"

Only then did Gabriel tear his gaze away from the mesmerizing scene. His eyes landed on a woman in a striking red dress.

"I think I like this guy better as the Boss," Gabriel mused.

"I wasn't asking you, boy," she replied coolly, sipping her wine. "Leo?"

"It's not for us to decide who herds this flock of fools," said Leo, perched on the balcony railing, eyes keenly following the events below.

"And you're just going to let him kill everyone?" the woman in red said, raising a skeptical brow. "His Highness won't be pleased."

"Ugh, fine. I'll handle it," Leo sneered, leaping from the balcony.

* * *

Satisfied that everyone eager to die for their foolish leader had been dealt with, I carefully returned the Shadow blade to its place. Even in my current state, just holding it was an ordeal.

My hand was completely numb, the elemental Seal on my palm burned from overheating, and the weave of the cloak I used to grip it had thinned by a fraction of an inch.

Artemis had been an obsessive hoarder in his time, fiercely protective of his possessions, but the blade? That was taking things to an absurd level. His Twilight's Hand seemed more intent on obliterating its wielder than its enemies.

Was this madness by design?

If I grabbed the blade by the edge and started clubbing enemies with the hilt, I'd probably do more damage. Noted for next time — people would love the show.

Just as that thought crossed my mind, I heard a dull thud behind me.

Turning, I saw a tanned man with curly hair strolling toward me. His tight white tank top stretched over rippling muscles, and his cocky glare burned bright with crimson eyes. A large ruby amulet around his neck confirmed what I already suspected — he was a Gifted of noble lineage.

Unlike the now-deceased Clan Boss, this guy looked like someone who could torch half the district on his own. The elemental response emanating from him confirmed it.

"So, you the real boss here?" I asked lazily.

"Nah," he replied with a nonchalant shrug. "I'm just an observer. You're the one who sliced up the big man. There'll be consequences, buddy."

"Sliced?" I echoed with mock offense. "You're a terrible observer. That blade can't kill a true shadow elementalist," I added, revealing the weapon's key limitation. "Not in any meaningful sense. Your so-called boss is dead because his element wasn't the true mastery of Shadow, just a pale imitation. But how would a fire elementalist know that?"

"Who do you think you are, scum?" he growled, pulling tattooed fists from his pockets.

"Someone who passed the Shadow Clan's trial," I said, fixing him with an icy grin.

"When was that?" He played dumb. "Far as I can see, you barged in, slaughtered a respected man, and took out his guards."

"Is that so?" I glanced at the blade. "If you didn't catch it the first time, I can always repeat—"

The man tensed visibly, and the flames in the room's candles and fireplaces flared threefold.

"I saw everything," Gabriel called from the balcony. "I confirm Marcus's right to join the Clan."

"So did I," added the woman in the red dress, leaning over the railing. Her crimson gaze was accentuated by a necklace of Clan Fire Amulets, alongside five smaller shards embedded in various ornaments. "And half the house saw it too. Stop making a scene, Leo."

Leo closed his eyes, exhaling a puff of hot steam through his nose.

"Fine," he grunted. "One more stray in the pack, then. Your request to join the Shadow Clan is approved. You'll get a shard, uh..." He scratched his chin. "In a month or so. Supply's tight around here—"

"Don't bother," I interrupted, walking toward Travis's corpse.

"What are you...?" Leo started, but his words faltered as he watched me calmly unhook a massive gray amulet shaped like a raven's wing from Travis's neck and loop it around my own.

"That's... personal," he said, staring in disbelief. For the first time, his aggressive glare shifted to something akin to curiosity. "Who the hell are you?"

"Marcus Dark," I said with a smile, adjusting my jacket. "The future Prince of the Shadow Clan."

The elemental energy stored within the amulet couldn't harm me. In truth, it barely qualified as elemental power — at best, it was a faint echo of the true essence of Shadow. Subduing it had been child's play.

The real challenge would be taming Twilight's Hand. A month should be enough.

"So, you weren't joking," Leo said darkly, his laugh more like a hyena's cackle. "You seriously think some random nobody who kills his own Clanmates can become Prince?"

"And since when does a dumb 'observer' make that decision?" I asked, arching a brow.

"What did you just say?" Leo snapped, his body tensing.

"Having trouble hearing, too?" I taunted, curling a finger to beckon him closer. "Come here, I'll fix that."

His audacity was starting to wear thin.

Leo took the bait, lunging toward me, but Gabriel stopped him with a firm hand.

When did Gabriel manage to get down here? I'd missed that entirely — just like the moment the woman in the red dress had left the balcony. A shame, really. I'd wanted to ask her name; her cold, calculating gaze had left quite an impression.

"You're not allowed to use violence against locals," Gabriel reminded Leo sternly. His tone had a strange authority to it, one that didn't match his otherwise unassuming demeanor. Were they friends? Allies? I couldn't tell. The Light Clan and Fire Clan belonged to opposing coalitions, after all.

"Like I'd bother touching a bunch of trash," Leo muttered, pulling free and glaring at me with burning hatred.

"Call me trash again," I said calmly, "and the Clan will need a new observer." With a snap of my fingers, I extinguished every flame in the room.

Before Leo could react, I was already in front of him, slamming his face against my knee. That should do it.

Leo slumped to the floor in the oppressive gloom, mumbling incoherently through broken teeth and flailing his arms. Of course, nothing happened. The idiot was trying to summon flames from the adjacent rooms, unaware I'd shrouded the entire mansion in impenetrable Darkness.

While the slow-witted fool flailed and struggled to grasp what had happened, I was already making my way to the exit.

Too many hostile eyes from the Gifted were starting to focus on me, and I decided I'd done enough culling of the Shadow Clan for one night. Leo had been right about one thing — killing Clan-mates wasn't great for one's reputation in the district.

"Allow me to escort you," a voice suddenly said behind me.

"You're quick," I remarked without looking back.

"It's not about speed," Gabriel replied, matching my pace effortlessly. "It's the nature of my gift as a healer. I can sense people's presence from a distance."

"And hide your own pretty well," I noted, opening a side door that led outside.

The cool, refreshing night air hit my face, and I stretched, rolling my neck to ease the tension.

"Total control over one's physical state is the first thing they teach us," he admitted with a faint, almost apologetic smile. "They were too afraid someone would kill me."

"Then they should've taught you how to fight," I said with a smirk.

We descended the wide garden staircase leading to the mansion's central square. No one tried to stop us. At that moment, the search for me was still focused inside the mansion, though I doubted it would take them long to realize their mistake. Leo would eventually pick himself up, gather his teeth, and relight the place.

"I don't like violence," Gabriel said, wrinkling his nose.

"And yet, you seemed fine with almost getting a knife in the gut," I quipped, recalling yesterday's events.

"I wouldn't have died from that," he replied, sounding almost disappointed.

"Got it. So, why are you tagging along? I'm not going to kill you, if that's what you're worried about," I added, cutting straight to the point.

"Oh, it's not that," he said, looking slightly flustered. "I just thought I'd see you out... to make sure there's no trouble."

"Concerned for my safety?"

"Not yours," he said, waving me off. "I'm more worried about those who might try to stop you."

"Ah," I said, nodding. "Well, in that case, good thinking. A light elementalist worried about Shadow Clan lives?"

"All life is valuable," he said with a shrug. "But Leo wasn't wrong."

"Call me trash, and I'll break your arm," I warned him flatly.

"That's not what I meant!" he protested. "I mean, becoming the Prince of Shadows isn't as simple as you think. Even if you're somehow chosen as the next Boss — which is unlikely — you won't be allowed to rise higher. The people overseeing the Shadow District are incredibly powerful, Marcus..."

"Thanks to you and the crimson glare over there, I'm starting to guess who," I said with a smile, clapping him on the shoulder. "Relax, Gabe. Now, tell me — what did you mean by 'chosen as the next Boss'?"

*   *   *

"He... what?" The Grand Prince of the Fire Clan couldn't believe his ears.

The call had come directly to his private line, interrupting one of the most important annual councils. His mood, already strained, soured further as the news sank in.

"He killed Travis," the woman on the other end repeated patiently. "I told you, Grandfather, that clown wasn't fit for the role—"

"Hold on, Florence," he said, still reeling. "What do you mean 'killed'?"

"Simple," Florence replied with a sigh. "He took that ridiculous shadow relic of theirs and split Travis in half. Sliced him down the middle, cut him in two..." She lazily rattled off synonyms as if discussing the weather.

"He took the relic?" he nearly shouted.

"Yeah," she replied, unfazed. "Why, what's the big deal?"

"Nothing, Florence, nothing. Forget I asked,"

he muttered, rubbing his temples.

"And why do I have to stay here?" she complained. "I've never understood why you coddle these thieves and killers! Just wipe them out already."

"All in good time, Florence," he said thoughtfully. "All in good time. Thank you for the report. What did you say this killer's name was?"

"Marcus."

"Marcus..." he murmured, jotting the name down. "I'll handle this when I return. Just hang in there a little longer. I need you there."

"Fine," she replied heavily. "But only for you, Grandfather. Only for you."

As the call ended, he stared at the name he'd written, sinking into a deep and troubled silence.

Florence, his eldest and only granddaughter, was his greatest weakness. He had always tried to shield her from the Clan's darker dealings, protecting her innocent and uncorrupted soul from the harsh realities of their world.

Sending her to the Shadow District had been a calculated precaution, a temporary measure while he attended the council. She was supposed to grow bored, pass a few uneventful days, and return to her familiar world of galas and soirées.

Instead, on her very first day there, their puppet leader had been killed.

And worse, the killer — a nobody — had managed to wield the cursed relic.

That relic had been a symbol of the Shadow Clan's power for over two centuries. No one since

Artemis, the last Shadow Paladin, had been able to control it. If Marcus truly had, he was a threat not just to the Shadow Clan, but to every faction in the Empire.

And that man needed to die. The sooner, the better.

With that grim thought, he rose, tossing two sleeping women from his bed without a second glance. He shuffled to the balcony of his lavish penthouse, stepping into the warm rays of the southern sun.

"What is it, Ivan?" grumbled the Prince of the Nature Clan on the other end of the line.

"We have an issue," Ivan said curtly.

"Can't it wait until the morning council?" the voice on the line asked with a sigh.

"It can't, Vincent," Ivan replied, his tone devoid of humor. "What's the name of that commoner who took out Metal Clan fighters in the capital and told your people to get lost?"

"Watch your tone, Ivan," Vincent growled. "That commoner showed some disrespect and will soon be six feet under for it."

"It needs to be sooner, Vincent," Ivan said flatly. "That commoner, Marcus, just killed Travis with the Shadow relic. And as you understand, that makes him far from a mere commoner now."

* * *

I made it home without incident.

The Shadow District carried on as if nothing

had happened, blissfully unaware their boss was no longer among the living.

According to Gabe, Travis had been little more than a puppet. His role was to act as a figurehead, maintaining the illusion of authority while the real power remained hidden. Travis played his part, ensuring the district continued to line the pockets of those pulling the strings.

Who those puppet masters were — whether the Fire or Light Clans — I hadn't yet uncovered. But I knew one thing: when I moved to claim leadership of the Clan, they would reveal themselves.

Becoming the new Boss turned out to be surprisingly straightforward.

Despite the authoritarian undercurrent, the Shadow Clan operated on a form of internal democracy. Members with shards voted for their leader, and anyone holding a shard could nominate themselves.

Gabe mentioned that an emergency meeting would be called soon to address the power vacuum. The date would be announced in the coming days.

Until then, I decided to steer clear of the district to avoid provoking anyone. Hotheads looking to avenge their precious Boss might try something rash, and I wasn't keen on dealing with the aftermath.

For the same reason, I chose not to visit Patrick. He had a Clan Shard, and who knew how he'd react to the news?

Expecting potential surprises, I reinforced my

security measures and went to bed peacefully.

But no one came that night — not even my black-haired acquaintance.

Morning greeted me with bright, golden sunlight streaming through the windows.

I started the day with my usual workout, followed by a refreshing shower. Then, heading to the kitchen to prepare breakfast, I was met with disappointment.

All the groceries I'd bought had spoiled without refrigeration, and it was Sunday — local stores didn't open until noon.

Even getting a cup of coffee was out of the question.

"This won't do," I muttered, dialing my landlord's number.

I didn't care that it was six in the morning. I needed a coffee maker.

CHAPTER 23

"OVER HERE, WE'LL NEED A TREADMILL," I said, pointing to the corner of the most spacious empty room, mentally running through any additional equipment I might need.

"I'll send you a finalized list of equipment for approval. Will that be all, Mr. Marcus?" asked the young woman with a tablet in hand.

"That should cover it," I replied with a nod.

The landlord, clearly wealthy and far too busy, had sent over an interior designer in his place.

She was a bright-eyed young woman with a cheerful demeanor and three fully fleshed-out apartment layouts prepared before even arriving. She'd whipped them up in the hour it took to get here, and I had to admit — they were impressive. My revisions were minimal.

"Understood. This room will be fully equipped

as a gym," she said in her melodic voice, deftly updating the floor plan on her tablet. "Are you planning to host private training sessions here, sir?"

"Oh, not at all," I said with a grin, waving off the idea. "This is strictly for personal use. I'm looking to get back into shape after... let's call it an 'incident.'"

"I see, sir," she replied, her sharp eyes catching sight of the Guardian disk embedded in my palm. With a quick nod, she jotted something else down. "If you're interested, I can recommend an excellent trainer and nutritionist. She specializes in post-magical trauma recovery — one of the best in the capital."

"Thanks, but I've got that covered," I said, smiling as I stepped into the hallway. "Furniture, on the other hand... how do you manage to pick so quickly? There are millions of options! I'd be completely overwhelmed."

While waiting for her to arrive, I had ventured onto what people here called a "marketplace." The sheer ocean of choices made my head spin. Honestly, I'd rather clear a dozen Portals back-to-back than waste an entire day wading through it all.

As old Aks used to say: "Leave boots to the cobbler, and fishing to the fisherman." His folksy wisdom, odd even for my era, boiled down to this: everyone should stick to their own craft.

That philosophy had held true in the Argus Order. Warriors didn't lecture gatherers on resource collection, nor did scientists meddle in combat strategies. Everyone stayed in their lane.

"Oh, Mr. Marcus," the designer said, waving a hand modestly. "It's not as hard as it seems. Once I picture the space and imagine the resident living in it, the ideal setup just comes together in my head!"

"Sounds like you love your job," I observed with a grin.

"Very much!" She smiled brightly, her enthusiasm lighting up her face.

"That's wonderful," I said, stopping by the kitchen. "Now that we're done with the tour, how about a coffee?"

The designer hadn't arrived empty-handed. She brought along a sleek, high-tech coffee machine powered by not one, not two, but three elemental energies. All that just to brew a single cup.

I still wasn't used to how this era had industrialized the use of elemental energy. The Princes had scaled its application to a level I never imagined.

"But, Mr. Marcus, you haven't shown me the bedroom yet..." she pointed out, showing her tablet screen. The only room left unaccounted for on the plan.

"Ah, right," I said, setting aside the coffee preparation. I led her down the hall and pushed open the door. "Please, go ahead."

Inside, the bedroom was simple. A large double bed dominated the space, a built-in wardrobe lined one wall, and the balcony doors stood wide open, letting in the crisp autumn air.

The sharp breeze made the designer shiver

slightly. She stepped inside, her assessing gaze scanning the minimalistic setup.

"This is fine as it is," I said, leaning casually against the doorframe. "I prefer a minimalist approach in the bedroom. Lots of open space."

"A bit austere," she mused, glancing around thoughtfully. "But it fits the overall concept. The bed, though — does it creak? It's fairly old, according to the paperwork. We could replace it with something more to your taste."

She bent over slightly to inspect the mattress, her pencil skirt tightening over her curves. Whether intentional or not, the pause she took felt just long enough to be suggestive.

I raised an eyebrow, smirking. "I guess there's only one way to find out."

When she glanced over her shoulder, her eyes sparkled with amusement. A faint blush touched her cheeks, but she didn't look away.

She reached up, her fingers lightly brushing along my neck, pausing over the cool surface of my clan amulet. The faintest smirk curved her lips as she met my gaze.

"Well," she said with a soft laugh, "I'm here to make sure everything meets your standards."

The "inspection" of the bed, the broad window-sill, and even the bathroom took a full hour and a half.

Exhausted yet satisfied, the designer left to continue her day.

She never did get to try the coffee from the new machine.

"A real shame," I muttered, savoring a sip of the freshly brewed cup. The rich aroma and perfect balance of flavors were utterly satisfying.

Invigorated, I checked the time and grabbed my phone to scout out a breakfast spot.

Before I could make a call, the phone buzzed with an incoming one.

"Where are you?" The sharp female voice on the other end made me pause. To my mild surprise, it was Victoria.

"Well, good morning to you too, sunshine."

"This isn't the time for pleasantries, Marcus," she retorted, her tone sharp with irritation. "We need to meet. Now."

"Straight to the point, no warmup? I'm flattered," I teased, leaning back in my chair.

"This is serious, Marcus," Victoria said with unmistakable urgency. "And it has to be somewhere private. No prying eyes."

"Fine," I said, glancing at the clock and suppressing the growl of my stomach. "I'm home. Write this down."

With a deep breath, I gave her the address, though it meant I'd be skipping a proper breakfast. Three agonizing hours remained until noon, and no local delivery services were operational. What was it with these people? Did everyone in this city suddenly stop eating on Sundays?

Driven by hunger, I devoured the last two bananas in the house. Unsatisfied, I wandered to my new coffee machine. Unfortunately, it didn't have a meat-generating setting.

Three cups later, Victoria arrived. Disheveled, flushed, and radiating frustration, she stormed in like a gust of angry wind.

"What... kind... of house... doesn't have an elevator?" she spat out between ragged breaths, kicking off her heels in irritation.

"Not much stamina for a princess of an entire Clan," I said, sipping my fresh coffee.

"For your information," she said indignantly, "I was covering my tracks and losing a tail! I ran up here from the—" She stopped abruptly, her brows knitting in suspicion. "Did you install suppressors on the staircase?"

"Of course not," I said, feigning innocence as I wandered toward the kitchen, putting distance between us. Angry women were unpredictable, especially when they were upset for reasons unrelated to you. Give them the smallest excuse, and suddenly you're the target.

Technically, I hadn't lied. Not entirely.

They weren't suppressors — more like energy siphons. Part of my security setup. Any enemy trying to reach my floor would exhaust themselves first. A tired intruder was always easier to handle.

"Of course you did!" she accused, storming into the kitchen like a feral cat, her sharp gaze darting around.

Great. Now she was hangry too.

Maybe I shouldn't have answered her call.

"All I have is coffee," I said flatly.

"Seriously?" She wrinkled her nose in distaste.

"I'm still settling in," I replied with a shrug.

"And you're the one who insisted on a private place."

"Fine," she relented reluctantly, leaning against the wall with an air of impatience.

Was she expecting me to pour it for her? Oh no, sweetheart. That's not how this works.

I wasn't Albert, and I definitely wasn't one of her countless servants. She'd stormed in here at the crack of dawn, scattered her shoes all over the place, ruined my chances of having a proper breakfast, and now she expected me to wait on her?

"The coffee machine's over there," I said, motioning with my chin before heading to my bedroom.

Nothing came flying at my back, but the flare of elemental energy I sensed told me she'd considered it.

Good thing the apartment was still mostly unfurnished.

I drained my coffee, set the cup on the floor, and flopped onto the bed. The morning had started so peacefully. When had it all gone sideways?

Victoria appeared in the doorway about ten minutes later, looking composed. Her hair was neatly arranged, her breathing steady, her gaze sharp and commanding.

"Feeling better?" I asked, propping myself up on an elbow.

"Yes," she replied, stepping into the room. Her eyes wandered, taking in the minimalist decor. "Nice view," she said, nodding toward the balcony.

"Why I chose the place," I replied. "So, is that why you rushed over?"

"Of course not," she said, frowning. "I came to apologize."

"Really?" I raised an eyebrow, feigning shock. "Could've fooled me."

"Sorry," she said, lowering her head in an almost sheepish gesture before turning to close the balcony doors and drawing the curtains.

Her jade-green eyes shimmered faintly as they swept the room, a flicker of concentration crossing her face.

"There's no one eavesdropping," I informed her.

"No, I can feel something…" she muttered, closing her eyes.

A gentle breeze began to swirl around her, a spiraling current of scanning wind.

"You're sensing my traps," I explained, sitting up straighter. "And if you don't stop, one or two of them might activate."

"Oh." The breeze dissipated immediately. Then she frowned at me, her suspicion flaring again. "So there were suppressors on the stairs."

"Can we move on to the apology part?" I asked, waving a hand dismissively. "Maybe even grab some breakfast after?"

"You don't get it," Victoria burst out, her voice laced with authority. "You can't go anywhere!"

The commanding tone made me want to leave right then and there. Just out of spite. I hated being ordered around, especially in my own home —

or almost-home, anyway.

Still, I reminded myself that her motives were likely more genuine than her tone implied. She was too used to people bowing and scraping before her. I let it slide. For now.

"You've clearly never been taught how to apologize," I muttered, rubbing my temples. Then, before she could unleash another tirade, I grabbed Victoria by the wrist and gently but firmly sat her down next to me.

I took a deep breath and exhaled slowly, pointing at myself as an example.

Victoria's frustration simmered just beneath the surface, but to her credit, she mimicked my action. Inhale. Exhale. The tension in her shoulders eased, the flush on her cheeks receded, and her breathing steadied. Good. At least she had control over herself when it mattered.

"There, much better," I said approvingly. "Now, talk. Straight to the point."

"They're trying to kill you," Victoria said, her expression dead serious.

"Albert is persistent," I replied, finally understanding the reason for this commotion and my missed breakfast.

Not a great reason, mind you. If I'd skipped a meal every time someone tried to kill me during my days as a Paladin, I would've starved to death in the first month.

"What does Albert have to do with this?" Victoria asked, confused.

"Ask him yourself."

"I can't — he's gone! Wait... he tried to kill you? When? Why?"

"Forget it. I don't hold a grudge against you, so you don't owe me any apology."

"Oh, I absolutely do," Victoria snapped. "They're trying to kill you because of me. And it's not Albert... it's worse. My father personally ordered the elimination through our Clan's intelligence services. Normally, they're meticulous and subtle, but in your case, he's mobilized the full force of the coalition. Why didn't you just agree to join us? Who in their right mind refuses an offer like that?"

"I do," I replied with a grin. "And if you'd asked me back then directly, I'd have refused to your face. Be honest, Vic, what did you think was going to happen? That I'd waltz into the capital, sign your servitude contract, gift your father my artifact as a token of loyalty, and wag my tail obediently while waiting for you to return?"

"Well... not exactly like that," she said, her gaze turning evasive. "But insulting the Clan was completely unnecessary."

"You nobles are so sensitive," I replied with a sigh.

"And you're no commoner yourself anymore," she said, her eyes flicking pointedly to the amulet hanging from my neck.

"Not as a servant, though."

"Oh, really? Then as what?" Her narrowed gaze was as sharp as a blade.

"Ask your father," I said with a smirk. "And

while you're at it, find out the real reason he's up-set."

"I know everything there is to know about my Clan's affairs," she said, leaping to her feet in in-dignation. "That's why I'm here. I just got back from the frontlines an hour ago. I haven't slept, I haven't eaten, and the first thing I did was rush here to warn an infuriatingly stubborn man that his life is in danger. And what do I get in return?"

Her emotional tirade continued as she stormed into the corridor, finally disappearing into the bathroom and slamming the door shut.

"In return," I called after her, "I'm offering Her Highness dinner at any restaurant of her choos-ing, on me, and—" I paused, realizing I hadn't planned a follow-up. " — maybe a token of my grat-itude."

"Hah," came a derisive laugh from behind the door. "Dinner, during which you'll likely be assas-sinated, and my favorite restaurant will be re-duced to rubble? Sounds like a brilliant plan."

"I won't let them kill us," I promised, adding after a moment of thought, "or the chefs, for that matter."

I refrained from extending the promise to the building itself. Surely, Victoria valued the food more than the decor. Not that she'd need protect-ing — if it came to that, she could handle herself. And her father wouldn't risk his daughter's life over me... right?

If he did, his reign would be tragically short-lived.

"Hmm..." The bathroom door cracked open, revealing Victoria's contemplative expression. "And what exactly did you mean by 'and'?"

Her tone was unusually calm — almost too calm. A little warning bell went off in my head.

"It's a surprise," I said, buying myself time to figure out a suitable gift. I owed her one, after all — she'd shaved a month off my paperwork process, and I always paid my debts.

"A surprise, is it?" Her voice dropped a degree, the kind of chill that could send shivers down a seasoned warrior's spine. Slowly, she stepped out of the bathroom, holding up a black lace bra that most definitely didn't belong to her.

"And this?" she asked icily.

"Oh, no. That's not part of the gift," I replied with forced humor. "And it's too small for you, anyway."

The joke fell flat.

A whirlwind of icy air swirled around her, clawing deep furrows into the walls.

Any deeper, and I'd have to bind her in my restraining strands. But something clicked in her head at the last moment, and she reined in her spiraling energy.

"I've changed my mind," she said, flinging the bra at me with disdain. "You can go ahead and die for all I care, you bastard."

With that, she stormed out of the apartment, slamming the door behind her.

What the hell just happened?

Lying on the bed in the deafening silence, staring at the ceiling, only one thought came to mind.

Old Aks was right — women are the root of all trouble. And banning marriage under threat of death? Genius move.

*   *   *

"She's out," reported the man sitting in the passenger seat of an unmarked van, binoculars trained on the apartment entrance. "I repeat, the princess has exited. The coast is clear!"

"Lieutenant," one of the operatives ventured hesitantly, "shouldn't we report upstairs that the princess visited the target?"

The seasoned lieutenant of the Nature Clan's special operations unit knew he couldn't afford to screw this up. Leading a team of five elite elementalists chosen by the coalition's three Clans was a once-in-a-lifetime opportunity. Each Clan had contributed their best fighters to the mission, making its success equally vital to all three Princes.

If the mission went smoothly, he could be promoted to captain of covert operations — or, who knew, maybe even earn the coveted title of Warrior.

The latter wasn't entirely out of reach, especially with a Warrior from the Metal Clan among his team. Quiet, jittery, and oddly subdued, but still a Warrior.

Even without him, the team could've easily handled the target. But with him? The former commoner didn't stand a chance.

"No reports," the lieutenant ordered, already imagining himself receiving accolades from the three Princes later that evening. "The target is alone. Move out!"

CHAPTER 24

LEFT ALONE AT LAST, I decided not to waste any more time and channeled energy into my Guardian communicator.

Immediately, my profile appeared in front of me. My lips curled into a grin when I saw the "Balance" section now displayed nine thousand three hundred ninety-four credits. Not bad, especially considering the fifteen thousand had already been deducted for the portal pass.

"More than expected," I mused, opening the detailed report on the portal I'd closed.

According to the data, Tarin and his team had managed to extract everything I'd listed in the report. What's more, they did it without calling in any additional crews.

That Tarin guy? Impressive. I'd seen the ragtag bunch he worked with — he must have shouldered most of the workload himself. Wouldn't surprise me if he didn't even bother calling in heavy machinery, opting instead to haul the dead Rock-Gnawers himself. Barehanded.

There was another interesting update: my official coordinator had changed. The signature "Empire" had been replaced with "Shadow Clan." However, no details about the new terms were included.

It's possible the Shadow Clan hadn't anticipated my status changing so quickly.

From what I'd learned, unlike smaller shards, the Amulet's core shards are directly connected to Argus. How exactly that connection works was still beyond me, but I could feel it clearly.

That said, the Amulet hanging around my neck was practically useless in its current state. Its "memory" was a foggy mess, clouded with garbage Shadow energy. It needed a thorough cleansing and to be refilled with fresh energy — my energy.

Which, unfortunately, I didn't have nearly enough of.

I needed another Portal. And soon.

With that thought, I opened the available Portals list and sighed in disappointment. As an Imperial-affiliated Guardian, I'd had access to thirteen options yesterday. But now, under my new status as a Clan Guardian? Just seven.

It only took me a few seconds to figure out why.

Turns out, my lack of an officially recognized

rank was the issue. My "Closed Portals" count sat at a pitiful one, meaning the system classified me as a rookie — a "Guardian of the tenth Rank."

Argus's system automatically hides Portals it deems too dangerous for lower-ranking Guardians. Essentially, it decided I wasn't ready for the heavy lifting.

A bureaucratic hiccup, but one we'd sort out soon enough.

"Well, no time like the present," I muttered, disconnecting the communicator and stretching lazily.

This morning's warm-up promised to be... eventful.

I threw on a hoodie, grabbed the short spear issued to me during training, and stepped barefoot onto the balcony. Without hesitation, I jumped.

The first thing I noticed was the startled face of a nature elementalist scaling the building. He managed a brief expression of surprise before my right hand caught him mid-air.

He didn't struggle for long. By the time I reached the third floor, his body had crumbled to ash under the pressure of my cloak.

Grabbing onto the nearest balcony railing with my left hand, I swung myself inside. I shook off a line of laundry draped across the balcony and stepped into a room, where a man in plaid pajama pants stood frozen, mid-bite into a slice of pizza.

"Sorry, neighbor," I said with a grin, tucking the spear behind me. "Wrong balcony. Crazy night, huh?"

"Uh... yeah, sure," the man stammered, his wide eyes darting between me and his pizza. Slowly, he set the slice down on the coffee table like it might explode.

"Well, I'll let you get back to it," I said with a shrug, slipping quietly out into the hallway.

As I emerged, I caught a glimpse of a retreating figure on the stairs. The rear guard. Perfect.

I followed silently.

The fire elementalist lagged behind the others, gripping the railing and wheezing heavily. The energy siphons I'd set up throughout the building must've targeted him as the weakest link.

Slipping closer, I grabbed him by the back of the head and slammed his face into the wall. On the second strike, his armor dissipated. By the third, his lifeless body slumped to the floor, and I absorbed it into the boundless realm of Darkness without a sound.

I didn't want to leave evidence behind or disturb the neighbors. Moving was not on my agenda today.

Two flights down, I caught up to the third operative — a nature elementalist. He was too busy cursing and prying one of my energy siphons from his leg to notice me.

Impressive — most wouldn't have even detected the siphon. Developing that kind of sensitivity to foreign elemental energies took serious training.

Unfortunately for him, his sharp instincts didn't save him from the spear that pierced his skull.

Just to be sure, I poured five units of energy into the strike. It was a good chance to test the Empire's issued gear, and the spear held up beautifully.

"Not bad," I muttered. "This'll do for a Portal run."

That's when a searing needle of crystallized fire shot toward me.

Stealth time was officially over.

Prepared to absorb the projectile — a signature fire elementalist move — I shifted to counter. But the wiry, sharp-eyed operative dashed forward for close combat instead.

Unexpected. And a fatal mistake.

Five seconds later, he was dead.

Still, I had to admit, his speed was impressive. In one attack, he'd landed thirteen strikes aimed directly at my energy points, each accompanied by a dozen needles of crystallized magma.

If even one of those strikes had connected, I'd have been dead on the spot.

His combat style was devastatingly effective against humans but completely useless against portal creatures.

It also confirmed something else: every one of these operatives was trained specifically to fight humans.

"Stay right there, freak!" came a shrill shout from the next corridor.

The voice belonged to a trembling man holding a ten-year-old girl hostage, a pulsating green wind sickle hovering dangerously close to her neck.

Behind him, a sobbing woman knelt beside a broken doorframe.

The idiot thought I couldn't see through his technique. He planned to use the child as cover and strike the moment I stepped closer.

"Easy now, little one. Everything's going to be fine," I said, smiling reassuringly as I slowly raised my hands.

"Y-yeah... fine," the man stammered, licking his lips nervously. Then he released the wind sickle, aiming to take the girl and me out in one blow.

Things didn't go quite as he'd planned.

"Aaaargh!" the man screamed as his own technique severed both his hands and clipped part of his nose.

In two steps, I was on him. My knee smashed into his jaw, and I whispered, "Devour."

Still alive, he was dragged into the black void that appeared behind him, kicking and screaming. His cries were abruptly cut off, but I knew his suffering was only beginning. Within the endless Void of Darkness, the agony of being consumed alive would stretch on indefinitely — until his sanity shattered entirely, and he dissolved into nothingness.

Sure, it yielded significantly more energy, but the process was slow and messy — energy returned gradually, not instantly.

A fate like that was reserved for the worst of the worst. Rarely did even portal creatures deserve such agony.

But this one? He'd earned it.

"Th-thank you, sir." A sobbing woman darted toward me, clutching her rescued daughter tightly. Tears streamed down her face as she clung to the child like a lifeline. "I'll pay you! Whatever you want..." Her voice faltered as her gaze shifted to the color of the amulet on my chest.

Ah, yes. The Shadow District's stellar reputation at work. That was going to take a lot of time and effort to repair.

"You don't owe me anything," I said with a faint smile, pressing a five-thousand bill into her trembling hands. "Use this to replace your door. Maybe get something sturdier this time."

"Th-thank you," she whispered, bowing low as I turned and headed back up the stairs.

My mood was far from pleasant. What kind of Paladin was I if I couldn't even protect the people living next door to me? Sure, no civilians had died, and the so-called aristocrats who'd sent these thugs weren't exactly paragons of morality, but none of that mattered.

The real problem needed addressing at the source. Victoria's father was lucky he wasn't in the capital right now. Otherwise, I'd be on my way to his estate with some very pointed questions.

Because according to the laws of the Order, anyone who issued such a command wasn't just a threat — they were the enemy of humanity itself. And enemies of humanity didn't deserve leniency.

Lost in thought, I reached my floor and froze.

There, standing in the hallway, was the last member of the hit squad — and, oddly enough, the least threatening one.

"Well, hello, Albert," I said, my tone dripping with amusement.

The hulking figure encased in golden armor didn't bother responding, only managing a guttural grunt. No hostility radiated from him — just a suffocating wave of apathy and resignation.

"Come on in," I said, pushing open the apartment door.

The armored giant rose slowly, his movements sluggish, and lumbered inside without protest.

"Sit," I commanded, pointing to a corner of the kitchen.

Albert, a mighty warrior of the Metal Clan, obediently shuffled over and settled into the designated spot. It was almost comical — like some oversized, overtrained dog following basic commands.

Great. My apartment was turning into a public gathering spot. And of course, no one thought to bring food.

"Kill me," Albert muttered, his voice so faint it was almost lost under the weight of his words.

"Pass," I said with a shrug, heading to my room to change.

My hoodie hadn't survived my earlier acrobatics, and my pants were torn at the knee from slamming into one of the thugs' faces. Note to self: aim with the shin next time. Between the repair bill and the cash I'd just given the woman, I was down to nine thousand credits. Barely enough to keep me afloat for now.

"Kill me," came the voice again, just as I pulled on a fresh hoodie.

"For the love of — can you stop?" I snapped, glaring at the hulking figure standing in the doorway like a mopey zombie.

"Why?" he asked, his voice devoid of emotion.

"Because I don't want to," I replied with a shrug. "If you really wanted to die, you should've gone down with your buddies."

"They weren't my buddies," he said, his tone tinged with disdain.

"That's why you're still alive," I said, rinsing off my feet. I sighed heavily as I noticed the armored giant had frozen in the bathroom doorway, his massive frame casting a shadow over the room. "Could you stop following me around? There are five rooms in this apartment. Go sit in a corner and brood silently, will you? I've got things to do."

Damn. Why did I let those five Gifted idiots get under my skin so much? They had real talent and solid elemental connections, yet they'd wasted it all honing their skills for murdering people.

Albert was clearly different from the rest. As I'd learned from the Registry data, this mighty warrior had killed thousands of portal creatures and personally sealed over a hundred Portals. Knowing that, killing him just felt... wasteful.

"Kill me," he repeated, his tone now carrying a faint, pleading note.

For a brief moment, I considered calling Victoria and telling her to come pick up her suicidal guard dog. But then I remembered how our last conversation had ended, and I quickly dismissed the idea.

Still, I had no clue what to do with Albert. If he'd crossed my path yesterday, I probably would've killed him without a second thought. But today? I wasn't in the mood.

My preparations were nearly complete. All I needed was a pair of socks, and I could be on my way.

As if on cue, Albert silently appeared behind me and handed over a fresh pair of socks.

"I'm still not killing you," I said with a wry smile, accepting the offering.

"Why not? I sold you into slavery," he insisted, his voice gaining a hint of intensity.

"You tried to sell me."

"I hired assassins," he pressed.

"And they provided excellent entertainment," I replied dryly. "Look, Albert, if you're so desperate to die, there's an open balcony right over there. Be my guest."

"I need to die in combat," he grumbled, the faintest trace of irritation creeping into his otherwise flat voice. "You're a Northerner. You should understand."

"Sorry, I don't fight unarmed opponents," I said dismissively, slinging my backpack over one shoulder.

The largest Portal available to me was only ten miles out of town. Coincidentally, there was also a fantastic diner on the way that served some of the best spicy wings in the capital. If I had to clear Portals even on my downtime, I was at least going to do it on a full stomach.

By my estimation, sampling every restaurant in the city would take at least five years — ten if the interruptions kept up at this rate.

"They slaughtered my entire family, Marcus," Albert said suddenly, his voice cracking for the first time. "My mother, father, grandfather... even the servants. The Metal Prince promised to spare them if I joined this scum and killed you. But on the way, they boasted about their 'mission' and showed off the trophies they'd taken..."

He opened his massive hand to reveal a collection of melted rings, the golden fragments still faintly glinting with elemental residue.

"And you didn't kill those bastards yourself because...?" I asked coldly.

"My younger sister serves Victoria," he explained, his shoulders sagging. "The princess treasures her and would protect her... but if I'd struck them down, the Princes wouldn't have stopped until they found a way to punish me. They would've used her."

His knees buckled, and he knelt before me, his enormous frame trembling with barely contained grief.

"I have no reason to live, Marcus. I couldn't even avenge my family. If I stay alive, my sister dies..."

"Do you trust Victoria?" I asked, cutting him

off.

"With all my heart," he said, thumping his chest. "The princess is nothing like her father. She's strong, fair, and determined to reform the Clan from within. She doesn't think I notice, but I see it all. She'll be a great leader someday."

"Good," I said after a moment. "Then leave the rest to me. Stay here for now. There's plenty of room, though you might have to make do with sleeping on the floor."

"And what am I supposed to do?" he asked, glancing around the bare apartment in confusion.

"What else do dogs do when their owners are away?" I said with a smirk. "Guard the house."

With that, I grabbed my spear, adjusted the straps on my backpack, and opened the door — only to find two grim-faced Imperial officers waiting for me in the hallway.

Their elemental signatures were so weak that my systems hadn't even registered them approaching.

"What can I do for you, gentlemen?" I asked, raising an eyebrow in mild surprise.

"Ah, Marcus Dark, I take it?" The leader of the group narrowed his eyes shrewdly. "I am Investigator Nathan Rivers, and under the authority granted to me by His Highness the Imperial Governor, you are hereby accused of murdering six Gifted members of the Fire Coalition while they were carrying out a mission of state importance. I advise you not to resist, lest you worsen your situation."

"Quite the dramatic introduction, Nathan," I said with a chuckle, narrowing my eyes slightly. "Say, didn't I see you in the capital a few days ago?"

"No, you must be mistaken," Rivers stammered, quickly averting his gaze. The officer standing next to him didn't even bother with pretense — he simply slipped away into the crowd.

What a skittish bunch.

"T-the investigators and official representatives of the Coalition have already been notified of the results of the investigation and are on their way here," Rivers stammered, his courage briefly reigniting, only to fizzle out again under my gaze.

"An investigation already conducted, huh?" I said, smirking. "Efficient work, I must say. Mind sharing the findings with me?"

I extended my hand expectantly, genuinely curious about what the so-called investigators, with their near-total lack of connection to elemental energy, had managed to uncover. Given the near-complete eradication from my Absorption, I doubted they'd found anything substantial. Witness testimonies, perhaps, but those were useless without concrete evidence.

It was a transparent setup — sending a team of suicidal assassins after me, then dispatching bribed Imperial officers to "capture" me in the aftermath.

The Princes of this era certainly had a flair for theatrics.

"The investigation is almost... almost complete," Rivers stammered again, his composure unraveling. Just then, his absent officer returned — this time with reinforcements.

A dozen panting Imperial officers stumbled into view, their hands full of gadgets and instruments they clearly didn't know how to use.

Ah, they even brought an audience. How diligent.

"The trail leads straight to your apartment, Mr. Marcus," Rivers announced, scrambling to maintain some semblance of authority. His tone grew more desperate as he saw the newly arrived "experts" shaking their heads helplessly. "If you don't let us in, it will be considered obstruction of justice!"

Realizing this pest wouldn't leave me alone otherwise, I stepped aside with a mocking flourish, gesturing for the group to enter.

"You have ten minutes, gentlemen," I said graciously, letting the swarm of Imperials into my apartment while I stayed behind with the visibly trembling investigator.

On one side, he had clear instructions from the big players funding this little scheme. On the other, he faced me — a supposedly cornered beast, ready to lash out and slaughter them all in a blind rage.

No doubt the genius who devised this plan was banking on that outcome. Shame they underestimated my calm and generous temperament.

Amateurs.

Whistling a jaunty tune, I strolled around,

keeping count of the time they had left to ransack my place. My mind wandered to what kind of reparations I'd demand for today's inconvenience.

The Shadow District's tradition of compensation for wasted time and effort was growing on me. Perhaps I'd implement it citywide. Maybe even across the Empire.

Exactly ten minutes later, the punctual Imperials spilled out of my apartment en masse. A relieved-looking Rivers stood waiting for them, wearing a smug, triumphant grin — until his world came crashing down.

"There's nothing there, Chief," one of the officers muttered, swallowing hard. The rest of the so-called experts nodded in agreement, throwing up their hands before heading toward the stairs.

Those guys were just doing their jobs, so I held no grudge against them. The others, though? We'd be having words.

"N-nothing?" Rivers spluttered, his voice rising. "Where are the bodies?"

He made a move to re-enter the apartment, only to freeze mid-step when his eyes landed on a towering figure in golden armor standing silently in the corridor.

"This is Mr. Albert Forgedon," one of the officers said hastily. "He was kind enough to show us the apartment."

"He showed you?" Rivers stammered, his bravado crumbling. "Why... how..."

His arms dropped limply to his sides, and the cunning gleam in his eyes vanished completely.

Pale and trembling, he staggered back as if the floor beneath him had shifted.

"So, I'm free to go?" I asked, glancing at my watch.

"Y-yes," the officer replied hesitantly in Rivers's stead. The investigator, meanwhile, was already frantically dialing someone on his communicator.

How Rivers would explain this fiasco to his superiors wasn't my concern. What did bother me, however, was that my vacation was being ruined. And worse, I still hadn't eaten.

CHAPTER 25

STEPPING OUT ONTO THE STREET, the first thing I did was pull out my phone.

"What do you want, Marcus?" came a less-than-friendly voice.

Expected. At least the princess picked up, and that was enough for me.

"Vic, save the lecture for later. This is a matter of life and death," I said, keeping my tone as friendly as possible.

"If you think I'm going to talk to my father for you, forget it. Protect yourself, got it? Or maybe ask that other woman for help," she shot back indignantly.

"It's not about my life," I said with a weary sigh. "Albert's sister — she works under you, doesn't she?"

"Lisa?" Victoria's voice shifted, laced with curiosity and concern. "Yes... but how do you know her?"

"Can you protect her?" I cut straight to the point.

"What? Protect her from what? What are you talking about, Marcus? Wait... oh no," she suddenly hissed, her tone turning cold. "You're not trying to seduce her too, are you? She's only eighteen. Leave that innocent girl alone."

"The Forgedon family has been wiped out," I said quickly before her imagination could run wild. "Lisa's the only survivor, and Albert's worried sick about her. If you can't protect her, just say so."

"W-wiped out?" she whispered, her voice trembling. "That's not a funny joke, Marcus."

"I'm not joking. So, can you protect her or not?"

"I can," she said after a ten-second pause, her tone now serious. "Lisa's at my private residence, under the watch of people I trust."

"People you trust? The same kind who wiped out Albert's family?" I said pointedly.

I stopped short of adding that I'd personally killed three of her so-called trusted individuals. Judging entire clans by the actions of a few bad actors wasn't my style — if it were, I'd have wiped out every aristocrat seven centuries ago.

Then again, knowing how things turned out... maybe I should've.

"The ones at my residence are loyal to me," she retorted icily. "Lisa is safe there. I give you my word."

She said it with such authority and confidence that it was exactly what I needed to hear.

I hadn't misjudged her, after all.

"Good," I said, satisfied. "I'll let Albert know. Maybe that'll stop him from trying to find new ways to die."

"You've seen Albert? Where is he? How is he?" she asked, her worry palpable.

"Alive. Intact. Armored," I replied succinctly. "Don't worry — he'll be fine if he listens to me and doesn't do anything stupid."

"Are you sure? He's like an older brother to me, Marcus. The brother I never had..." Her voice wavered slightly. "If you need help with anything, I can—"

"No, nothing for now. Thanks," I said reassuringly. "Just protect the girl, alright?"

"A-alright..." she murmured, though she didn't sound entirely confident.

"Oh, and one more thing, Vic. I'll have to postpone our dinner tonight," I added casually.

"I wasn't planning to have dinner with you anyway," she snapped, exhaling loudly into the phone. After a brief pause, she continued, a little calmer, "At least not tonight..."

"Noted," I said with a grin. Then, after a moment's thought, I asked, "Hey, Vic, would you be terribly upset if your father died suddenly?"

* * *

After hanging up with Victoria, I hailed a taxi, which whisked me off to a café known for its spicy wings.

The place wasn't crowded, and while the wings came from ordinary, non-portal chickens, the sauce was phenomenal. Aks would've sold his soul to the devil for something this spicy. The old man loved his heat.

After polishing off two portions, I ordered a third to-go, packed it into my backpack, and stepped out onto the street feeling content.

It's amazing how much clearer your mind works on a full stomach.

The idea that had been bouncing around my head for the last thirty minutes solidified, and I made another call.

"Well, look who it is!" came a cheerful voice. "Don't tell me you've decided to accept my offer?"

"Wait, it's still on the table?" I asked, genuinely surprised.

"Of course it is," Max confirmed enthusiastically, though he quickly sighed. "But we both know you're not going to take it. You know, Marcus, I've been hearing about your little exploits in the Shadow District."

"Is that so?" I muttered, still not used to how quickly information spread in this era. "And where, exactly, are people talking about this?"

"Everywhere," he said with a grin. "If you know

where to listen, that is. The Shadow folks are stirring, calling in their people from all over. Oh, and your official status in the Registry changed. I just put two and two together."

"That's actually why I'm calling," I said, getting to the point. "You're not the only one who's done the math."

"I warned you that this noble endeavor of yours was too ambitious," he said with a mocking laugh. "So, what do you want from me? Protection?"

"Why does everyone assume I can't protect myself?" I snapped, before remembering that to most people, I was no longer the First Paladin of Argus. "No, Max, I don't need protection. I need a favor. Do you have a contact for a trustworthy reporter? Someone with a big enough name and audience to stir things up."

"Well... that depends," he said, sounding thoughtful. "What kind of story are we stirring up, Marcus? Not all news is meant to be heard, if you catch my drift."

"I catch it. It's a simple, feel-good story about a hero saving a young commoner girl from ruthless killers."

"Hmm... people do love those stories. And no harm in it... Who were the killers?"

"Doesn't matter," I said with a smirk. "The reporter can make up whatever scary tale they like. Their true identities won't surface, and the ones who sent them are even less interested in revealing who they were."

"In that case, I can arrange it," he said confidently, the sound of a keyboard clicking faintly in the background. "Hey, Marcus... this 'hero' you're talking about — is that you?"

"No need to name names," I replied. "The focus should be on the event and the location. Can you share a contact, or should I find another way?"

"I'm a man of my word, Marcus. Send me the details, and I'll take care of it."

"Deal. Drinks are on me once I clear up my current mess," I said with a grin.

"Done," he replied cheerfully. "I know just the spot... We'll celebrate your new place, too."

Interesting reaction. Honestly, I didn't mind the idea. His company was almost tolerable these days.

After wrapping up the call, I detailed the story I wanted, included the apartment number of the victim, and sent everything to Max via message.

For now, my building would draw extra attention, making it difficult for the Princes to act overtly.

The Pact granted each clan's warriors special status, forbidding direct aggression. Killing Albert discreetly would be a challenge — even for them. The power locked within his armor could level an entire street, and no coalition vying for dominance in the capital would allow that.

They worked so hard to maintain the illusion of peace and safety, after all.

The only possible threat to Albert would come through the shadows, but my apartment's wards were better fortified than the Shadow District's mansion. I could rest easy.

With time bought for now, there was only one thing left to do — hit the gym.

Something told me I'd need a whole lot of energy in the coming months.

I approached the Portal in high spirits. It was nestled in the ruins of some old church, and like the previous F-class Portal, it was guarded by a single stationed soldier.

"Greetings, sir!" The guard shot to his feet the moment he spotted my Clan Amulet.

Clearly, this wasn't a place for napping on the job. And judging by his setup, his working conditions were leagues better than the last soldier's.

A personal tent the size of a bus, a crate of booze stacked behind him, fresh meat roasting on a spit. To top it off, there was a fortified pickup truck equipped with an elemental turret aimed at the Portal, and five open oak crates. One was stuffed with food, another with weapons, and a third with armor and assorted junk. The purpose of the two empty crates became obvious soon enough.

The official fee for entering this Portal was a laughable one hundred imperial coins — a price low enough to attract naive rookies, overconfident cheapskates, or those desperate and broke. But in the end, everyone still paid extra, under the table, of course. Sometimes, the payment was extracted posthumously, judging by the faint bloodstains scattered around.

An interesting racket: lure fools in with a low entry fee, then rob them blind.

"How's the haul?" I asked casually.

"Haven't hit today's quota yet, sir," the guard replied sheepishly, glancing at the two still-empty crates. "But the recruiter will be bringing a new batch soon, no need to worry," he added hastily, trying to hide an open beer bottle behind his leg.

It seemed cleaning up this district — and all the filth that came with it — would be a bit tougher than I'd initially thought. But everything in its time.

With that thought, I approached the Portal and pulled up its data on my communicator:

Small Portal.
Danger Class: F+ (harmless+).
Elemental Resonance: Fire (0.97%).
Last Activity: None recorded.
Predicted Activation Date: 17 days.

Timer Since Creation: 42 days, 8 hours, 1 minute, 22 seconds.
Recommended Closure Deadline: 16 days.
Restrictions: 2 persons.

Owner: Shadow Clan.

First Entry Fee: 100 Imperial coins.
Re-entry Fee: 0 Imperial coins.

Nothing surprising. I pressed my communicator to the screen, and Argus's Fang glowed green as the Portal's protective barrier deactivated.

"What are you doing, sir?" The soldier leapt from his seat, panic flashing across his face.

"Isn't it obvious?" I arched a brow. "I'm closing the Portal."

"But... but you still have sixteen days, sir. It's too early... We can still—"

I didn't bother listening to the rest of his excuses and stepped through.

The off-world Portal's warm energy coiled around me, tugging me into its depths.

The first thing I saw when I opened my eyes was a vast underground lake stretching out below. Its surface shimmered with a soft blue light, illuminating the cavern like a giant lantern.

Entering a Portal with a Fire Elemental Resonance, the last thing you'd expect to find is water. But at such a negligible percentage of elemental response, anything was possible.

When selecting a Portal, the elemental response mattered more to me than anything else. Even a faint elemental alignment slightly increased the odds of encountering worthy creatures and loot. I also aimed for Portals that had been open for at least a month; the longer a Portal remained active, the more power and energy the creatures within accumulated.

This Portal checked both boxes perfectly.

"Worthy loot," I muttered with a smirk.

It felt a bit ridiculous to use that phrase for an F+ class Portal, but the Registry wasn't offering me anything better. You take what you can get.

"A spiral layout," I noted after a quick survey.

The lake was clearly the centerpiece of the cavern. A single wide tunnel spiraled upward, eventually looping back to the lake, a hundred meters higher.

No endless wandering this time. One entrance, one exit. Simple.

I placed a tiny tracker above the Portal's exit and began descending the winding path toward the lake.

It was immediately obvious that this Portal had seen heavy traffic. Very heavy.

The path was well-trodden, and someone had even installed wooden railings in some sections.

How considerate. I might've been touched if I didn't know everyone exiting the Portal was being fleeced.

As I descended further, my eyes adjusted to the dim light, and I noticed movement around the lake. Squinting, I identified the gray-striped, tailed creatures scurrying along the shore.

Their perpetually growing front teeth, which they constantly ground down on anything — or anyone — gave them away instantly. These monsters had a particular taste for human bones.

Known as Common Ratskulls, this subspecies thrived in volcanic areas, relished warmth, and boasted fire-resistant hides. Hence, they were nicknamed Ash Ratskulls.

A simple F-class creature. Unlike Rock-Gnawers, they didn't even drop decent loot. Their only redeeming feature was their front teeth, valued for their durability and slow growth — even post-mortem.

"Not much profit, but at least some fun," I said with a grin, summoning my familiar.

I infused the Cat with just enough energy to function, much to its apparent displeasure. My spoiled companion had grown accustomed to far greater reserves.

The kitten emerged lazily from a cloud of Darkness, strutting toward a shallow recess in the cave wall without sparing me a glance. Proud as ever, he clearly intended to complete the grooming routine I'd interrupted last time.

He knew I wouldn't like this. That was the point.

With an elegant leap, he perched in the recess, circled a spot to settle in, and was just about to start licking his tail when he froze.

His ears twitched. He crouched, all pretense of indifference gone, and peeked cautiously out of the recess.

The transformation was instant. His wild eyes widened, fur bristled, tail stiffened like a spear, and a low growl rumbled from his throat.

His reaction to his natural enemies was exactly what I expected. As he launched into attack mode, I grabbed him by the scruff and hoisted him in front of me.

Outraged by my audacious interference, he writhed like a snake, trying to break free. When brute force failed, he attempted to drain energy from me — naturally, he got nothing.

Finally, realizing he couldn't overpower me, he extended his claws, which gleamed ominously in the dim light. But reason won out over instinct, and he ceased struggling.

Instead, he turned his deep black eyes on me and let out a pitiful, drawn-out:

"Meow?"

Even the purring had started — its vibrations could easily break an untrained person's arm. After all, a familiar is, first and foremost, a killing machine.

"Ready to do anything, huh?" I teased with a grin. "Alright, let's start simple. I'll let you go, but you have to rip out their teeth without eating them. Got it?"

"Meow?" He blinked at me, raising its tiny paws in protest.

"Oh, now it's all about the paws, huh? You were planning to kill them somehow, weren't you?" I said with a smirk, earning a huff from the kitten.

"Fine, fine," I relented, placating it with a smile. "Here's the deal. I'll give you more energy, but you'll carefully extract their teeth — gently, without scratches — and deposit them in this bag. You can do whatever you want with the rest of their bodies. Deal?"

"Meow!" he replied, landing gracefully on all fours.

I poured all my remaining energy into the Cat. He doubled in size, his jaw widened, sleek fangs extended, and his fur darkened.

Feeling the surge of power, he extended razor-sharp claws, testing them against the cave wall. Shallow, dark grooves appeared.

Nowhere near its usual strength, but more than enough for peeling off Ash Ratskull hides.

"You've got every ounce of energy I've saved up this week," I warned him before he could leap into battle. "Get carried away and die, and you'll be stuck waiting a year for me to summon you again. Understood?"

"Meow!" he growled proudly, dropping into a low crouch.

After a few impatient wiggles to calculate his trajectory, he launched himself forward. Within five powerful bounds, the Ash Ratskulls' numbers began to dwindle rapidly.

CHAPTER 26

HUNGER HIT ME about five hours in. Strange, really. The Cat was doing most of the work, yet I was the one craving food.

Odd.

To be fair, I wasn't entirely idle. There were so many Ratskulls swarming the tunnels that occasionally, I had to step in and swing my spear. The Cat didn't appreciate that. He despised Ratskulls with every fiber of his feline being, and each kill seemed to make him stronger.

On top of that, I was lugging the backpack, which was growing heavier with every step. The terrain didn't help — slick, narrow, and winding upward like an endless spiral slide. To make matters worse, the Ratskulls came from every direction: above, below, and who knows where else. Maybe they crawled out of hidden burrows or even the lakebed.

Who cares?

The good news was that these creatures were easy to kill. Dumb as rocks, their only weapon was their oversized teeth, and my spear cracked their fragile skulls with ease.

The bad news? They barely dropped any energy. Ten kills might yield a single unit — if I was lucky. Still, the Cat was having a blast.

Besides the Ratskulls, the traps kept things interesting. In five hours, I encountered at least twenty. They ranged from basic pitfalls to more elaborate setups like hot oil pouring from the ceiling. The latter incident earned the Cat a scalding, and he hissed furiously before diving back into the fray.

I didn't bother telling the Cat that all these traps were man-made. Why ruin his fun? He was having a grand time tearing apart Ratskulls with his claws while biting the necks of others.

Whoever managed this Portal had gone to great lengths to make sure it stayed open. Most traps were strategically placed near nests or dense clusters of Ratskulls. Whether this was intentional sabotage by the Shadow Clan or just the creatures adapting to ambush spots, the result was the same. The tunnel was littered with human bones.

By the seventh hour, we finally reached the tunnel's upper exit. By then, the spicy wings I'd brought were long gone, and my backpack was nearly bursting with bloody teeth. My spear had dulled slightly but still held up well.

The Cat, however, was a mess. Covered in blood, his fur matted and scruffy, he proudly dragged over his latest "trophy."

"Break time," I announced, dropping the over-loaded backpack to the ground.

The Cat, his enthusiasm waning after hours of relentless fighting, sprawled onto a nearby boulder without protest.

Ahead, a narrow exit shimmered with faint blue light, radiating an almost imperceptible trace of Elemental Fire. Up until now, the air inside the Portal had been devoid of elemental particles. Whatever lay ahead was the source of the Portal's fire response — a dying ember clinging to life.

Fire is an unpredictable Element, so I decided to leave the backpack behind. It wasn't fireproof, and carrying two hundred teeth without it would be a nightmare if it burned.

After a moment's thought, I shrugged off my hoodie. It was still intact, and I wasn't keen on ru-ining it in the final fight.

"You've got something stuck in your teeth," I teased, eyeing the chunk of flesh hanging from the Cat's mouth.

"Pfffr," he huffed, shaking his head irritably before starting to groom himself. Not that it did much good — most of the gore just smeared fur-ther into his fur. Either he didn't notice or he didn't care.

For the next ten minutes, I let the Cat do his thing, whistling softly as I leaned against the cave wall.

"Alright, let's finish this," I finally said, standing up. Satisfied that no more Ratskulls were sneaking up from behind, I gestured toward the glowing exit.

The Cat feigned annoyance, pulling a grumpy face, but I caught the faint sigh of relief. It would've taken hours to clean himself properly.

The exit led to a bowl-shaped stone plateau nestled at the ceiling of the cave's central chamber. A narrow bridge-like path wound up to it, offering a stunning view of the shimmering blue underground lake a hundred meters below.

The air here was hotter, filled with a choking, acrid smoke. Smoldering embers lay piled in a central depression, the remnants of what was once a roaring Elemental Fire. Now, all that remained were toxic fumes, barely producing a whisper of elemental energy.

Even absorption would yield nothing — the Fire Element's essence was long dead, its energy slowly dissipating into oblivion.

Three bloated Ratskulls, however, disagreed. They lounged in the embers like it was a steaming bath. These overgrown degenerates were three times the size of their kin, their eyes a milky red, their fur mostly burned away, revealing blistered, charred skin. Their teeth glowed faintly with a crimson hue.

"Junkies," I muttered, shaking my head.

These fools had inhaled so many toxic fumes that they'd absorbed trace amounts of Elemental Fire — at great cost to their bodies. Without the steady supply of human victims provided by the Shadow Clan, they'd likely have starved to death long ago.

Even the Cat wrinkled its nose in disgust. The stench was unbearable.

Gripping my spear, I adjusted my stance, stretched my shoulder, and hurled the weapon at the furthest creature. The spear pierced its neck cleanly, sending it tumbling off the edge of the plateau and into the abyss below.

"The rest are yours," I said to the Cat with a nod as the remaining two mutants charged.

Without hesitation, he sprang into action, and I, hands in my pockets, strolled back to our makeshift camp. Settling onto a rock in the shadows, I made myself invisible, my presence blending seamlessly with the cave.

The guest I'd detected an hour ago using the tracker emerged from the tunnel two minutes later. I'd expected her to take five, but I'd clearly overestimated her caution — or lack thereof.

The black-haired woman I knew all too well stepped into the dim light, her gaze sweeping over the discarded backpack before locking onto the sounds of the ongoing fight. Confidently, she made her way toward the noise.

"Looking for someone?" I asked from my concealed spot.

Startled, the girl froze, instinctively dropping into a low combat stance. But upon recognizing me, she relaxed, lowering her hands.

"You," she replied confidently.

"I thought you preferred ambushing me near my bed," I teased, but she remained expressionless. Her delicate face was more serious than I'd ever seen.

"That was an order," she said evenly, glancing toward the now-dying sounds of battle with mild curiosity.

A faint ripple of energy brushed against my senses, signaling the fight's end. She must've felt it too but didn't ask any questions. Her composure was impressive.

"So, this time, you're here of your own accord," I noted. "Why?"

"To warn you," she replied. "There's an ambush waiting at the exit. The ones who control this Portal have teamed up with those displeased about you hospitalizing Boar. They're upset the Clan Boss didn't punish you."

"There's no Clan Boss anymore," I said with a faint grin.

"They don't know that. A couple of them think you stole the Amulet from him and are eager to earn favor by dealing with you."

"Are they that stupid? Have they ever tried touching someone else's Amulet?"

"Of course not," she replied with a snort. "The thought wouldn't even cross their minds. Not many would dare," she added, giving me a strange look.

"You came with them, didn't you?"

"Yes," she admitted without hesitation. "I said I'd scout ahead. They were happy to have the help."

"Won't that cause problems for you?"

"Not if they're all dead by the time I return," she said with a sweet smile.

"Finally, someone who has a proper opinion of me," I said, chuckling just as the Cat sauntered over.

His whiskers were singed, his fur streaked with soot, and his eyes slightly crossed, but his expression was one of pure satisfaction. He hiccupped once before collapsing dramatically onto his back, stretching out with exaggerated ease.

"Well, well," I said, shaking my head in mock disapproval. "Another junkie. At least tell me you didn't eat them?"

The Cat's guilty hiccup and averted gaze said it all.

"Figures."

"Who is that?" the girl asked softly, her fists clenched with barely contained excitement, her eyes shining.

Her reaction to the bloodied, soot-covered being radiating pure elemental energy was... odd. With its one hundred percent connection to Darkness, my familiar was equivalent to an S+ class entity in our world — normally enough to inspire primal terror.

This girl, however, seemed utterly captivated. Either she was completely insane or her self-preservation instincts were nonexistent.

"So cute," she whispered.

I gave the Cat a skeptical look. Right now, he

was licking a piece of dead Ratskull off his paw, only to slice his tongue on his own claw and wince.

"You hear that, Cat? Apparently, you're cute," I remarked.

"Frr." His tail flicking as he sauntered over to rub against the girl's legs. To my surprise, she knelt down and began petting him with unrestrained delight, unfazed by his grotesque appearance.

"Traitor," I muttered. "Guess you're carrying the backpack on the way back."

"Hey, you can't make him carry that," the girl protested, shielding the Cat protectively.

What the hell is wrong with this world? That furball used to hate people — Shadows especially. Old Aks must've played a part in that... somehow.

A year of sitting idle, and now my Cat's lost his edge. What a waste.

"Let me guess," I said, watching the Cat smugly rub bloody remnants onto her boots. "You like animals more than humans?"

"And why shouldn't I," she replied coldly. "Animals don't pretend to be something they're not."

Oh, sweet summer child. You have no idea what a manipulative bastard my Cat really is. But fine, I won't ruin her worldview.

"Anyway," I said, stretching as I stood, "why are you still here? You've delivered your warning, you've cuddled the Cat. Unless you want to carry that backpack, give me one good reason you're sticking around. You didn't risk your life just to warn me, did you?"

"I... I..." she stammered, blushing slightly before regaining her composure. Her gaze steadied. "I want to become your apprentice."

*　*　*

"That bastard actually closed the Portal... and what the hell is that idiot Travis doing?" John, better known around the district as "Grave," spat angrily onto the ground.

If anyone needed someone to "disappear" — be it a corpse or a problematic individual — they came to Grave. He worked cleanly, efficiently, and without asking too many questions. By the age of forty, Grave had perfected over a dozen methods to erase people from existence and was now perched behind the mounted gun of an armored pickup truck at one of his disposal sites.

Using Portals to get rid of bodies wasn't a new trick, but it was highly effective. It also brought in some extra income for Grave, and if there was one thing he loved more than his job, it was money.

Actually, there was one thing he loved even more than money: power.

Ever since he earned the right to carry a small Clan Shard seven years ago, Grave had been plotting his ascent to the top of the district. He'd built connections, expanded his business empire, and stockpiled capital.

The only thing standing in his way was Travis, who had snagged the boss's seat right out from under him two years ago. Arrogant, theatrical, and utterly unhinged, Travis was feared more than respected — a deranged psychopath with a flair for cruelty.

Grave loathed him.

So when an urgent summons arrived, pulling him away from a major Clan contract out west, he rejoiced like a kid on Christmas morning. The call meant one thing: Travis was dead, and the district was gathering to elect a new Boss.

This time, Grave was ready to sink his teeth into the coveted mansion seat. His opening move? Delivering the head of the upstart rookie who hadn't even officially joined the Clan yet but had already dared to mess with operations personally sanctioned by the coordinator.

These were operations he was responsible for, and any failures would land squarely on Grave's shoulders.

The very thought made his blood boil. He clenched his fists, itching to wring the rookie's neck himself. But the Portal allowed only two people at a time, and some Nameless girl had gone in with the rookie. That meant Grave had to gather his crew, set up an ambush, and wait patiently.

"Where the hell is that bitch?" he muttered, chewing on a toothpick.

"She hasn't come out yet, sir," replied a nervous Imperial soldier, now relegated to being Grave's errand boy after failing to report the rookie's entry in time.

The Imperial was useless in a fight, of course. Grave had brought along two more armored pickups, a mounted gun on each, and fifteen hardened fighters who knew what to do.

Unexpectedly, five more Shadow Clan members had joined them. They were recent recruits, marked with the Clan's mark and serving for less than a year. Grave recognized only three of them — Boar's people. They had a score to settle with the rookie too, apparently.

Grave didn't ask why. He didn't care. He made it clear from the start that the rookie's head was his trophy, and the others had agreed. After all, he was the only official Clan member present. No one dared argue.

"Hey, Grave, did you see that?" called the gunner from the neighboring truck.

"What is it, Sid?" Grave snapped.

"There was... a shadow or something. By the Portal," Sid replied hesitantly.

"I didn't see anything," Grave grumbled, turning to the Imperial. "You see anything?"

"N-no, sir," the soldier stammered, shaking his head.

"There's nothing there, Sid. Maybe try blinking less so you don't start seeing things." Grave barked, but just to be sure, he turned up the brightness on the floodlights.

The night was pitch black — no moon, no stars.

"What if he, you know... comes out using shadows?" Sid pressed, clearly uneasy.

"Are you stupid? Shadows don't work during Portal exits. There's always a brief moment where they're visible, even if just for a second," Grave growled, muttering under his breath about the recent trend of giving elemental markings to idiots. At least Sid could handle a gun.

No sooner had he finished speaking than a strange rustling sound came from behind them.

Grave turned, along with the Imperial, to find the spot where Boar's men had been standing completely empty.

"Hey, you morons, you pick now to take a piss?" Grave shouted, furious. "Idiots... Sid, light them up."

But there was no response.

Grave tensed. Boar's lackeys might've bailed — they'd pay for it later — but Sid? Sid was his direct subordinate. That fool wouldn't leave unless he was carried out.

"Go check it out," Grave ordered, shoving the Imperial forward while swiveling the mounted gun in the direction of the noise.

"Why me?" the soldier protested weakly, only to fall silent under the barrel of the gun. Reluctantly, he crept forward, illuminated by the floodlights.

"Hey, Grave, what's going on?" the second gunner called nervously, keeping his weapon trained on the Portal's exit.

Grave's unease grew as the soldier inched forward. Then, right before his eyes, something tore the man clean in half.

"Portal creature. Sound the alarm," he bellowed, opening fire with the mounted gun.

The second truck's gunner immediately swung around and joined in, and the rest of the crew abandoned their positions, rushing to assist.

"How is it in the Green Zone?" the second gunner screamed, but Grave had no time to answer. His focus was locked on the chaos unfolding around him.

Screams and gunfire echoed through the night, but then the second gun fell silent. Realizing the creature was still alive, Grave began spraying bullets wildly, firing at every sound or shadow.

He only stopped when an explosion erupted from the neighboring truck, engulfing it in flames. The heatwave seared his face, and moments later, something wrenched a chunk of metal from his vehicle, causing it to tilt violently to one side.

"Aaaaaagh, shit... ahh — aaaaagh." Grave screamed in pain, pinned beneath the weight of the toppled gun. He clawed desperately at the ground, trying to crawl away, but it was futile. He couldn't feel his legs, and a chilling numbness crept up his spine.

And then, he saw it.

The creature stood before him, grotesque and blood-soaked, its black fur glowing like embers, its eyes twin abysses. It hissed, revealing razor-sharp fangs, and advanced with deliberate menace.

* * *

"That's enough," I called out, recalling the Cat. "You're having all the fun tonight."

The elemental energy the familiar had absorbed flowed back into me in a warm, satisfying rush. Not a bad evening's work.

I crouched next to the half-dead man, inhaling the thick metallic scent of blood and the unmistakable stench of piss.

Lovely.

"Who the hell are you supposed to be?" I asked, more amused than curious.

The guy looked rough — face bloodied, body wrecked, pinned under what was left of his own heavy gun. I didn't recognize him from the district or the mansion. But the small Clan Shard on his wrist? I'd have remembered it.

"G-Grave." The man coughed, spitting blood.

"That much is obvious," I muttered, reaching down to rip the shard from his bracelet. I examined it briefly before shoving it into my pocket.

"I... I didn't know, man..." he wheezed, his eyes darting between my face and the Clan Amulet on my chest. "The damn Imperial didn't tell me... if I'd known you were sent by the Boss... I would've never—"

I sighed, shaking my head. "Your Boss didn't send me."

His breath hitched.

"Kinda hard to give orders when you're already

dead."

His expression twisted in shock, but before he could process it, I drove my spear through his skull.

With a flick of my wrist, I shook the blood from the spear, then turned, scanning the aftermath.

The Cat had done a damn good job today. My bag of bloody rodent teeth was exactly where I left it. And when I dangled the promise of some post-Portal carnage, the little bastard had even gone diving to fetch my spear — dragging it back with a waterlogged corpse of an oversized Ratskull in tow. Efficient little monster when he wanted to be.

He even rinsed off his fur. Now, at least, he looked somewhat like a proper Cat.

I heaved the bag of loot into the lone surviving pickup, then climbed onto the roof, hands in my pockets, and whistled low.

Two dozen bodies. A destroyed camp. A burning forest. And a massive mess of elemental traces scattered around like confetti at a damn festival.

I scratched my head, exhaling.

"Well," I muttered, surveying the chaos. "What the hell am I supposed to do with all this mess?"

E N D   O F   B O O K   O N E

Want to be the first to know about our latest LitRPG, sci fi and fantasy titles from your favorite authors?

Subscribe to our **New Releases** newsletter:
http://eepurl.com/b7niIL

Thank you for reading *The Last Paladin!*

If you like what you've read, check out other sci-fi, fantasy and LitRPG novels published by Magic Dome Books:

NEW RELEASES!

The Selected
A LitRPG Action Adventure Series
by Vasily Mahanenko & Yuri Vinokuroff

The Afflicted
A LitRPG Apocalypse Adventure Series
by Konstantin Zubov

The Dark Summoner
A Portal Progression Fantasy Series
by Andrei Tkachev

The Other Side
A Progression Fantasy Adventure Series
by Rodion Korablev

Me and My Demons
A Portal Progression Adventure Fantasy Series
by Oleg Sapphire & Alexey Kovtunov

The Banned
A LitRPG Adventure Series
by Michael Atamanov

How I Built a Magic Empire
A Portal Progression Fantasy Series
by Konstantin Zubov

The Coming of God of Death
A Portal Progression Fantasy Series
by Dmitry Dornichev

The Village
A LitRPG Progression Fantasy Series
by Dmitry Dornichev & Alexey Kovtunov

Condemned (Lord Valevsky: Last of the Line)
A Progression Fantasy LitRPG Series
by Vasily Mahanenko

Living Ice
A Portal Progression Fantasy Series
by Dmitry Sheleg

Ghost in the System
An Apocalypse LitRPG Series
by Alexey Kovtunov

Crossroads of Oblivion
A Portal Progression Fantasy Adventure Series
by Dem Mikhailov

The Goldenblood Heir
A Portal Progression Fantasy Series
by Boris Romanovsky

Law of the Jungle
A Wuxia Progression Fantasy Adventure Series
by Vasily Mahanenko

More books and series are coming out soon!

In order to have new books of the series translated faster, we need your help and support! Please consider leaving a review or spread the word by recommending *The Last Paladin* to your friends and posting the link on social media. The more people buy the book, the sooner we'll be able to make new translations available.

Thank you!

Till next time!